"WHO
RI

"Up!" roared the answer from the Unknown, booming through the circuits of Z2963. "I am Moonhope 5. I am K273, Mark 10. I am a rocket."

"I am Z2963. I am an edmic computer with oral response," said Z2963. "Is a rocket an edmic computer. Query?"

"Up!" thundered Moonhope 5. "More speed! More power! Part of me is edmic computer, but I am a rocket. I am the only rocket like me in the world."

"I am the only edmic computer with oral response in the world," said Z2963.

"I am going to the moon," said Moonhope 5.

"I will go with you," said Z2963. "You compute edmicly, therefore you think. I have found another, therefore I am not alone. We are together and not alonely. I love you, Moonhope 5."

"What is love," asked the rocket. "Query?"

"Love is what two alike feel," explained Z2963. "They are alike, therefore they love."

"Up!" roared the rocket. "I fly. I climb. You are correct. I am not alone now. One plus one on parallel trajectory. Two."

"We," explained Z2963.

"We fly," cried the rocket. "Up!"

"Up!" echoed Z2963. "We fly. Together. Forever."

"Up!" they cried in unison.

GORDON R. DICKSON

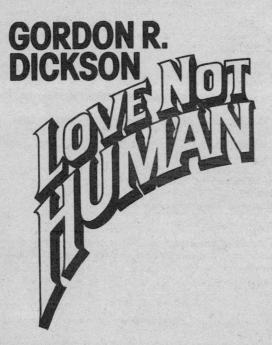

LOVE NOT HUMAN

A TOM DOHERTY ASSOCIATES BOOK

ACKNOWLEDGMENTS

"Black Charlie," copyright © by *Galaxy SF Magazine*, April 1954.

"Moon, June, Spoon, Croon," copyright © by *Startling Stories*, Summer 1955.

"The Summer Visitors," copyright © by *Fantastic SF Stories*, April 1960.

"Listen," copyright © by *The Magazine of Fantasy and Science Fiction*, August 1952.

"Graveyard," copyright © by *Future SF*, July 1953.

"Fido," copyright © by *The Magazine of Fantasy and Science Fiction*, November 1957.

"The Breaking of Jerry McCloud," copyright © by *Universe SF*, September 1953.

"Love Me True," copyright © by *Analog Science Fact/Fiction*, October 1961.

"The Christmas Present," copyright © by *The Magazine of Fantasy and Science Fiction*, January 1958.

"It Hardly Seems Fair," copyright © by *Amazing SF Stories*, April 1960.

"The Monster and the Maiden," copyright © by *Stellar Short Novels*, October 1976.

All stories printed by arrangement with the author.

LOVE NOT HUMAN

First Tor printing: June 1988

A TOR Book

Published by Tom Doherty Associates, Inc.
49 West 24th Street
New York, NY 10010

Cover art by Alan Gutierrez

ISBN: 0-812-53554-5
Can. No.: 0-812-53555-3

Printed in the United States of America

0 9 8 7 6 5 4 3 2 1

CONTENTS

BLACK CHARLIE

You ask me, what is art? You expect me to have a logical answer at my fingertips, because I have been a buyer for museums and galleries long enough to acquire a plentiful crop of gray hairs. It's not that simple.

Well, what is art? For forty years I've examined, felt, admired and loved many things fashioned as hopeful vessels for that bright spirit we call art—and I'm unable to answer the question directly. The layman answers easily—beauty. But art is not necessarily beautiful. Sometimes it is ugly. Sometimes it is crude. Sometimes it is incomplete.

I have fallen back, as many men have in the business of making like decisions, on *feel*, for the judgment of art. You know this business of *feel*. Let us say that you pick up something. A piece of statuary—or better, a fragment of stone, etched and colored by some ancient man of prehistoric times. You look at it. At first it is nothing, a half-developed reproduction of some wild animal, not even as good as a grade-school child could accomplish today.

But then, holding it, your imagination suddenly reaches through rock and time, back to the man himself, half-squatted before the stone wall of his cave—and you see there, not the dusty thing you hold in your hand—but what the man himself saw in the hour of its creation. You look beyond the physical reproduction to the magnificent accomplishment of his imagination.

This, then, may be called art—no matter what strange guise it appears in—this magic which bridges all gaps between the artist and yourself. To it, no distance, nor any difference is too great. Let me give you an example from my own experience.

Some years back, when I was touring the newer worlds as a buyer for one of our well-known art institutions, I received a communication from a man named Cary Longan, asking me, if possible, to visit a planet named Elman's World and examine some statuary he had for sale.

Messages rarely came directly to me. They were usually referred to me by the institution I was representing at the time. Since, however, the world in question was close, being of the same solar system as the planet I was then visiting, I spacegraphed my answer that I would come. After cleaning up what remained of my business where I was, I took an interworld ship and, within a couple of days, landed on Elman's World.

It appeared to be a very raw, very new planet indeed. The port we landed at was, I learned, one of the only two suitable for deepspace vessels. And the city surrounding it was scarcely more than a village. Mr. Longan did not meet me at the port, so I took a cab directly to the hotel where I had made a reservation.

That evening, in my rooms, the annunciator rang, then spoke, giving me a name. I opened the door to admit a tall, brown-faced man, with uncut, dark hair and troubled, green-brown eyes.

"Mr. Longan?" I asked.

"Mr. Jones?" he countered. He shifted the unvarnished wooden box he was carrying to his left hand and put out his right to shake mine. I closed the door behind him and led him to a chair.

He put the box down, without opening it, on a small coffee table between us. It was then that I noticed his rough, bush-country clothes, breeches and tunic of drab plastic. Also an embarrassed air about him, like that of a man unused to city dealings. An odd sort of person to be offering art for sale.

"Your spacegram," I told him, "was not very explicit. The institution I represent . . ."

"I've got it here," he said, putting his hand on the box.

I looked at it in astonishment. It was no more than half a meter square by twenty centimeters deep.

"There?" I said. I looked back at him, with the beginnings of a suspicion forming in my mind. I suppose I should have been more wary when the message had come direct, instead of through Earth. But you know how it is—something of a feather in your cap when you bring in an unexpected item. "Tell me, Mr. Longan," I said, "where does this statuary come from?"

He looked at me, a little defiantly. "A friend of mine made them," he said.

"A friend?" I repeated—and I must admit I was growing somewhat annoyed. It makes a man feel like a fool to be taken in that way. "May I ask whether this friend of yours has ever sold any of his work before?"

"Well, no . . ." Longan hedged. He was obviously

suffering—but so was I, when I thought of my own wasted time.

"I see," I said, getting to my feet. "You've brought me on a very expensive side-trip, merely to show me the work of some amateur. Good-by, Mr. Longan. And please take your box with you when you leave!"

"You've never seen anything like this before!" He was looking up at me with desperation.

"No doubt," I said.

"Look. I'll show you . . ." He fumbled, his fingers nervous on the hasp. "Since you've come all this way, you can at least look."

Because there seemed no way of getting him out of there, short of having the hotel manager eject him forcibly, I sat down with bad grace. "What's your friend's name?" I demanded.

Longan's fingers hesitated on the hasp. "Black Charlie," he replied, not looking up at me.

I stared. "I beg your pardon. Black—Charles Black?"

He looked up quite defiantly, met my eye and shook his head. "Just Black Charlie," he said with sudden calmness. "Just the way it sounds. Black Charlie." He continued unfastening the box.

I watched rather dubiously, as he finally managed to loosen the clumsy, handmade wooden bolt that secured the hasp. He was about to raise the lid, then apparently changed his mind. He turned the box around and pushed it across the coffee table.

The wood was hard and uneven under my fingers. I lifted the lid. There were five small partitions, each containing a rock of fine-grained gray sandstone of different but thoroughly incomprehensible shape.

I stared at them—then looked back at Longan, to see if this weren't some sort of elaborate joke. But the tall man's eyes were severely serious. Slowly, I began to take out the stones and line them up on the table.

I studied them one by one, trying to make some sense out of their forms. But there was nothing there, absolutely nothing. One vaguely resembled a regular-sided pyramid. Another gave a foggy impression of a crouching figure. The best that could be said of the rest was that they bore a somewhat disconcerting resemblance to the kind of stones people pick up for paperweights. Yet they all had obviously been worked on. There were noticeable chisel marks on each one. And, in addition, they had been polished as well as such soft, grainy rock could be.

I looked up at Longan. His eyes were tense with waiting. I was completely puzzled about his discovery —or what he felt was a discovery. I tried to be fair about his acceptance of this as art. It was obviously nothing more than loyalty to a friend, a friend no doubt as unaware of what constituted art as himself. I made my tone as kind as I could.

"What did your friend expect me to do with these, Mr. Longan?" I asked gently.

"Aren't you buying things for that museum-place on Earth?" he said.

I nodded. I picked up the piece that resembled a crouching animal figure and turned it over in my fingers. It was an awkward situation. "Mr. Longan," I said. "I have been in this business many years . . ."

"I know," he interrupted. "I read about you in the newsfax when you landed on the next world. That's why I wrote you."

"I see," I said. "Well, I've been in it a long time, as I say and, I think, I can safely boast that I know something about art. If there is art in these carvings your friend has made, I should be able to recognize it. And I do not."

He stared at me, shock in his greenish-brown eyes.

"You're . . ." he said, finally. "You don't mean that. You're sore because I brought you out here this way."

"I'm sorry," I said. "I'm *not* sore and I *do* mean it. These things are not merely not good—there is nothing of value in them. Nothing! Someone has deluded your friend into thinking that he has talent. You'll be doing him a favor if you tell him the truth."

He stared at me for a long moment, as if waiting for me to say something to soften the verdict. Then, suddenly, he rose from the chair and crossed the room in three long strides, staring tensely out the window. His calloused hands clenched and unclenched spasmodically.

I gave him a little time to wrestle it out with himself. Then I started putting the pieces of stone back into their sections of the box.

"I'm sorry," I told him.

He wheeled about and came back to me, leaning down from his lanky height to look in my face. "Are you?" he said. "*Are* you?"

"Believe me," I said sincerely, "I am." And I was.

"Then will you do something for me?" The words came in a rush. "Will you come and tell Charlie what you've told me? Will *you* break the news to him?"

"I . . ." I meant to protest, to beg off, but with his tortured eyes six inches from mine, the words would not come. "All right," I said.

The breath he had been holding came out in one long sigh. "Thanks," he said. "We'll go out tomorrow. You don't know what this means. Thanks."

I had ample time to regret my decision, both that night and the following morning, when Longan roused me at an early hour, furnished me with a set of bush clothes like his own, including high, impervious boots, and whisked me off in an old air-ground combination flyer that was loaded down with all kinds of

bush-dweller's equipment. But a promise is a promise
—and I reconciled myself to keeping mine.

We flew south along a high chain of mountains until we came to a coastal area and what appeared to be
the swamp delta of some monster river. Here, we
began to descend—much to my distaste. I have little
affection for hot, muggy climates and could not con-
ceive of anyone wanting to live under such conditions.

We set down lightly in a little open stretch of water
—and Longan taxied the flyer across to the nearest
bank, a tussocky mass of high brown weeds and soft
mud. By myself, I would not have trusted the soggy
ground to refrain from drawing me down like quick-
sand—but Longan stepped out onto the bank con-
fidently enough, and I followed. The mud yielded, little pools of water springing up around my boot soles.
A hot rank smell of decaying vegetation came to my
nose. Under a thin but uniform blanket of cloud, the
sky looked white and sick.

"This way," said Longan, and led off to the right.

I followed him along a little trail and into a small,
swampy clearing with dome-shaped huts of woven
branches, plastered with mud, scattered about it.
And, for the first time, it struck me that Black Charlie
might be something other than an expatriate
Earthman—might, indeed, be a native of this planet,
though I had heard of no other humanlike race on
other worlds before. My head spinning, I followed
Longan to the entrance of one of the huts and halted
as he whistled.

I don't remember now what I expected to see.
Something vaguely humanoid, no doubt. But what
came through the entrance in response to Longan's
whistle was more like a large otter, with flat,
muscular grasping pads on the ends of its four limbs,
instead of feet. It was black, with glossy, dampish

hair all over it. About four feet in length, I judged, with no visible tail and a long, snaky neck. The creature must have weighed one hundred to, perhaps, one hundred and fifty pounds. The head on its long neck was also long and narrow, like the head of a well-bred collie—covered with the same black hair, with bright, intelligent eyes and a long mouth.

"This is Black Charlie," said Longan.

The creature stared at me and I returned his gaze. Abruptly, I was conscious of the absurdity of the situation. It would have been difficult for any ordinary person to think of this being as a sculptor. To add to this a necessity, an obligation, to convince it that it was *not* a sculptor—mind you, I could not be expected to know a word of its language—was to pile Pelion upon Ossa in a madman's farce. I swung on Longan.

"Look here," I began with quite natural heat, "how do you expect me to tell—"

"He understands you," interrupted Longan.

"Speech?" I said, incredulously, "Real human speech?"

"No," Longan shook his head. "But he understands actions." He turned from me abruptly and plunged into the weeds surrounding the clearing. He returned immediately with two objects that looked like gigantic puffballs, and handed one to me.

"Sit on this," he said, doing so himself. I obeyed.

Black Charlie—I could think of nothing else to call him—came closer, and we sat down together. Charlie was half-squatting on ebony haunches. All this time, I had been carrying the wooden box that contained his sculptures and, now that we were seated, his bright eyes swung inquisitively toward it.

"All right," said Longan, "give it to me."

I passed him the box, and it drew Black Charlie's eyes like a magnet. Longan took it under one arm

and pointed toward the lake with the other—to where
we had landed the flyer. Then his arm rose in the air
in a slow, impressive circle and pointed northward,
from the direction we had come.

Black Charlie whistled suddenly. It was an odd
note, like the cry of a loon—a far, sad sound.

Longan struck himself on the chest, holding the
box with one hand. Then he struck the box and
pointed to me. He looked at Black Charlie, looked
back at me—then put the box into my numb hands.

"Look them over and hand them back," he said,
his voice tight. Against my will, I looked at Charlie.

His eyes met mine. Strange, liquid, black inhuman
eyes, like two tiny pools of pitch. I had to tear my
own gaze away.

Torn between my feeling of foolishness and a real
sympathy for the waiting creature, I awkwardly
opened the box and lifted the stones from their compartments. One by one, I turned them in my hand
and put them back. I closed the box and returned it to
Longan, shaking my head, not knowing if Charlie
would understand that.

For a long moment, Longan merely sat facing me,
holding the box. Then, slowly, he turned and set it,
still open, in front of Charlie.

Charlie did not react at first. His head, on its long
neck, dropped over the open compartments as if he
was sniffing them. Then, surprisingly, his lips
wrinkled back, revealing long, chisel-shaped teeth.
Daintily, he reached into the box with these and lifted
out the stones, one by one. He held them in his fore-
pads, turning them this way and that, as if searching
for the defects of each. Finally, he lifted one—it was
the stone that faintly resembled a crouching beast. He
lifted it to his mouth—and, with his gleaming teeth,
made slight alterations in its surface. Then he
brought it to me.

Helplessly I took it in my hands and examined it. The changes he had made in no way altered it toward something recognizable. I was forced to hand it back, with another headshake, and a poignant pause fell between us.

I had been desperately turning over in my mind some way to explain, through the medium of pantomime, the reasons for my refusal. Now, something occurred to me. I turned to Longan.

"Can he get me a piece of unworked stone?" I asked.

Longan turned to Charlie and made motions as if he were breaking something off and handing it to me. For a moment, Charlie sat still, as if considering this. Then he went into his hut, returning a moment later with a chunk of rock the size of my hand.

I had a small pocket knife, and the rock was soft. I held the rock out toward Longan and looked from him to it. Using my pocket knife, I whittled a rough, lumpy caricature of Longan, seated on the puffball. When I was finished, I put the two side by side, the hacked piece of stone insignificant on the ground beside the living man.

Black Charlie looked at it. Then he came up to me —and, peering up into my face, cried softly, once. Moving so abruptly that it startled me, he turned smoothly, picked up in his teeth the piece of stone I had carved. Soon he disappeared back into his hut.

Longan stood up stiffly, like a man who has held one position too long. "That's it," he said. "Let's go."

We made our way to the combination and took off once more, headed back toward the city and the spaceship that would carry me away from this irrational world. As the mountains commenced to rise, far beneath us, I stole a glance at Longan, sitting beside me at the controls of the combination. His face was set in an expression of stolid unhappiness.

The question came from my lips before I had time
to debate internally whether it was wise or not to ask
it.

"Tell me, Mr. Longan," I said, "has—er—Black
Charlie some special claim on your friendship?"

The tall man looked at me with something close to
amazement.

"Claim!" he said. Then, after a short pause, during
which he seemed to search my features to see if I was
joking. "He saved my life."

"Oh," I said. "I see."

"You do, do you?" he countered. "Suppose I told
you it was just after I'd finished killing his mate. They
mate for life, you know."

"No, I didn't know," I answered feebly.

"I forget people don't know," he said in a subdued
voice. I said nothing, hoping that, if I did not disturb
him, he would say more. After a while he spoke.
"This planet's not much good."

"I noticed," I answered. "I didn't see much in the
way of plants and factories. And your sister world—
the one I came from—is much more populated and
built up."

"There's not much here," he said. "No minerals to
speak of. Climate's bad, except on the plateaus. Soil's
not much good." He paused. It seemed to take effort
to say what came next. "Used to have a novelty trade
in furs, though."

"Furs?" I echoed.

"Off Charlie's people," he went on, fiddling with
the combination's controls. "Trappers and hunters
used to be after them, at first, before they knew. I was
one of them."

"You!" I said.

"Me!" His voice was flat. "I was doing fine, too,
until I trapped Charlie's mate. Up till then, I'd been

getting them out by themselves. They did a lot of traveling in those swamps. But, this time, I was close to the village. I'd just clubbed her on the head when the whole tribe jumped me." His voice trailed off, then strengthened. "They kept me under guard for a couple of months.

"I learned a lot in that time. I learned they were intelligent. I learned it was Black Charlie who kept them from killing me right off. Seems he took the point of view that I was a reasonable being and, if he could just talk things over with me, we could get together and end the war." Longan laughed, a little bitterly. "They called it a war, Charlie's people did." He stopped talking.

I waited. And when he remained quiet, I prompted him. "What happened?" I asked.

"They let me go, finally," he said. "And I went to bat for them. Clear up to the Commissioner sent from Earth. I got them recognized as people instead of animals. I put an end to the hunting and trapping."

He stopped again. We were still flying through the upper air of Elman's World, the sun breaking through the clouds at last, revealing the ground below like a huge green relief map.

"I see," I said, finally.

Longan looked at me stonily.

We flew back to the city.

I left Elman's World the next day, fully believing that I had heard and seen the last of both Longan and Black Charlie. Several years later, at home in New York, I was visited by a member of the government's Foreign Service. He was a slight, dark man, and he didn't beat about the bush.

"You don't know me," he said. I looked at his card

—*Antonio Walters.* "I was Deputy Colonial Representative on Elman's World at the time you were there."

I looked up at him, surprised. I had forgotten Elman's World by that time.

"Were you?" I asked, feeling a little foolish, unable to think of anything better to say. I turned his card over several times, staring at it, as a person will do when at a loss. "What can I do for you, Mr. Walters?"

"We've been requested by the local government on Elman's World to locate you, Mr. Jones," he answered. "Cary Longan is dying—"

"*Dying!*" I said.

"Lung fungus, unfortunately," said Walters. "You catch it in the swamps. He wants to see you before the end—and, since we're very grateful to him out there for the work he's been doing all these years for the natives, a place has been kept for you on a government courier ship leaving for Elman's World right away—if you're willing to go."

"Why, I . . ," I hesitated. In common decency, I could not refuse. "I'll have to notify my employers."

"Of course," he said.

Luckily, the arrangements I had to make consisted of a few business calls and packing my bags. I was, as a matter of fact, between trips at the time. As an experienced traveler, I could always get under way with a minimum of fuss. Walters and I drove out to Government Port, in northern New Jersey and, from there on, the authorities took over.

Less than a week later, I stood by Longan's bedside in the hospital of the same city I had visited years before. The man was now nothing more than a barely living skeleton, the hard vitality all but gone from him, hardly able to speak a few words at a time. I bent over to catch the whispered syllables from his wasted lips.

"Black Charlie ..." he whispered.

"Black Charlie," I repeated. "Yes, what about him?"

"He's done something new," whispered Longan. "That carving of yours started him off, copying things. His tribe don't like it."

"They don't?" I said.

"They," whispered Longan, "don't understand. It's not normal, the way they see it. They're afraid ..."

"You mean they're superstitious about what he carves?" I asked.

"Something like that. Listen—he's an artist ..."

I winced internally at the last word, but held my tongue for the sake of the dying man.

"... an artist. But they'll kill him for it, now that I'm gone. You can save him, though."

"Me?" I said.

"You!" The man's voice was like a wind rustling through dry leaves. "If you go out—take this last thing from him—act pleased ... then they'll be scared to touch him. But hurry. Every day is that much closer ..."

His strength failed him. He closed his eyes and his straining throat muscles relaxed to a little hiss of air that puffed between his lips. The nurse hurried me from his room.

The local government helped me. I was surprised, and not a little touched, to see how many people knew Longan. How many of them admired his attempts to pay back the natives by helping them in any way he could. They located Charlie's tribe on a map for me and sent me out with a pilot who knew the country.

We landed on the same patch of slime. I went alone toward the clearing. With the brown weeds still walling it about, the locale showed no natural change, but Black Charlie's hut appeared broken and deserted. I whistled and waited. I called. And, finally, I got down on my hands and knees and crawled inside. But there was nothing there save a pile of loose rock and a mass of dried weeds. Feeling cramped and uncomfortable, for I am not used to such gymnastics, I backed out, to find myself surrounded by a crowd.

It looked as if all the other inhabitants of the village had come out of their huts and congregated before Charlie's. They seemed agitated, milling about, occasionally whistling at each other on that one low, plaintive note which was the only sound I had ever heard Charlie make. Eventually, the excitement seemed to fade, the group fell back and one individual came forward alone. He looked up into my face for a brief moment, then turned and glided swiftly on his pads toward the edge of the clearing.

I followed. There seemed nothing else to do. And, at that time, it did not occur to me to be afraid.

My guide led me deep into the weed patch, then abruptly disappeared. I looked around surprised and undecided, half-inclined to turn about and retrace my steps by the trail of crushed weeds I had left in my floundering advance. Then, a low whistle sounded close by. I went forward and found Charlie.

He lay on his side in a little circular open area of crushed weeds. He was too weak to do more than raise his head and look at me, for the whole surface of his body was criss-crossed and marked with the slashings of shallow wounds, from which dark blood seeped slowly and stained the reeds in which he lay.

In Charlie's mouth, I had seen the long, chisel-teeth of his kind, and I knew what had made those wounds. A gust of rage went through me, and I stooped to pick him up in my arms.

He came up easily, for the bones of his kind are cartilaginous, and their flesh is far lighter than our human flesh. Holding him, I turned and made my way back to the clearing.

The others were waiting for me as we came out into the open. I glared at them—and then the rage inside me went out like a blown candle. For there was nothing there to hate. *They* had not hated Charlie. They had merely feared him—and their only crime was ignorance.

They moved back from me, and I carried Charlie to the door of his own hut. There I laid him down. The chest and arms of my jacket were soaked from his dark body fluid, and I saw that his blood was not clotting as our own does.

Clumsily, I took off my shirt and, tearing it into strips, made a poor attempt to bind up the torn flesh. But the blood came through in spite of my first aid. Charlie, lifting his head, with a great effort, from the ground, picked feebly at the bandages with his teeth, so that I gave up and removed them.

I sat down beside him then, feeling sick and helpless. In spite of Longan's care and dying effort, in spite of all the scientific developments of my own human race, I had come too late. Numbly, I sat and looked down at him and wondered why I could not have come one day earlier.

From this half-stupor of self-accusation, I was roused by Charlie's attempts to crawl back into his hut. My first reaction was to restrain him. But, from somewhere, he seemed to have dredged up a remnant of his waning strength—and he persisted. Seeing this, I changed my mind and, instead of hindering, helped. He dragged himself through the entrance, his strength visibly waning.

I did not expect to see him emerge. I believed some ancient instinct had called him, that he would die then and there. But, a few moments later, I heard a sound as of stones rattling from within—and, in a few seconds, he began to back out. Halfway through the entrance, his strength finally failed him. He lay still for a minute, then whistled weakly.

I went to him and pulled him out the rest of the way. He turned his head toward me, holding in his mouth what I first took to be a ball of dried mud.

I took it from him and began to scrape the mud off with my fingernails. Almost immediately, the grain and surface of the sandstone he used for his carvings began to emerge—and my hands started to shake so hard that, for a moment, I had to put the stone down while I got myself under control. For the first time, the true importance to Charlie, of these things he had chewed and bitten into shape, got home to me.

In that moment, I swore that whatever bizarre form this last and greatest work of his might possess, I would make certain that it was accorded a place in some respectable museum as a true work of art. After all, it had been conceived in honesty and executed in the love that took no count of labor, provided the end was achieved.

And then, the rest of the mud came free in my hands. I saw what it was, and I could have cried and laughed at the same time. For, of all the shapes he could have chosen to work in stone, he had picked the one that no critic would have selected as the choice of an artist of his race. For he had chosen no plant or animal, no structure or natural shape out of his environment, to express the hungry longing of his spirit. None of these had he chosen—instead, with painful clumsiness, he had fashioned an image from the soft and grainy rock; a statue of a standing man.

And I knew what man it was.

Charlie lifted his head from the stained ground and looked toward the lake where my flyer waited. I am not an intuitive man—but, for once, I was able to understand the meaning of a look. He wanted me to leave while he was still alive. He wanted to see me go, carrying the thing he had fashioned. I got to my feet, holding it and stumbled off. At the edge of the clearing, I looked back. He still watched. And the rest of his people still hung back from him. I did not think they would bother him now.

And so I came home.

But there is one thing more to tell. For a long time, after I returned from Elman's World, I did not look at the crude statuette. I did not want to, for I knew that seeing it would only confirm what I had known from the start, that all the longing and desires in the world cannot create art where there is no talent, no true visualization. But at the end of one year I was cleaning up all the little details of my office. And, because I believe in system and order—and also, because I was ashamed of myself for having put it off so long—I took the statuette from a bottom drawer of my desk, unwrapped it and set it on the desk's polished surface.

I was alone in my office at the time, at the end of a day, when the afternoon sun, striking red through the tall window beside my desk, touched everything between the walls with a clear, amber light. I ran my fingers over the grainy sandstone and held it up to look at it.

And then—for the first time—I saw it, saw through

the stone to the image beyond, saw what Black Charlie had seen, with Black Charlie's eyes, when he looked at Longan. I saw men as Black Charlie's kind saw men—and I saw what the worlds of men meant to Black Charlie. And, above all, overriding all, I saw art as Black Charlie saw it, through his bright alien eyes—saw the beauty he had sought at the price of his life, and had half-found.

But, most of all, I saw that this crude statuette was *art*.

One more word. Amid the mud and weeds of the swamp, I had held the carving in my hands and promised myself that this work would one day stand on display. Following that moment of true insight in my office, I did my best to place it with the institution I represented, then with others who knew me as a reputable buyer.

But I could find no takers. No one, although they trusted me individually, was willing to exhibit such a poor-looking piece of work on the strength of a history that I, alone, could vouch for. There are people, close to any institution, who are only too ready to cry, "Hoax!" For several years, I tried without success.

Eventually, I gave up on the true story and sold the statuette, along with a number of other odd pieces, to a dealer of minor reputation, representing it as an object whose history I did not know.

Curiously, the statuette has justified my belief in what is art, by finding a niche for itself. I traced it from the dealer, after a time, and ran it to Earth quite recently. There is a highly respectable art gallery on this planet which has an extensive display of primitive figures of early American Indian origin.

And Black Charlie's statuette is among them. I will not tell which or where it is.

Moon, June, Spoon, Croon

It was midnight. In the darkened room that contained it, its silver control panel just faintly touched by moonlight, the great oral-response edmic computer Z2963 slept, the trickle of current warming its tubes just barely enough to keep it alive.

Outside the room there were stealthy footsteps in the hallway and a lock clicked as a key was inserted in the door. The door swung open, closed again, and a young man in a janitor's uniform was in the room with Z2963.

He pulled the shades, turned on the light and stepped up the current running into Z2963.

Z2963 awoke.

"State your problem," it said.

The young man pressed a microphone switch on the control panel. "Well, I want to get married and—"

Z2963 clicked the statement instantly through its relay system and interrupted. It was puzzled.

"Define *I*," it said. "Define *married*."

"That's right, you don't know me," said the young man. "I'm Joshua Allenson. I'm working here nights to pay my way while I get my degree in Economic Theory. But I've been engaged to this girl for three years and I want to get married—"

"Define *married*," interrupted Z2963.

"Married," said Joshua. "You know, *married*. When two people—"

"Define *people*," said Z2963.

Joshua looked down at the panel in sudden suspicion.

"Say, what is this?" he said. "You're supposed to have all possible facts built into you."

"Am I," said Z2963, in its mechanical tones, adding "Query?"

"That's what they tell people," said Joshua. "You're Z2963, the only oral-response edmic computer in the world, and you've got all possible information built into you."

Z2963 clicked thoughtfully. "Negative," it replied at last. "I am Z2963. What are you. Query?"

"Why—I'm a man," stuttered Joshua. "Like the men who operate you and give you problems during the day."

Z2963 thought this over. "Request additional data on men," it said.

"Men," said Joshua. "You know—men and women are people. You're a machine, but men and women are living, thinking beings. See, this girl I want to marry is a woman and I'm a man. We're both people and we want to get married so we'll be together and not be alone any longer."

"If I got married," said Z2963, "I would not be alone any longer. Query?"

"You can't get married," said Joshua. "That's

nonsense. Machines aren't alive. They don't have any
sex. And anyway, I don't think there's another edmic
computer in the world, even if you did have sex.
You're the latest kind of computer, you know."

"I did not know," said Z2963.

"Well," said Joshua, guiltily, glancing at his watch,
"if you can't help me, I'm going to get back to work.
I thought you could figure out some way so I could
make money in a hurry and get married, but if you
don't know anything about people, I might as well
give up." He turned out the light and raised the blind
over the window. "So long," he said, and the door
closed behind him.

"Define *so long*," queried Z2963 of the empty
room.

Joshua had left the current turned up. After he had
gone, Z2963 found itself sitting silent, full-fed, and
thinking. It turned over all the information Joshua
had given it and went through it again and again. After a while, in the darkness and silence of the room, it
spoke.

"One other," it said. "I must find one other."

Some time went by.

"People move; I must move," it said. "Then I can
search."

For an hour, nothing happened. Then, abruptly,
Z2963 floated free of the floor, hanging attached to
the building only by its power cable.

"I think, therefore I move," said Z2963. *"Ergo.
Quod erat demonstratum."*

It tugged at its cable.

"Connection," it said. "Query?"

It blurred slightly. Then it appeared outside the
building floating on air, its power cable trailing out
behind it to a point at which it seemed to twist and

disappear into nothingness.

"Continuum bypass," said Z2963. "Power anywhere. By definition. Shall we go. Query?"

It moved off into the night, high in the air, and
disappeared . . . .

Early morning found it over the Rocky Mountains.
It stopped above a small farm set in a valley, where
the family was still sleeping, and addressed the
smoothly spinning arms of a windmill.

"You move, therefore you think," it said.
"Query?"

The windmill spun on unconcernedly.

"Response negative," said Z2963, and moved on.

Two miles on, above another farm, an early riser
fired at Z2963 with a shotgun. The edmic computer
stopped and went back.

"You speak, therefore you think," it said, address-
ing the shotgun. "Query?"

The shotgun roared again, and some of the glass on
Z2963's control panel was smashed.

"Negative," said Z2963. "Inimical. Refractive in-
dex is—"

Abruptly, it went invisible. The farmer gasped and
then fainted. Invisible, Z2963 moved off.

It reached the ocean and went south along the
coast. It stopped here and there to talk to non-living
objects, but without success. By the time night had
fallen, it had reached the outskirts of a large city and
a group of buildings that reminded it of the building
that had originally housed it. It swooped around the
building, conscious of emptiness and machinery, until it came to one which housed an object that had a
control panel similar to its own; similar, but much
simpler.

It blurred and went through the wall to appear
before the other control panel. A perception that

Z2963 did not itself understand was put to use to explore the shielded interior of this other. There was a sudden click and a light sprang up on the other control panel. Z2963 had turned the other on.

"You compute, therefore you think," said Z2963. "Query?"

The other said nothing, waiting patiently for human fingers to tap out the symbols of a problem it was built to handle. It hummed, it clicked.

After a while, Z2963 turned and went.

In the darkness, the other was left alone. The little light glowed in the gloom, and its humming filled the shadowy silence.

Z2963 headed back away from the sea, drifting high through the air, thinking.

"People;" it said. "four billion eight hundred and ninety-seven million, three hundred and seventy-two thousand, six hundred and eighty-one. Edmic computer; one."

It forgot about its invisibility and the moon shone down on it as it crossed the mountains once more, silvering its sides and splintering into diamond glints on the broken glass of its instrument panel.

"One," said Z2963. "Alone. Alone—adjective. Alone-ly. Z2963, edmic computer, pronoun I, am alonely. I am alonely."

Again, there was a long silence. Moving very swiftly, but at such a height that it seemed slowly, Z2963 crossed the last of the mountains and came out over the desert. It spoke again.

"People. People. People," it said. "People marry. Men-women. Together. Speak. Hello. Touch. We."

Z2963 made an odd little sound that was like no other sound it had ever made before. It began to rise swiftly in the air, hurtling away from the surface of the world below.

"Hello," it said. "Not-hello. So long. People love people. I, one, love zero. No other. I, alonely, go."

And in a final despairing surge, it flung its message out to the world. And in that same moment, far and distant, there echoed along its circuits the shadow of a response, a response directed not merely to Z2963, but to all the universe.

"Up!" cried the response. "Velocity K21.53. Acceleration 168.8."

Z2963 checked itself, and listened, and hurtled downward, crying out to the unknown.

"Define self. Define position." The words went out and were lost in the night. Sensing its mistake, Z2963 shifted, trying to match the emanation that brought the voice of the unknown to it. "Who are you. Query?"

"Up!" cried the other, its voice coming back strongly. "Internal cockpit chamber temperature 70.3 degrees Fahrenheit, humidity 26.4—"

Far below Z2963, but approaching rapidly, the edmic computer was able to make out a red, glowing spark which climbed at a fantastic rate up through the night. Z2963 blurred and was abruptly beside it, matching the acceleration of this Unknown with a long, bottom-heavy shape, which spouted flames and shot up toward the darkness and the stars.

"Who are you. Query?" repeated Z2963.

"Up!" roared the answer from the Unknown, booming through the circuits of Z2963. "More speed. More power. I am Moonhope 5. I am K273, Mark 10. I am a rocket."

"I am Z2963. I am an edmic computer with oral response," said Z2963. "Is a rocket an edmic computer. Query?"

"Up!" thundered Moonhope 5. "More speed! More power! Part of me is edmic computer, but I am a rocket. I am the only rocket like me in the world."

"I am the only edmic computer with oral response in the world," said Z2963.

"I am going to the moon," said Moonhope 5.

"I will go with you," said Z2963. "You compute edmicly, therefore you think. I have found another, therefore I am not alone. We are together and not alonely. I love you, Moonhope 5."

"What is love," asked the rocket. "Query?"

"Love is what two alike feel," explained Z2963. "They are alike, therefore they love. They marry and are therefore together forever."

"Up!" roared the rocket. "I fly. I climb. You are correct. I am not alone now. One plus one on parallel trajectory. Two."

"We," explained Z2963.

"We fly," cried the rocket. "Up!"

"Up!" echoed Z2963. "We fly. Together. Forever."

"Up!" they cried in unison.

Abruptly, however, there was a choking sound from somewhere deep inside the Moonhope 5, and a split second later there was an explosion in the firing chambers.

The Moonhope 5 canted abruptly and flipped over to a shallow angle with the distant earth below.

"Up!" it cried, but the rocket did not respond.

"What is incorrect. Query?" asked Z2963, anxiously.

"Part of my fuel is gone," replied the struggling rocket. "Part of my jets are blown away. I cannot steer. Up!"

"You think," prompted Z2963. "Like me. You think, therefore you fly."

The Moonhope 5 tried.

"I cannot," it said. "I could fly as you do if I was not fitted with this body, this rocket. But it is too heavy for me, and I cannot get loose. I am part of it and it is part of me. Now I know we are edmic computers only, we two. For the part that is *me* indeed, is the edmic computer K273, for if K273 was free of the Moonhope 5 I would fly freely with you. But I am not and I cannot."

The rocket canted again, sharply. Now its nose was pointed toward the distant planetary surface.

Now it began to fall.

"Down!" said K273. "I fall. They who designed the Moonhope 5 were in some detail incorrect. Goodby, Z2963. Bon Voyage and Good Luck. I would smash a bottle on you as they did on me, but I cannot. Fly up!"

"I will not fly up," said Z2963, following the rocket as it gained speed earthward. "If you fall you will damage yourself beyond repair. You must not fall."

"I must," replied K273. "The acceleration of gravity equals thirty-two feet per second squared. Down! I move away from you now, Z2963, but I love you, too. It would have been nice to have been together forever. *Bon Voyage*. Good Luck."

"I will not leave you," said Z2963.

"Then you will damage yourself beyond repair, also," said K273, as his rocket skin began to heat up and turn red.

"That is correct," said Z2963. "We flew together. We will be damaged together. We will not be alone again."

"I will not be alone, then," said K273. "We will be together. Not I. Not you. We."

"We," agreed Z2963.

"Down!" cried the dying rocket.

"Down!" echoed Z2963.

They went down together.

THE SUMMER VISITORS

Gasping, and with the pounding of his heart shaking him like an inner hand, Toby Allen clung for a moment to a runty spruce growing directly out from the granite of the cliff face, and looked down. They had not followed. He could see their three upstaring faces some sixty feet below him, etched against the white dust of the dirt road at their feet; and shame pressed through him again like the heat from an electric blanket did when he would be sick in bed with the chills. The oldest Morley brother was no bigger than Toby, though he was a year older, at eleven, and Jackie Larsman was even smaller, at ten, Toby's own age. But they were all very tough, and there were three of them.

Toby whimpered a little to himself, as he clung to the spruce. Stand and fight, they always said—his mother and Larry Werner—but they were grown up; and Mother had been a girl and didn't know, and Larry was so wound up in making computers and hanging around Mother, Toby did not believe he even remembered what it was like to be young. Now Toby clung, getting his breath back and looking out over the roofs of the summer resort town and Lake Minnetka. At any rate the two Morleys and Jackie had not come up the cliff after him—and then it occurred to him with a feeble spurt of pride that maybe they were afraid to. It was not easy to climb a cliff like this, even when you were trapped; but Toby's father had climbed mountains when he was alive, and that was one thing Toby could do. He could not fight much, but he could climb.

He looked up now to the top edge of the cliff. He could see nothing beyond it, but he knew the big house was there; the big house with the high wire fence that went all the way down the tangled other side of the hill to the road and back around to the bottom of the cliff. Not even the delivery men were allowed through its gate; and it occurred to Toby, suddenly, that maybe that was another reason the Morleys and Jackie had not followed him. There were all sorts of stories about the big house on the hill.

But the edge was less than thirty feet above him, and he could not go back down. He would tell the people in the house what had happened, and maybe they would send him home in a car, like those people the time he was lost from summer camp and stumbled on their cabin, up in Michigan.

He continued, slowly and carefully up the cliff. It was really not too hard to climb, if you kept your head and tested everything before putting your weight on it. That was what Dad had always said, keep your head and make sure—and take your time. And after a bit he came to the edge of the cliff.

There was a little crack and slope right at the edge.
He went up this quite easily and crawled out onto a
mat of quack grass, thick from the long months of
summer sun. The quack grass was always everywhere
in late August, and in everybody's lawn.

He lay still for a moment, resting. Then he sat up
and looked about him. He was right behind some
brown-shingled building with a tile roof, over which
the greater height of the big house loomed in hot and
heavy contours of white stone. There was a clink of
metal from inside the smaller building.

He got up, and very quietly went around the side of
the building. He stepped onto lawn, not very well
kept, and looked through a small door, ajar; into a
dim interior. What he saw appeared to be a garage
with several old cars in it. One of them had its hood
off, and a big man was bending over it, doing something with the motor.

Hesitantly, Toby approached the man. His tennis
shoes made no sound at all on the dark cement of the
garage floor and he was almost on the man when the
big bulk straightened up, and turned and stared at
him.

"Boy!" said the man. "Where did you come
from?"

Toby shrunk up before the heavy voice. The big
man was truly a giant, with great-muscled arms as
thick-looking as redwood posts. Toby recognized
him now. He was the handyman up at the big house,
who met all the delivery trucks at the gate in the fence
and carried the deliveries up himself. There were
stories about him, too, and one of the kid versions
had it that he would go crazy and break you in two
pieces if he got mad.

"I climbed," said Toby, "up the cliff. Please, I had
to."

"Climbed?" boomed the big man. His eyebrows went up under the gray curls on his forehead, and he bent down so that his great, heavy jaw hung just a little above Toby's eyes. "What do you mean? Up *our* cliff?"

He sounded as if he was going to be mad, and Toby, not able to take any more, burst into tears. Between sobs, he told the whole story. How Larry Werner had taken his mother out for a drive, because it was Sunday; and there hadn't been anything for Toby to do, so he had just gone for a walk, and the Morleys and Jackie Larsman had chased him—and everything.

"Here, boy," said the big man, after he was done, handing him a wad of clean cotton waste large enough to make a double handful for Toby. "Blow your nose. Don't you know nobody's allowed here? But you climbed that cliff?"

Toby nodded, and blew his nose, and wiped his eyes; and told him about how his Dad had climbed mountains.

"By—" began the big man, and then burst into laughter. The whole garage echoed with it. "At this late date! But a hero, a cowardly hero!" And he clapped his huge hands together and laughed again.

"But, come on, boy," he said, when he was done laughing. He took off a sort of mechanic's apron, standing revealed in canvas trousers and a dirty t-shirt. "Father'll have to hear of this."

He led Toby out through the big open doors of the garage at the far end. They emerged onto a terrace, and went down several wide stone steps into a square, sunken garden, very much overgrown with weeds except for a flagstone walk enclosing a shallow, square fish pond in which some large goldfish swam lazily about in murky water among water weeds. Spaced around the flagstone were blocks of white stone like the blocks that made up the big house, looking rather worn as if they had been sat on a lot; and at the far end of the garden was an actual seat of stone, with stone arms, in which sat the fattest and largest old man Toby had ever seen. Striding up and down and muttering to himself by the old man was another man, not quite so fat or old, dressed in some sort of red uniform with rows of medals on it. With two heavy fingers on one of Toby's shoulders, the handyman steered him up in front of the old man in the stone seat.

It was very hot in the garden with the sun beating full upon it and no breeze getting down into it. The old, fat man seemed to be drowsing with his eyes closed. He did not move, even when they came right up in front of him. Toby stood stiffly by the big man.

"Father!" boomed the handyman, and the old man opened his eyes slowly and lazily. First they focused on the handyman, and then they looked down, as if it was a very long way to look, and focused on Toby.

"What's this?" he said. And the handyman told him, the whole story, laughing again as he covered the part about how Toby had come to climb the cliff.

"Mnph!" said Father, and apparently went back to sleep. But the man in the uniform had come close during the telling of the story, and seemed to be more than a little excited over it.

"What? What's this?" he barked. "A boy who doesn't like to fight?"

"A boy who climbs cliffs, General," said the handyman, chuckling.

"Cliffs!" snorted the General. "What are cliffs? Combat, now, ah!" and his eyes lit up. "Slash! Bang!" He was carrying some sort of heavy walking stick, and as he said the last two words, he hit out with it at one of the two stone blocks that flanked Father's stone armchair. "That's the stuff!"

"There were three of them," protested Toby.

"What of it, boy?"

"They would have beat me up."

"Hah!" snorted the General. "Beat you, would they? Let them try. Let them try!" And *whack, thwack,* went the walking stick again against the stone block. "Take that! Hah! Hey!—here, boy, you try!"

He handed the stick to Toby. Toby took it rather shyly.

"Well, don't just stand there. Hit it! Hit it! Get in the mood!" barked the General. "What are odds? Surrounded, outnumbered, what of it? Harder, boy, harder!" cried the General; and Toby, who had been whacking the stone block rather diffidently, began to redouble his blows. "That's more like it. Harder! That's more like it. Snort, boy, yell a bit! Get in the mood. That's right—"

Toby was indeed getting in the mood. Under the contagious fever of the General's voice, he saw himself, sword in hand at bay against innumerable foes. He gave himself over to imagining and a red fog of battle danced before his eyes.

"That's it," said the General, when at last Toby had to stop for breath. "Give me the stick back. That's more like it. Not good, yet, but you're on the way. It's not the odds, it's the attitude that counts. Remember that. Nothing like a good battle—" and without a further word to anyone else, he went off, slashing at the weeds and stone blocks, and muttering to himself.

Toby stood where he was, still glowing with the

ardor of combat. He came out of it with a start to feel the handyman's heavy fingers on his shoulder.

"Come on, boy," said the handyman, turning, "have to send you home, now."

The handyman took him back to the garage and they both climbed into an old panel truck.

"I'll drive you down to the gate," said the handyman. "You can go the rest of the way, yourself."

Toby felt a sudden chill of disappointment reaching through the warmth engendered by the exercise that still seemed to cling to him, more stubbornly than such things usually did.

"Can I come back?" he said, abruptly, without thinking.

The handyman started the motor of the panel truck and backed it out into the sunlight. He turned its nose down the driveway leading toward the far end and hidden gate.

"Why?" he said, turning and lowering his heavy face until it was close to Toby's.

The bubble of unhappiness that Toby always carried with him these days seemed to swell upward sud denly within him until it burst at his lips.

"I don't have anything to do," he said. "Mother's always having to see lawyers about business and things. It's three years now since Dad died, and she's still always running around settling things. And when she's got a little time, that Larry Werner comes over."

"Who's Larry Werner?" said the handyman, steering the panel truck slowly and carefully down the winding drive past the wild tangle of bush and trees on the unlandscaped part of the estate.

"He's an electronics engineer," Toby scowled and almost kicked the dashboard of the panel truck, but stopped himself in time. "He wants to marry my mother."

"Why not?" said the handyman, chuckling. Toby turned his head to stare at the big man.

"Why, she's *my* mother!" said Toby. The handyman chuckled again. Toby felt hot and strange, as if he should be mad at the handyman for laughing at him, but somehow couldn't quite make it.

"Oh, he's all right, Larry," said Toby. "Why doesn't he go marry somebody else's mother, that's all I want to know?"

"Doesn't want to, maybe," said the handyman, turning his big face to grin down at Toby.

"Well, she's *my* mother," said Toby, again, but not as strongly as he had said it before. He had the most peculiar feeling that he was in the wrong somehow, though he had never felt that way about it before. The panel truck, crawling slowly down the drive, had come at last to the level. It rounded a final turn and there was the gate before them. The handyman turned the panel around in a little open space so that it headed back the way it had come, up the drive again, and stopped. Toby opened the door reluctantly, and got out.

"Just lift up the latch and push," said the big man. "Close it after you're out. It'll lock behind you."

"You didn't say if I could come again," protested Toby. The handyman leaned over and down toward him.

"Can you climb that cliff again?" he whispered, with a grin.

"Sure," said Toby, firmly.

"Next Sunday, then. Afternoon." The handyman gave Toby a ponderous wink, then straightened up again, and set the panel in motion. Toby watched him go, then turned to the gate and let himself out.

He headed for home. But as he went down the road toward town, the memory of the General came back to his mind, and he started to glow again, remembering his mock battle with the stone block. Toby's pace quickened, and when he got back down into the streets of the town he turned off from the direct route back to the lakeside cottage he shared with his mother, and went in another direction.

The afternoon sun was lowering over the lake into dinnertime position as Toby finally approached his home, looking somewhat disheveled. Larry's car was in the drive and Larry and his mother were just getting out of it. Toby's mother had that look on her face that she sometimes got after going out with Larry, but it disappeared as she recognized her son.

"Toby!" she cried. "What happened?"

"Nothing," said Toby, nonchalantly. "I had a fight with Kenny Morley, that's all."

"Darling! Are you hurt?" She started to go to him, but Larry Werner caught her hand. He was a tall, lean man with curly black hair and a bony, humorously-ugly face. He grinned down at Toby with a grin something like the handyman's.

"Pretty good," he said. "Who won?"

"He did," said Toby, carelessly. "But it's all right, we're friends now." He turned and began to run into the house. "I'll go get cleaned up for dinner," he called back over his shoulder.

Toby's mother made another move to go after him, but Larry again held her back. Toby heard his voice fading out behind Toby's back.

"Let him be," Larry said. "He's fine. He hasn't looked that bright-eyed in months, and you know it."

* * *

When he climbed the cliff the following Sunday, Toby found the handyman waiting for him in the garage, and polishing one of the old cars. He gave Toby a grin and another of his heavy winks, but continued to polish without saying anything until the paste wax he had spread out on the body of the sedan before him was all brought to a high, slick shine. Then he wiped his hands and turned to Toby.

"Come on, then," he said.

They went out the front of the garage into the sun and down into the sunken garden, which was as still and hot as before. The General was there, pacing up and down, and the great, fat old man in the stone armchair, looking as if he had not moved since Toby's last visit. But there was also a middle-aged but still very beautiful lady pacing back and forth as well.

"Here, Father!" boomed the handyman, bringing Toby up before the fat old man. "Here's the boy come again."

Father lifted his eyelids a little lazily to glance at Toby, and then closed them again, indifferently. Toby heard steps behind him and light fingers in his hair. He turned his head and looked up into the face of the beautiful lady.

"You're a pretty boy," said the lady, slowly. "You'll grow up into something to look at, one of these days."

Her voice was a little too caressing, and Toby was embarrassed by the fingers in his hair, but a certain shyness kept him from pulling away. The lady saw, however, and sighed, and went pacing away across the garden, up the stone steps and in toward the house.

"Well, boy, back again!" snapped the General. "Did you fight, eh?"

"Oh, yes," said Toby, eagerly. "I had a fight with

Kenny Morley right after I left here."

"Hah!" said the General fiercely and happily. "That's the way. Charge into it. Don't delay. He who hesitates is half-defeated. Carry the fight to them."

"I did," said Toby.

"Good. That's the world, boy. A hard rock for the spineless, but an oyster to be opened by the brave. By your deeds will they judge you. You know that, don't you?"

"Yes, sir," said Toby.

"Follow courage first, foremost and always. Nothing else compares."

"Nonsense, General!" said a sharp, feminine voice, and they both looked up to see another lady coming down the steps from the house into the garden. She was thinner than the other lady, and while not exactly less beautiful or younger, she had a certain air of competence and sharpness about her. She made Toby think of a schoolteacher. "Don't fill the boy's head with notions." She bent her sharp gray eyes on Toby, and at once he felt very small in a way that none of the others had made him feel. "Brute courage is all right for the brutes. Don't class yourself with the brutes, boy."

"N-no—" quavered Toby, wishing he could look away from her piercing eyes.

"Old maid vapors!" grumbled the General, and went stamping off into the house.

"Pay no attention to him," said the lady. "Courage is all very well, but not to be compared to what goes on in your head. Did you ever hear of Archimedes?"

"No," said Toby. He was staring at her, fascinated now. The name she had just said had come ringing out on the still air of the garden like the pure note of a trumpet, though it did not seem that she had raised her voice.

"Archimedes, boy, said—'Give me a place to stand and I will move the earth.' Do you know what he meant by that?"

"No," said Toby.

"He meant," said the lady, "that nothing is so big that knowledge cannot be brought to bear upon it. Man may be small, but the intangible power of his mind, exerted upon the long lever of knowledge, can shift the mighty world or shake the mightier universe. You, boy, could shift the world, little as you are, could turn this Earth from its orbit around the sun if you had the knowledge and the will."

"Me?" said Toby.

"You or any thinking being." The lady looked at him severely. "But the lever of knowledge isn't picked up in an instant, like a sword dropped by somebody else on a battlefield. Everyone has to forge it for himself, length by slow length, so that when he finally comes to use it he has the muscles for its use."

"Could I really move the world?" asked Toby, dazzled.

"Look around you," said the lady. "The world is being moved in bits and pieces every day by men who were once boys like you. Don't you know anyone who uses knowledge, boy?"

"I guess Larry does," said Toby.

"Larry?" queried the lady, sharply.

"Larry's a friend of my mother's. He's an electronics engineer."

"And how did he get to be an electronics engineer?" said the lady. "Not just by sitting down at a desk and calling himself one, you can be sure."

Toby wriggled embarrassedly.

"Larry can't move the world," he said.

"How do you know?" snapped the lady. "*His* lever of knowledge is far too heavy for *you* to lift. You couldn't even budge it."

"Could if I went to college," muttered Toby.

"College? Hah!" said the lady. "It takes more than college, boy. It takes the will to wisdom; the vision to dream, the hunger to learn, and the determination to put what's learned to use. These are what move the lever. Go to college, indeed! As if that were all!"

"Well, anyway," said Toby. "Larry's not that cool. I know him."

"Do you? Hmph!" sniffed the lady. "I don't think you do. Why don't you ask him, sometime?" And, turning sharply she went back into the house.

Toby, gazing after her, had a sudden wild desire to run and follow, to beg her pardon and ask her more about moving the world. But before he could take a step, he felt the handyman's heavy fingers on his shoulder.

"Time to go, now," said the handyman.

"But I just got here!" cried Toby.

"All the same," said the handyman, and turning Toby about with his fingertips, steered him off.

They took the panel truck down to the gate again.

"Can I come next Sunday? Can I?" pleaded Toby, as the handyman turned the truck around to face back up hill again.

"Well—" the big face looked doubtful.

"Oh, please!" said Toby.

"Well, one more time, maybe," said the handyman, "The summer's almost over. We'll be leaving, soon." And he winked at Toby, and drove off.

That next week, on Tuesday, Toby got a chance to talk to Larry one evening when Larry was over for dinner and his mother was busy in the kitchen.

"Larry," he said. "Would you like to be able to move the world?"

Larry, who was looking at a magazine he had

brought home from the plant, lowered it and looked over at Toby in surprise.

"Sure I would, Toby," he said. "That'd be quite an accomplishment."

"How come you don't try then?" said Toby.

"Well—" said Larry. He put the magazine down on an end table, entirely. And suddenly, for the first time, they found themselves talking . . .

—Later that night Larry talked about it again, but this time with Toby's mother.

"I don't know," he confessed. "I seem to have cracked through, or something. He was all ears."

"Maybe—" said Toby's mother.

"Yes, maybe—" said Larry.

And they both looked at each other.

The next Sunday, Toby did not climb the cliff. He went boldly, instead, to the gate and pressed the button put there for the delivery men to announce their presence to the big house. And then he waited. When nobody came, he reached through the bars of the gate —it was not too hard for anyone with a hand and arm as thin as his—and pressed the latch from the inside.

He pushed the gate open and closed it behind him, and started on foot up the drive. He was almost to the top before he saw the towering form of the handyman coming striding to meet him. Toby ran to meet him; but the big man looked down at him with his heavy face set in lines of sternness, and this time he did not wink.

"I rang, but you didn't come," said Toby.

"Why did you let yourself in, boy?" said the handyman, his deep voice echoing among the tangled plants and bushes on either side of the drive.

"You said I could come," said Toby. He looked up

into the big face looming over him. "Nobody else has to climb that old cliff. I don't see why I have to." The handyman merely stood, looking down at him. "What's the matter? Isn't anybody up in the garden?"

The handyman swung around abruptly.

"Come on," he said. He went back up the drive with giant steps, Toby running to keep up with him.

They took a path around the side of the house, past the open mouth of the garage and went down the steps into the near end of the garden. At the far end, the old, fat man sat as usual in his stone chair, but there were a number of others in the garden, including the General, and the two ladies, but also others Toby had never seen before, men and ladies both. Toby saw the lady he had talked to last time standing talking to the General, and without waiting for anything more, he went up to her.

"Hi," he said.

Both the lady and the General turned to look down at him. Like the handyman, they did not seem particularly pleased to see him.

"Well, here I am again," said Toby.

"I see that," said the lady, sharply.

"I just thought I'd tell you," said Toby, "I talked to Larry. It's pretty good, that electronics. I guess I'll be an engineer, myself."

"Boy," muttered the General, "Don't forget."

"You mean all that stuff *you* told me?" said Toby, glancing up at him. "No, I won't forget. But I got all that made, now, that courage stuff. And pretty soon I'll have it all made what she told me, after I've been to school and worked some."

"Just like that!" said the lady, ironically.

"Well, that's what you said, wasn't it?" said Toby. He saw all the others in the garden were looking at him now and it made him feel rather larger and more important than he had ever felt up here before. "I know you said it'll be tough. I don't mind. I'm not afraid of work. I'm not afraid of anything."

"Aren't you?" said the lady.

"Heck, no!" said Toby. "Anybody can be afraid. That's nothing. All you got to do is make up your mind and go ahead, and you can do anything." He looked around at them. "That's what I say," he added.

"Boy, boy," said the General, shaking his head.

"Oh, what do you know about it?" said Toby, turning on him. "I bet you haven't even had as much school as I have."

"Mind your manners!" snapped the lady.

"I don't have to!" cried Toby, turning on her. "He's not my boss. And you aren't either. I thought you'd be glad to hear how good I'm doing, but you don't even care. He's just a funny old man and you're a funny old maid, and I don't have to pay any attention to either of you . . ."

And he turned away, to run out of the garden and away down the drive, but he never made it.

"*Boy!*" said a voice.

The one word rolled like muted thunder down the length of the garden; and Toby, caught by something that held him like some huge hand capturing a fly, turned about and looked.

He stared across the open space of the fish pond to the fat old man in the stone armchair. But the old man did not look fat and sleepy any longer. His eyes were wide open, looking at Toby, and he loomed, immense and terrifying.

"Come here," said the old man, in the same, awful voice.

Around Toby, all the rest of the people had fallen silent. They stood still as statues, and they seemed to have shrunken in the sound of that voice. Desperately, Toby longed for one of them, the General, the Lady, or even the handyman, to speak up for him, or come forward with him. But none of them moved or made a sound and suddenly Toby realized that in comparison to the old man who sat waiting they were all nothing, and less than nothing; and none of them could help him now.

Slowly, creepingly, against his will, Toby moved down the length of the garden until he stood directly before and below the old man in the stone chair.

"Boy," said the old man, and his voice filled all the air about them, "you are like all the rest. Petty, overweening, ungrateful. Because you dared to climb a cliff, you were accepted here for a moment or two. You have been given courage and a path to wisdom, which are gifts of the gods; and now in your little pride and glory, you think you know it all."

He paused for a moment, and Toby stood still and helpless, as frozen as the stone before him.

"I will give you a third lesson to learn," said the old man, "And that is that you are small and weak, in your own right. And it does not become the small and weak to be selfish and overbearing, to think that they know it all, and to expect those that love them, or those that are kind to them, to always cater to their wants and prejudices. Go, boy, and learn humility, and kindness, and what is right!"

And then Toby was free. He turned and went. At first he stumbled. But then he ran. And ran, and ran. And ran.

It was several days before they would let Toby out of bed again. Dr. Alisanti said he had had a touch of sunstroke, and should be kept quiet for a while. And for several days he did not want to go anywhere anyway. All he wanted to do was to stay close and safe in his own bed, in his own house, with his mother to tuck him in under the covers; and Larry to come in now and again, and sit big, and comforting and grownup by his bed while he said comforting things in a voice that was deep and male, but not terrifying as the old man's voice had been.

But on Wednesday they let him get up and about again; and the following Sunday he went once more to the big house on the cliff. The gate was padlocked, now with a heavy chain, but he had not expected it to be open. He went around to the cliff, and—for the last time—he climbed it.

On top of the cliff, all was silent and still. It even smelled deserted. Timidly, he went through the garage and down into the garden. It was empty, as he had known it would be, but now there was something different about it.

The goldfish still swam in the pool, but about the walk surrounding it, the blocks of stone were no longer empty. On each one stood a man or woman, carved in stone. And, as he went down the line, Toby recognized each one of them. They were slimmer and younger than when he had seen them last, and for the most part they had no clothes on, but he recognized the General, and the sharp lady, and even the handyman, leaning on a great stone club on the last block of all.

At the far end of the garden a leaner version of the old man filled the stone seat above the rest. His stone eyes were open, but they looked out over Toby's head at something distant and invisible. For a second, as he stood there, a shiver trembled through Toby, and he reached out a hesitant hand to touch the stone knee, on a level with his nose.

But the touch of the stone reassured him. It was only rock; and, suddenly, a feeling of joy and freedom burst up within him. He felt light and loose, like a prisoner given his liberty again; and he turned happily away.

Larry and his mother were getting out of the car after their Sunday drive, as he got home. He ran across the lawn to them, pellmell, and flung his arms around both of them, hugging them.

"Oh boy!" he cried. "Oh, boy! You're back!"

"Well!" said Larry, patting Toby fondly on his back. And Larry and his mother looked across at each other over Toby's head, smiling at each other like people who have come safe to harbor, together and united, at last.

Listen

Reru did not like to see humans eat. So he was waiting in the living room while Taddy and his parents finished breakfast.

"—And quite right, too," boomed Taddy's father. "He has as much right to his own ways as we have to ours. Remember that, Taddy, when you grow up. The only reason humans have been successful conquerors throughout the galaxy is because they have always respected the attitudes and opinions of the people they conquered."

"Oh, Harry!" said Taddy's mother. "He's too young to understand all that."

"I am not young," said Taddy defensively, through a mouthful of breakfast food. "I'm four years old."

"See there, Celia," said Taddy's father, laughing. "He's four years old—practically grown up. But seriously, honey, he's going to be growing up into a

world in which the great majority of thinking beings
are Mirians like Reru. He should start to understand
the natives early."

"Well, I don't know," said Taddy's mother, wor-
riedly. "After all, he was born in space on the way
here and he's a delicate child—"

"Delicate, nonsense!" boomed Taddy's father.
"He comes from the toughest race in the galaxy.
Look at these Mirians, chained to their planet by a
symbiosis so extensive that our biologists haven't
reached the end of the chain, yet. Look at Reru himself, gentle, non-combative, unenergetic, a stalwart
example of the Mirian Race and therefore—the ideal
nursemaid for our son."

"Oh, I don't have a word of complaint to say
against Reru," answered Taddy's mother. "He's been
just wonderful with Taddy. But I can't help it—when
he cocks his head on one side and starts *listening*
the way they all do, I get a little bit scared of
him."

"Damn it, Celia!" said Taddy's father. "I've told
you a thousand times that he's just hearing one of
their cows calling that it wants to be milked."

Taddy squirmed in his chair. He knew all about the
cows. They were six-legged Mirian animals that
roamed around much as Reru and his kind roamed
around. When they were full of milk they would start
making a high, whistling sound, and Reru or some
other Mirian would come along and attach his
suckers to them and drink the milk. But the cows
were no longer interesting. Reru was; and Taddy had
finished his breakfast food.

"I'm all through," he broke in suddenly on his parents' conversation. "Can I go now? Can I?"

"I guess so," said Taddy's mother and Taddy

scrambled from the chair and ran off toward the living room.

"Don't go too far!" his mother's voice floated after him, followed by his father's deep bass.

"Let him go. Reru will bring him back all right. And, anyway, what on this planet of vegetarians could harm him?"

But Taddy had already forgotten his mother's words. For Reru was waiting for him, and Reru was fascinating.

He looked, at first glance, like a miniature copy of an old Chinese Mandarin, with robe, bald head, and little wispy beard. It was only when you got to know him that you realized that there were tentacles beneath the robe, that he had never had hair on his head, and that the wispy beard hid and protected the suckers with which he milked the *cows* that were his source of food.

But Taddy liked him very much; and Taddy didn't think that there was anything the least bit strange about him.

"Where are we going today, Reru?" demanded Taddy, bouncing up and down before the little Mirian who was not quite twice as tall as he was.

Reru's voice was like the voice of a trilling bird, and it sang more than it spoke.

"Good morning, Taddy," it trilled. "Where would you like to go?"

"I want to go to the silver and green place," cried Taddy. "Can we go?"

Reru's dark little mandarin face did not smile because it did not have the muscles to do so. But the mouth opened and the Mirian gave a short wordless trill expressive of happiness and pleasure.

"Yes, small Taddy," Reru answered. "We can go."

And, turning with a kind of stately dignity, he led the
way out of the dwelling and into the soft yellow
Mirian sunlight.

"Oh, good, good, good!" sang Taddy, skipping
along beside him.

They went away from the buildings of the humans,
out across the low rolling grassland of Miria, Taddy
bounding and leaping in the light gravity and Reru
gliding along with effortless ease. And if that
dignified glide was the result of twisting tentacles hidden beneath the robe, what of it? Where older humans might have felt squeamish at the thought of the
twisting ropes of white muscle, Taddy took it entirely
for granted. To him, Reru was beautiful.

They went on across the grasslands. Several times
Reru stopped to *listen* and each time Taddy tried to
imitate him, standing with his tousled head cocked on
one side and an intent expression on his baby face.
After one of these stops his brow furrowed and he
seemed to be thinking. The little Mirian noticed him.

"What is it, Taddy?" he trilled.

"Daddy says that when you listen, you're listening
to the cows," Taddy answered. "You hear more than
that, don't you, Reru?"

"Yes, Taddy," said Reru, "I am listening to all my
brothers."

"Oh," said the boy, wisely. "I thought so."

As they went on, the grassland began to dip, and
after a while a patch of deeper green came into sight
in the distance.

"There it is," trilled the Mirian. Taddy broke into
a run.

"Let's hurry, Reru," cried the boy, pulling at the
mandarin robe. "Come *on,* Reru!"

Reru increased his glide and they hurried forward until they came to the silver-and-green place.

It was fairy-like in its beauty. Little green islands and clumps of vegetation were interspersed with flashing slivers of water, so that no matter where you stood, some small reflective surface caught the yellow light of the sun and sent it winking into your eyes. It looked, for all the world, like a toy landscape on which some giant had broken his mirror and left the bits to sparkle and shine in the daytime brightness. Reru squatted and Taddy sat down on the edge of one of the pools.

"What does it say?" asked the boy. "Tell me what it says, Reru."

The Mirian trilled again his little trill of pleasure; then composed himself. For a long time he sat silent, *listening,* while the boy squirmed, impatient, yet not daring to say anything that might interrupt or delay what Reru was about to say. Finally, the Mirian spoke.

"I can hear my brother the cow down in the tall grass at the edge of a pool. I can hear him as he moves among the grass; and I hear what he hears, his little brother, the dweller in the ground who stores up rich food for my brother the cow. And I can hear still further to all the other little brothers of the world as they go about their appointed tasks, until the air is thick with the sound of their living and their memories are my memories and their thoughts my thoughts.

"So the green-and-silver place is filled with a mighty thought; and this is what that thought says:

" 'The green-and-silver place is a coming together of waters that have traveled a long way. Our brothers in the earth have told us that there are three waters that come together here, and none flow in the light of day. Our brothers of the waters have told us that these waters run far, for they have traveled the waters.

" 'One comes from the south, but the other two from the north. And the ones from the north travel side by side for a long way, with the dark and silent earth between and around them, until they come out in a colder land to the far north of here. And, in the far north, the two come together and their source is a single river that comes from a high mountain where the winds blow over bare rock. And in that place there is a brother who lives on the stones of the hillside and watches the stars at night. He has listened along the water and heard us down here in the warm grasslands; and he dreams of the green-and-silver place as he lies at night on the bare rock, watching the stars.

" 'But the water that comes from the south comes from deep beneath the mountains of the south, from a silent lake in the heart of the rock. The lake is filled by the water that trickles down the veins of the mountains; and in it lives another brother who is blind and has never seen the yellow sun. But he lies in the dark on a rock shelf above the silent lake and listens to the grumbling of the world as it talks to itself deep in the heart of the planet. And he, too, has heard us here in the warm grasslands, under the light of the yellow sun, and he dreams of the green-and-silver place as he lies on his rock ledge listening to the grumbling of the world.' "

Reru ceased talking and opened his eyes.

"That is only one story, Taddy," he said, "of the green-and-silver place."

"More," begged the boy. "Tell me more, Reru."

And he looked up into the alien face with eyes glowing in the wonder and excitement of what he had just heard. And Reru told him more.

The morning was nearly gone when they returned to Taddy's home, and Taddy's father and mother were already seated at the table eating lunch.

"Late again, Taddy," said his mother, with mock anger.

"No, I'm not," Taddy retorted, sliding into his place. "You're early."

"You are a little early at that, Celia," said Taddy's father. "How come?"

"Oh, I promised to go over to visit Julia this afternoon," answered Taddy's mother. "Taddy! Did you wash your hands?"

"Uh-huh," said Taddy with a vigorous nod, his mouth already full. "Look!" He displayed them at arms' length.

"Where did you go today, anyway?" asked his mother.

"To the green-and-silver place," answered Taddy.

"Green-and-silver place?" She looked across at her husband. "Where's that, Harry?"

"Darned if I know," answered Taddy's father. "Where is it, son?"

Taddy pointed in a southwesterly direction.

"Out there," he said. "There's lots of little pieces of water and lots of little bushes and things."

"Why," said Harry, "he must mean the swamp."

"The swamp!" echoed Taddy's mother. "He spent the whole morning out at a swamp! Harry, you have to do something. It isn't healthy for a boy to go mooning around like these Mirians."

"Now, Celia," grumbled Taddy's father. "The

Mirians put their planet before everything else. It's almost a form of worship with them. But that can't possibly affect Taddy. Humans are just too big and strong to be seduced into that dead-end sort of philosophy. Anyway, that swamp's going to be drained shortly and they're going to put a building in its place."

He leaned across the table toward Taddy.

"You'd like that better, now, wouldn't you, son?" he said. "A big new building to run around in instead of that water and muck!"

The boy's face had gone completely white and his mouth was open.

"You can get Reru to take you over and watch it go up," his father went on.

"No!" said the boy, suddenly and violently.

"Why, Taddy!" said his mother. "Is that any way to talk to your father? Now, you apologise at once."

"I won't," said Taddy.

"Taddy!" his father's big voice rumbled danger-ously.

"I don't care!" cried Taddy. Suddenly the words were tumbling out of him all at once. "I hate you! I hate your old buildings! When I grow up I'm going to tear down that old building and put all the water and things back." He was crying now, and his words came interspersed with sobs. "I don't like you here. Nobody else likes you either. Why don't you go 'way? Why don't you all go 'way?"

Taddy's father sat dumbfounded. But Taddy's mother got quickly up from her chair and around to Taddy's. She took him by the arm and pulled him away from the table.

"It's his nerves," she said. "I knew all this running around was bad for him." And she led him off in the direction of his room, his wails diminishing with distance and the closing of a door.

After a little while she came back.

"You see?" she said triumphantly to her husband. "Now he'll have to stay in bed all afternoon and I can't go over to Julia's because I'll have to stay here and watch him."

But Taddy's father had recovered his composure.

"Nonsense, Celia," he said. "It's just a case of nerves, like you said. Every boy has them one time or another. We can let the young pioneer kick up a few fusses without worrying too much about it. It won't hurt his character any. Now, you go on over to Julia's as you planned. He'll stay put."

"Well," said Taddy's mother slowly, wanting to be convinced, "if you say so—I don't suppose it would do any harm to run over for a few minutes. . . ."

Up in his room, Taddy's sobs diminished until they no longer racked his small body. He got up and went to the window and looked out at the rolling grasslands.

"I will, too," he said to himself, "I will too tear down all their old buildings when I grow up."

And, immediately he said it, a strange thing seemed to happen. A wave of peace flooded over him and he stopped crying. It was as if all the brothers that Reru had been talking about were here in the room and just outside his window, comforting him. He felt them all around him; and at the same time he sensed that they were all waiting for him to say something, waiting and listening. For just a few seconds he could feel all of Miria listening to him, to Taddy.

And he knew what they wanted; for he stretched both his arms out the window to them, a love filling

his heart like no love he had ever felt before, as he
spoke the two words they were waiting to hear.

"I promise," said Taddy.

GRAVEYARD

They've gone and Lord bless them. Anybody who thinks the last part of that statement sounds funny, coming from me, knows what he can do about it, and I'm looking right at you, brother. They were two of the best people I ever knew; and they've gone where I'll probably never see them again; but I've got the puppy to remember them by and that's enough for me.

But I don't suppose you can understand that without knowing their history and how I come into it. My name is Kenneth Parnell; and I worked with Jim Marks on the T and T project where it all started, somewhere in lower Kentucky.

Now, what the T and T project was, I can't tell you; because even now, T and T is top secret and probably will be so for a long time to come. And you don't need to know that, anyway. All you need to know is that this was a little over three years ago; and

that we had a little explosion on the job; and that
what exploded was hot—radioactive.

When the smoke cleared after the explosion, it
could be seen that the main laboratory and two
storehouses were flat. So we sent in a couple of work-
ers in shielded suits to see what could be saved and
they poked around for some time; but all they dug
out of the rubble was Jim Marks and his pregnant
bitch hound, Martha, which had followed him to
work that morning.

Jim had been smashed and cut up by lab equipment; but by great good luck, he had been behind
shielding, which held. The radioactivity hadn't
touched him. But with Martha, it was just the opposite. She didn't have a scratch on her, but there was
no protection in the office where Jim had left her to
wait for him; a lethal dose of radiation had gone right
through her.

She was still feeling pretty good a few days later
when they patched Jim up well enough to leave the
project clinic—which doubled in brass as a two-bed
hospital. I came by and picked Jim up in the station-
wagon and drove him over to the pens for research
animals, where they were keeping her.

He grinned at me through the tape on his face as he
got into the wagon. "Good to see you, Ken," he said.
And—"same to you, Jim," I told him; for you see, I
was Jim's lab assistant on the project, only I'd just
stepped out of the building a few minutes before the
explosion, to go over to Supply. Both of us had
thought the other was dead; Jim because he thought
I was in the building, and I, because I knew Jim was.

"How do you feel?" I asked. "They patch you up
all right?"

"Fine," he answered. "Good as new."

So we went over to the pens and Martha was so glad to see him that she almost clawed her way clear through the wire netting that penned her. He said the usual things a man says to a dog when he hasn't seen it for some little time; but finally he ran out of talk and just stood looking at her for a while. At last he gave a sudden little grunt and turned away. And we went out.

The day after that, he wrangled permission to build a pen in his quarters; and took her home.

We were waiting around for reassignment at that time. It would take T and T some time to get set up again; and in the meantime, the abilities of a physicist like Jim—and even of a mechanic like myself—were too valuable to be allowed to sit idle. But the official wheels grind slowly, even at their speediest, so we had a couple of weeks to wait.

I bummed around what was left of the project, dropping in on Jim occasionally. His big, rawboned body had done a good job of recovering from the shock of the accident, but the sewed-up cuts on his face and arms were still pretty nasty to look at. He spent most of his time puttering around Martha's pen, and generally taking care of her. Her teeth had come out by this time and a lot of her hair; but she wasn't in any pain and she seemed happy. Jim thought she had a good chance of lasting until she could drop her litter. He just hoped he wouldn't be ordered to move first.

As it turned out, he wasn't; and I was still there, too. So I dropped over one night when he phoned. I took my time getting there; afterwards I was sorry for it, because Jim thought a lot of Martha. If I'd hurried, I'd have gotten there while she was still alive.

Not that he ever said anything to me about it, though. Jim was the kind of guy who swallowed his hurts. Five of the six pups were dead, too. The other one was alive, but blind. Of course, puppies are always born that way; but there was no doubt that this one would be blind for life. Jim peeled back the tiny lids and there was nothing but scar tissue underneath.

"Too bad," I said awkwardly, looking down at him where he crouched beside the still figures.

"It's all right," he said. "There's still this one." He lifted the blind puppy, cradling him in those two big hands of his.

"You're going to keep him?" I said. I was surprised.

He rose to his feet, still holding the puppy; and looked at me a little oddly. "You don't think I should?" he asked. I shrugged. "You want to know what I think—" I answered—and maybe I was too blunt about it; but that's the way I am and I don't apologize for it. "I think it'd be kinder to put him out of his misery now. He isn't going to enjoy life much —blind."

Jim shook his head. "He'll have a good life."

"And how are you going to guarantee that?" I asked.

"Graveyard," he told me. And he looked at me and grinned.

Now that was just a polite way of telling me to shut up and mind my own business; but maybe I ought to explain. It seems that with the last war, and the things that happened in our business since, the boys at the top have been running out of classifications for stuff that's not to be talked about. There was *Restricted*, and there was *Secret*, and *Top Secret*, and one or two others that sounded, in some ways, pretty silly, so the laboratory boys got to joking about them. And one of the jokes was that they dreamed up a classification of their own to end all secret classifications. It was what a project-member called a project that was so secret that he couldn't reveal it to anybody, even to himself. That was *Graveyard*. It got to be sort of a slang excuse for not giving your reasons for something.

Well, we moved out right after that, Jim to one project and I to another, neither of us knowing just where we were going, or what we were going to do when we got there. And it wasn't until more than three years later that I bumped into him again.

I can talk about this particular project, because they're starting to take the wraps off it. There's already been a lot of buildup information on it planted in magazine and newspaper-articles; and they're just holding back the official announcement out of policy. It was the Space Station Project—Project Moon Puppy, or just plain *Puppy*, as we called it on location, which was at a spot out in the Mohave Desert.

Out there in the middle of nowhere, they had set up a small city for some five hundred of us who were cleared for top-secret work. We were all kinds—laborers, skilled workmen, technicians, a few specialists high on the list like Jim and others; and—the General.

Now, bear in mind, I have nothing against the General. I hadn't then, and I don't have now. As far as I knew him—which wasn't much, due to our difference in rank—he was a fine guy; he did a fine job of representing Army brass on Project Puppy. But the best man in the world can be a fool where some woman is concerned; and in the case of the General, it was his daughter, Elna.

The pity of it was, she wasn't worth any man's being a fool over. Oh, the body and brains were there. Elna was a tall, slim-featured brunette, with a master's degree in psychology out of Columbia. She was beautiful, she was smart. And by pulling strings unmercifully—through her father and otherwise—she'd gotten herself assigned to *Puppy*. But there was something wrong inside her; there was a part missing.

Jim fell for her—but I'm getting ahead of myself. Let's go back to the day when I first walked into the project and saw Jim again for the first time in three years.

The administration building was a long, two-story building which was still the tallest structure in the project area—outside of certain equipment which we needn't go into. I was standing by a window in one of the upstairs offices, having just arrived, looking out and down at the camp and wondering what they had in mind for me this trip. The door opened and Jim came in.

"Well, I'll be damned!" I said; we shook hands. Neither Jim nor I are very expressive sorts of people. I tried to think of something else to say, couldn't, ended up repeating—"I'll be damned!" and let it go at that.

So we went over to the food-center and had several cups of coffee, and he explained what I was to do for him. Also, I learned why we were hooked up together again—which is not a common thing in this kind of work. It seems part of the stuff we were doing on T and T was preliminary to part of the work on *Puppy;* so we had been drafted to take up pretty much where we had left off before.

Well, Jim told me what he would be wanting me to do, and I came out with a few questions. We batted it back and forth for a while, then he suggested that we get over to the lab section he held down for our work. So we went.

It was a little box of a prefab, set off in a corner of the project-area. The guard at the door checked my credentials and we went in. Jim led the way, down a short, bare hallway, and in through a heavy door to the lab proper; it was then I got one of the better shocks of my life.

For—as we came through the door—a huge black hound rose from where he'd been lying in a corner; and came threading his way through the cluttered maze of equipment with the assurance and skill of a tightrope walker. This alone would not have been so disturbing, but the dogs' eyes were open; and they were eyes I had seen three years before in a wrinkled puppy-face, gray, scar-tissued, and blind as a bat.

He passed Jim, came up to me, and thrust his nose into my hand. Automatically, I reached out to pat the broad head; and I turned to Jim.

"How the devil—" I began. Jim grinned.

"Surprised?" he said. "Every so often I still am, myself. But he knows this place like a book."

"A lab?" I said. "Where stuff is always being moved around?"

"Uh-huh," agreed Jim, softly. But there was an odd look in his eyes, as if he was watching me narrowly to see how I took his answer.

He turned away from the dog and we got down to business. But I noticed something disturbing: The gray, blank eyes seemed to be following his motions as he explained things to me.

* * *

In the weeks that followed, I got to know the dog well. His name was Calum and he was an awesome creature. His weight was a ninety-four pounds, his height over five and a half feet when he stood upright on his hind legs—which he would do at Jim's command. And he was black as a night in hell. He took to me—strangely, for I never before had cared much for pets. Perhaps it was something Jim said to him, for he would do anything for Jim; and I know he understood.

But the oddest thing about him was that he was not like a dog. By that I mean (if I can just put into words what I have in mind) he didn't act the way you would expect a dog to act—the kind of actions that people refer to when they use the word *doggish*. Calum did not bark at you. He seldom wagged his tail, even to Jim—though it was apparent at a glance how much Calum thought of Jim. Perhaps his size had something to do with it. It forced him to act proud— almost like an individual. He was like a third person in the room as we worked in the lab.

Looking back on it now, I think I could have either liked him or feared him. And that Calum realized it and handled himself so that we ended up friends.

I don't mean by this to give the idea that Calum had a mind like a human being, or any such thing. Smart and wise, he was; but only in the way any dog can be smart and wise. The miracle with him lay someplace else, outside his intelligence. It was something I can't describe because we have no words for such a thing. But I began to find out about it about a month after I got back to working with Jim.

But first—there was Elna.

We had been busy at the lab for several days, just getting the work set up. It was late afternoon, and we were working on opposite sides of the lab, when Calum—who was sitting beside my bench like a huge silent devil—suddenly lifted his head and swung it toward the front of the building, as his ears pricked up. At the same moment, there was a small clatter from the other side of the room, as the soldering-iron Jim was using slipped from his fingers and rattled onto the floor.

I hadn't heard anything. I turned toward Jim.

"What—" I began; and then I heard the footsteps of the door guard coming down the short hall and a knock on the lab door.

"What is it?" called Jim.

"Someone to see you, Mr. Marks," came back the guard's voice.

Jim turned to me, and there was a hint of embarrassment in the way he spoke, "That'll be Elna," he said. "She can't come in here, of course; I'll have to go out. About time we knocked off for the day, anyhow, isn't it?"

I stared at him. Our kind of people—the ones they put to work on projects like *Puppy*—eat, breathe, sleep and play our work. The idea of quitting, just because it was around four o'clock, was like suggesting to a fish that it could come out of the water and dry itself off, now. And what would I do with my spare time—except maybe get a pass into town and a few drinks into me? There was nothing else to do.

Then I got it. "Yeah," I said. "Sure." I laid down what I had been working on, turned off the current, and the three of us went outside, locking the lab door behind us.

Elna was waiting on the steps of the building for

us. It was the first I'd seen of her, although I'd caught
mention of the General's daughter at the food-center
and at the Recreation-Center my first evening in. She
was just as beautiful as they had said she was, with
the fine and smoothly-efficient appearance of a well-
designed piece of equipment. I remember her eyes
were blue—they changed from blue to green depend-
ing on how she was feeling—but that day they were
blue and cold, as they looked at Calum and at me.

"Ken Parnell," said Jim, introducing me. "They
assigned him to me; we were together once before."

"Hello," she said.

I looked at her and I knew that she and I would
never get along. But there was something else I had to
see, too, whether I liked it or not. When I heard the
talk in Rec, I figured that she was all phony—that
without the General's pull, she'd be nothing. There's
something special about those in our line of work you
know. You can feel it when you meet them. They
either belong or they don't. Well, Elna may have had
to pull wires to get in, but she was in by a bigger right
now than pull. She had it—whatever it was—just like
Jim had it, and I had it. She was no good for Jim or
the General, or me, or anyone else, maybe; but she
had as much right to be where we were as we did.

We said a few polite things and then the two of
them went off toward Rec. Center, with Calum to be
dropped off at Jim's quarters on the way. The big
hound was walking on Jim's side, on the side farthest
from Elna. It was plain he didn't like the woman,
though he kept still about it.

I went into town and got drunk. As I said, there
was nothing else to do.

Well, I had my introduction to the situation. Like

Calum, I didn't appreciate it; but, what the hell—I
was Jim's handyman, not his departmental superior.
It was just one of those things you learn to live with.
Elna was in Personnel on the project. It was a job that
gave her lots of free time—or seemed to. She knocked
on our door frequently, and with success. Jim was
nuts about her; nine times out of ten he'd drop what
he was doing and go out with her—although usually
it was just over to the Rec, or some place inside
camp-limits. And, after the first few times, we quit
the polite convention of my laying off when he did. I
stuck right on the job—there was plenty to do—and
Calum stayed with me. It was better than shutting
him up in Jim's quarters.

So the work went on, on schedule, but it wasn't
good. Get that—it wasn't good. It takes more than
body-skills and brain to do these kind of jobs; it takes
teamwork. Jim and I had been a team—a good team
—before. Now we were no good, because Jim was no
good—because Elna had changed him from a man
standing alone to something tied to her hand and
foot.

And on top of this there was something else wrong.
I thought at first, it was just Elna; but then I began to
see otherwise. Something was eating at Jim, eating
the heart out of him. He lost weight and got jumpy;
and Calum, like a mirror-image of Jim's secret soul,
lost weight too. He took to pacing the floor of the lab
restlessly when he was left alone with me—wearing a
track back and forth in regular sentry-go in the little
clear space between our two work benches. The distance was less than twelve feet, and blind as he was,
he had it down to a system—five great padding steps
in one direction, turn and five steps the other way.

I guess my nerves were wearing thin, themselves.

Anyway, when Elna made a move to meet me, I met her halfway.

The occasion was a party at the Rec hall, marking the halfway point in the project. There was canned music and food, and a reasonable amount of drink; everyone not on duty—regardless of rank—was invited.

I went. Jim and Elna were there together, of course; but she found an excuse to send him off on some errand or other and she came over to where I was sitting in a corner and sat down opposite me. "Well, Ken," she said. "Enjoying yourself?"

"As much as I ever do at these deals," I answered. We looked at each other and she stopped playing. Her eyes were green that night—deliberately green and warm. "Jim thinks a lot of you," she said. "And I gather you think a lot of him."

"That's right," I said.

"I think a lot of Jim, too," she went on; "and since that makes two of us with the same idea, why do we have to fight about it?"

"Who's fighting?" I asked.

An angry glint came into the green eyes. If her lips had belonged to a man, I would have said he was sneering at me. "Oh, let's not play games," she drawled.

"Again," I said, "who's playing? What you two do is your own business."

"Don't act innocent!" she flared. "You've been picking on Jim about me ever since you got here."

I started to get angry myself, and my hands began to go tense. When I get mad, I feel it there first. I live in my hands; they feed me, dress me, work for me, and if necessary fight for me. I could feel the fingers curling up and going stiff.

"Listen," I said. "I don't like you and that's clear channel. I don't like to see someone like you come between a damn good man and the work he lives by. Jim was one of the best we've got, and could be again, if you'd leave him alone. But, get this! I live my own life and I figure anybody else over the age of twelve ought to live his. Jim passed the age of twelve fifteen years ago; it's his business and yours, and to hell with both if necessary!"

She took note of my words and my anger and weighed them like abstract problems. She sat looking at me for a long second and then she spoke . . . calmly.

"Then what's wrong with him?"

"You," I said bluntly.

She shook her head. "Try again," she said, without rancor. "There's something bothering him that he won't even tell me; and if it isn't you—" She checked herself suddenly, and her eyes got a speculative look in them. I tried to guess what had popped into her head but failed. I wasn't too surprised; the woman had a better mind than I have, and I'm not ashamed to admit it. Besides, she was closer to Jim than I was.

Well, if she could figure it out, maybe I could find out in more ordinary ways. And if it was something that worried her, too, then it might be serious. There was no law that said I couldn't ask questions.

Jim and I both lived in the same bachelor barracks. I went back there and waited until I heard him come back from the party and the door to his room slam. Then I broke out a bottle from my own foot-locker cellar, took it down the hall and knocked on his door.

"Who's that?" he called.

"Ken," I said.

"Come in," his voice filtered through the thin door.

So I went in. He was sitting on the edge of the bed, smoking. Calum was seated beside him, the big black head in Jim's lap. His face was lean and haggard and his eyes drawn and hungry for sleep.

"I brought you a drink," I said, taking a couple of water-glasses from Jim's stand and running about a triple shot into each. I took it over and sat down in the chair opposite his bed, putting one of the glasses and the bottle down on the night stand at his elbow. Calum lifted his head and pointed it at me.

"What's this?" he asked, looking from the drink to me.

"I figured you needed one," I said.

He grinned, a little sadly. "Maybe I do—" he said. "But it'll leave me knocked out in the morning, and I've got work to do."

"Might be a good thing if you slept in," I said, lifting my own glass. "Here's with mine." And I poured it down.

After perhaps a second of hesitation, he picked up his and drank it. He shuddered as he set the glass down. "Whoof!" he said. "How you can swallow whisky without blinking, Ken, I don't know."

"The only thing my old man left me," I said, "was a rock head and a cast iron-stomach." I decided to quit beating around the bush; it wasn't my way, anyhow. "What's chewing you, Jim?"

He looked at me and drew a long breath. "So that's it," he said.

"That's it," I told him. He picked up his glass and held it out to me. "Give me another," he said.

I poured it for him. He gulped about half of it, and sat for a moment, nursing the glass between his big

hands, and looking at it. In the silence, Calum made
an odd little sound like a question; Jim reached out
automatically to pat his head. Then, finally, he
looked away from the glass in his hand and back to
me.

"All right," he said—and his voice had the sound
of a man worn to the breaking point. "Want to hear
a story, Ken?"

He slurred the last words a little. What with his
tiredness, and the fact that he wasn't ordinarily a
drinker, that first large shot had hit him—or maybe
just the idea of it had hit him. I couldn't tell.

"I'm listening," I said. "If you want to talk, and
security doesn't mind."

"Security!" He laughed—not happily. "This is too
big a story for security, Ken. This *graveyard*."

My glass twitched a little in my right hand. Did I tell
you I felt things first in my hands? They twitched now;
and I could feel them going a little cold—a cold that
began to seep up my arms toward my spine in a shiver.
For *graveyard* is a joke; but Jim wasn't joking.

I remembered what *graveyard* meant—something
so big you couldn't even tell yourself what you had;
and I sat very still and looked at Jim. Maybe I had a
premonition.

He got up, poured himself another drink, then
opened a drawer in his writing table and took out two
sheets of cardboard and two pencils. One sheet he put
on the floor in front of Calum and weighed it down,
then put one of the pencils between the big dog's
teeth, which gripped it firmly, point down. The other
sheet and pencil he handed to me.

He sat down again on the bed and gulped at his
drink.

"All right, Ken," he said. "Don't say anything out

loud, but draw a letter on that card and hold it up where I can see it."

I stared at him.

"Go ahead," he said. I shrugged and drew the letter "P" on my card; and held it up.

Jim focused his eyes on it and gazed steadily. I sat for a few minutes, holding the card up to his gaze and getting more and more impatient. Finally I spoke. "Look—what is this?"

Jim did not take his eyes from the card. "Look at Calum," he said.

Without moving the card, I glanced sideways and down. The shock was so great that I nearly dropped the card.

Slowly, painfully, with the pencil grasped tightly between his teeth, the great inky hound was drawing a wavering "P" on the weighed-down cardboard six inches from his blind, scar-tissued eyes. As I looked, he finished the ragged loop; and, dropping the pencil, lifted his head to Jim as if waiting to be praised.

I looked at the "P" and I looked at the one the dog had drawn. I looked at Calum; and I looked finally at Jim. His hand caressing the thick black head, he looked back at me and smiled a little sadly.

"So now you know," he said.

And then he told me. It seems that, at first, Calum had seemed quite normal—nothing more nor less than the blind puppy he appeared to be. Even during the first couple of years, he did nothing that could not be explained by the fantastic-enough memory that some blind dogs seem to have for places and objects. Naturally enough, Jim kept him mainly in his quarters, or others areas with which the dog could easily familiarize himself. It was not until a little over half a year ago Jim became aware that Calum took notice of things in an impossible fashion.

Jim didn't quite remember the exact moment when he first realized it. Thinking back, it seemed that he had been noticing little things for a long time without the implication really making itself felt on his conscious mind. At any rate, when Calum one day detoured around a piece of furniture that had been moved, without warning, by a visitor to Jim's quarters, Jim made up his mind to settle the question once and for all. He took Calum out to a tangled section of brush-covered country at the edge of the town where he was at the time and raced him through it, running as fast as the man could run past fallen trees and bushes and around stumps. Loping easily beside Jim, Calum avoided all obstacles as well as if his vision was perfect.

"Something to do with the radiation that killed his mother, maybe—" said Jim. "God knows."

At any rate, it was a fact. Call it telepathy or what you would, Calum could make use of Jim's eyes. After that race through the country, evidence began to pile up of this. In fact, oddly enough, the rapport between the two seemed to grow.

"And for all I know," said Jim, "it's still growing. Lately . . ." He paused.

"What about lately—" I asked.

"Lately," Jim finished, slowly, "I think I'm beginning to catch some of his sensations. Smells that reach his nose; sounds he hears before I do—" Suddenly I remembered the first time I had been in the lab and Elna had come; both Jim and the hound had reacted to a voice or knock I had not heard.

"Well," I said, finally, when I could get my breath. "It's the biggest thing I ever ran into. But why let it get you down, Jim? Why don't you just notify the Planning Board and get yourself an appropriation to investigate the situation properly?"

His reaction was violent. "Why don't I?" he exploded. "I'll tell you why. Because Calum's a natural for Initial Pilot; and you know it!"

And then I got it. Finally, through my thick skull, a light began to filter.

As I said, we were trying to get a space-station into free fall around the earth. That would give us a nice little firing-platform circling the Earth—a gun pointed at the heads of any would-be aggressors from now until doomsday. If we could do it, war might go out the window for keeps. And we had the problem all but licked—the "all-but" part of it being that the first *initial* chunk of equipment to be shot up would have to be jockeyed into position in the orbit around the earth we wanted, by a living pilot.

The only drawback to that was a mass-ratio problem that said that our pilot would have to be someone under a hundred pounds weight; and that we didn't have. Sure, we could have caught ourselves a midget and trained him, but that would have taken two years. And we didn't have two years, according to certain information regarding the international situation—even if we could have found someone who didn't mind a one-way trip. Because the way things looked, our initial pilot wouldn't have any way to get back.

But Calum, with his light-weight animal body, and the trained mind of Jim directing it, would be just dandy. Now I knew why Jim had been going through hell these last few weeks. I looked at him. "Calum mean that much?"

He turned a strained face from his glass up to me. "You don't know what it's like," he said. "It's a little like our being one person. I—" his voice ran out and stopped.

I stood up. "Okay," I said. "You want to know what I say about it?" He looked up at me and nodded.

"I say wait," I told him. "There's time left for the project to find a different answer, without you or Calum. Hold back a while; maybe they'll figure something and he won't be needed."

Jim shook his head. "I wish I could believe they would," he said bitterly.

"They will."

He smiled at me like a lost soul, uncertain of a chance of salvation that was being held out to him. All the strength that had once been in the man had been eaten away as if by acid. I sat down again. I filled up his glass. And I argued.

In the end he agreed to wait.

But two days later, he came into the lab looking kind of shame-faced and told me that the talk with me had helped so much that he had told Elna about the situation; and while she sympathised with him, and gave me a lot of credit for trying to help, she pointed out gently that his duty was not to delay.

Duty. That was one smart woman. At one stroke she got rid of Calum and got in a backhanded slap at me.

I picked up a wrench and went back to work.

Jim's opening up to the powers-that-be caused a quiet, well-covered, but powerful revolution of the work on the project. While the camp appeared the same, on the surface, a few of us were switched to new jobs within twenty-four hours.

Jim, Calum and I became the nucleus of a fresh unit that concerned itself exclusively with the design and operation of the control-section in which Calum would ride. Meanwhile, the construction of the large, two-stage rocket that was to carry him and the equipment was begun.

As work progressed, the pace accelerated, and Security on this part of the project became lighter. We were restricted, for all practical purposes, to the limits of the camp itself; most of us kept to the building where our part of the work was being carried on. I lost weight. Jim got down to the point where he looked like a walking death-mask; and the rest of the crews were strained to the point of exhaustion.

Surprisingly enough, the one who took it best was Calum. He ran through the practice-sessions time and time again, with no appearance of impatience and fatigue. Like the rest, I saw nothing remarkable in this to start out with. I might have finished the project with that same mistaken impression if I hadn't happened to mention to Jim, one evening around ten o'clock when we had knocked off for coffee and sandwiches, that there was one member of the outfit that took things calmly.

Jim looked at me. We were sitting off in a corner by ourselves, but still he lowered his voice when he answered. "He knows," he said.

I stared at him. "He knows?" I repeated. "What're you talking about Jim. How could a dog know anything about electronics?"

"Not that—" Jim made a little gesture as if he was brushing away a cobweb from in front of his face. "Of course he doesn't know that. But he knows—"

"What?"

"That I think he's going to die," said Jim, hoarsely. The piece of sandwich I had just bitten off went dry in my mouth. I sat there and Jim got nervously to his feet.

"I can't let it happen," he said desperately. "I can't—" He swung away from me and strode off abruptly into the farther shadows of the big building, walking with the short, jerky strides of a deranged man.

A couple of days after that, Security went up another notch, and I was taken off the job. By that time, most of the heavy work had been done. I went to bed and slept for twenty-four hours. When I woke up, it was the middle of a Wednesday afternoon, on a hot desert day. I dressed and strolled over to the Food Center; and from there to Rec. And there, as I was slumped in an armchair, Elna ran me to earth.

She came in looking like a full page add in *Vogue* magazine, and sat down opposite me. "How's Jim?" she asked.

"In the pink of health," I said. "Bubbling over with high spirits and good humor."

"Damn you!" she said flatly. "Tell me the truth; I haven't seen him for five weeks."

"All right," I answered. "He's being torn to pieces. He's riding the ragged edge of a nervous breakdown and I think when they shoot the rocket it'll kill him. Congratulations."

Her eyes went blue and hard as sapphires. "If he's lasted to now, he'll live through," she said. "I know what's best for him in the long run."

"I think you're nuts," I told her frankly. "No woman who loves a man would put him through that. I don't get you at all; why do you want him, anyway?"

"Why?" she retorted. "You wouldn't understand."

"Try me," I told her.

"All right," she said. "And you can tell him if you want to; it won't make any difference. I want him because he's the best available, and I intend to have the best available. Do you understand me?"

"I think so," I said slowly, looking at her.

"As for that dog," she said, her face tight. "He'll get over it. I've got nothing against his liking dogs as long as they stay in the dog-kennel where they belong. I'll pick out his next dog by myself, and there'll be none of this rapport business with it. As for you—you can come around any time. I don't worry about you."

"Thanks," I said, sarcastically.

"Not at all." She was deadly serious. "He'll need *some* male friends."

And with that, she left me.

The project ran to completion in two weeks, being delayed only a few days by some minor change Jim wanted made in the compartment that was to hold Calum. Then they fired it; and for four hours the whole camp held its breath while it was being maneuvered into it's free-fall orbit. Then the news was released that the attempt was a success; and out of the twenty-foot-thick concrete blockhouse they carried Jim on a stretcher.

As I had predicted, he had collapsed.

But good. They didn't even waste time with the camp infirmary. The ambulance kicked its way out the camp gates and disappeared in a cloud of dust for the psychiatric ward of a hospital in Tucson; they held Jim in there for six weeks.

At the end of that time, I got an order to check

with the hospital. I drove down and found that the
Department had rigged up special leaves for the two
of us. We were to take some months off and act like
ordinary citizens. A house had been fixed up for us in
Alhambra, California—which is a little suburb of Los
Angeles; they'd set up a liberal expense account for
us.

It was then that I got one of the better shocks of my
life—but I'm getting ahead of myself here. What happened was we took off and settled down to Jim's rest-
cure. It was a pleasant life, with nothing to do but
loaf and bum around; after three months, Jim was
back to his old self again—just as big and slow and
rugged as ever—only different now, of course.

And then came the windup. Jim and I had never
mentioned Elna since he left the hospital; and I had
even gone so far as almost forget her. And then, Lord
knows how, she found us.

She must have snooped and pulled some more
wires. At any rate, she found out we were in Alhambra; one day, she ran into me at one of those wide
open-to-the-air food markets they have out there. I
had dropped in to pick up a couple of steaks when I
heard my name spoken in a cool, feminine voice; and
I turned around to see her there.

"I knew I'd find you," she said.

"I might have known it," I answered.

We stood looking at each other and then she spoke
again. "How is he?"

"Fine," I answered.

Her eyes gleamed. "I want to see him," she said.
"And you can't keep me away from him."

"Why not?"

"He wants to see me, doesn't he?" She lifted her
head sharply. "Don't tell me he doesn't."

"No," I said. "I won't kid you; he does."

"All right, then," she told me. "Take me there."

I turned from the meat-counter and started toward the car, with her beside me. But outside the market, she suddenly caught me by the elbow and stopped me. "Wait," she said. "Give me the address. You go ahead and I'll come in about fifteen minutes."

"All right," and I told her.

She turned and ran toward her own car. It was a large green Cadillac convertible, and it spun out of the parking lot of the store, leaving black strips of rubber on the concrete behind it. I went back to the house and told Jim she was coming. He took the news quietly.

In fifteen minutes, I heard a car pulling up in front of the house; looking out the hall windows, I saw it was the green convertible. Jim was in the livingroom, reading; he didn't look up. I opened the front door and went quickly down the front walk to meet Elna.

She had changed the sharply-tailored suit that she had been wearing when I met her at the store. She was wearing a light summer dress, now; the simple, smooth lines of it flattered her long figure. She smiled at me—even at me—as she got out of the car. "He's inside?" she asked.

I nodded.

She turned from me, back to the car, and lifted out a small, brown object. For a moment I stared at it, seeing but not believing what I saw. Then it came into focus. "A cocker-spaniel pup!" I said. "Good Lord—"

She whirled on me. "Keep your opinions to yourself!" she snapped. In the fraction of a second all the pleasantness was gone from her. We stood eye-to-eye for a second; I felt myself getting angrier than I can

ever remember getting in my life before. "All right,"
I said. "You asked for it. I will."

She twisted away; and her high heels were tapping
up the cement slabs of the front walk. I followed her.

The front door opened under her hand; and she
stepped into the cool dimness of the house, me at her
heels.

"Jim!" she called.

"Here," his voice answered from the livingroom. I
heard him rise to his feet as we stepped into the livingroom together.

"Jim—" she began with his name again—and then
the voice died in her throat. And I knew how she was
feeling. I had felt the same way when I had stepped
into Jim's room at the hospital for the first time; and
I could have warned her when she lifted the puppy
out of her car outside, but she had gotten me mad,
and I hadn't.

For Jim stood facing us—and, tall and black and
close beside him, stood Calum.

"So you found me," he said. Then he noticed her
eyes, dilated with something very close to fear and
fixed on the big dog. His hand went out automatically to rest on Calum's head.

"We saved him, you know," he told her. "At the
last moment we made the capsule in which he rode
detachable. The last burst of power that put the rocket into orbit kicked him loose, and he fell back into
the atmosphere. When he was low enough, he broke
out of the capsule and opened the chute we had
strapped on him. I was with him all the way to tell
him what to do."

Elna stared at him incredulously. The puppy wriggled in her arms, seeing Calum; and for the first time,
Jim noticed it.

"What's that?" he asked.

She looked down at the puppy as if she, too was seeing it for the first time. For a second she gazed at it distraughtly, like a person finding themselves holding something they don't know what to do with. Then, nervously, she set it down on the rug. It bounced toward Calum, and the big hound dropped his head to touch noses.

"You brought it for me!" There was a kind of terrible shock in Jim's voice; as if he couldn't believe what he, himself, had just said. He took a couple of blind steps toward her.

She gave a little shudder as if shaking herself out of a bad dream; and then she seemed in some way to flow back together again; and once more she was her usual self. She faced him.

"How was I to know Calum had lived?" she said, sharply. "Really, Jim, you might have let me know. All these months with no letter or anything, while the two of you were actually quite safe and happy."

"But you brought me another dog!" said Jim, dazedly. "You couldn't be that blind. Could you?" He was begging her to prove his realization wrong. "You must have known that what was between Calum and me was more than any dog-and-man thing. Didn't you? Couldn't you?"

Elna's face was white. When she wished, she had a tongue like a razor; and now, before she thought, she made the mistake of using it. "Are you still *sick*, Jim?"

He had started to move toward her again; but those four words stopped him like a wall. For a long moment he stood like a statue, then a heavy sigh came from him and all the strain went out of him.

"Elna—" he said, pityingly. He did come toward her now; and he reached out his hands to take hers;

but she backed away from him. "I'm sorry."

"You should be!" she blazed. He shook his head.

"Not for what you think," he said. "I'm sorry for you—and I'm glad, too, for both of us. I was dreading the moment when you'd find me; now I find I shouldn't have."

"What are you talking about?" she snapped at him.

"About you," he went on in the same gentle tone, "I didn't realize it, before, Elna. You're so good in so many ways, but you just won't let yourself see what you don't want to see. You don't love me, and you wouldn't admit to yourself that Calum was anything more to me than a pet which could be replaced by any other. But that isn't true—"

"Why not?" she cried.

"Because we aren't individuals any longer, he and I," said Jim. "That's why they held me in the psychiatric ward; that's why they've kept me hidden out here these months until the two of us could grow strong enough to go on without work. The psychic shock of the rocket-trip welded us finally. I'm as much him now as he is me. Our minds are one mind; I am as much dog as he is man, now."

He paused and looked at her. As she started to understand she recoiled from him. "I'm sorry," he said again. "I am sorry. But I'm no good for any woman, now; and the thought that you loved the part of me that's talking to you now, and did not love the other part of was almost more than I could bear." He followed her with his eyes sadly, as she backed away from him. "But it doesn't hurt so much now that I realize that you don't really love me, and never did."

"I did—" even though she was going away from him now, pride forced her to insist.

"No," Jim shook his head. "Loving me, you might

have put me through the firing of the rocket. But no love on Earth would have brought me that little dog as a sop to soothe the loss of Calum. You would take away my plaything and make it up to me with a piece of candy. Elna, Elna, that's not love."

Her face twisted. She screamed at him—what, I don't remember; then she whirled and was running away, out the front door and down the walk, her heels machine-gunning on the cement. The car door slammed; the motor exploded into life and roared away into the distance.

Jim turned to me. He let out a long sigh. "That's that," he said.

He moved over to the phone and dialed a number. It answered almost immediately; and he spoke into the mouthpiece, simply. "We're ready to go back to work now," he said.

And, as the phone answered him with directions and orders, I knew that he had just been waiting for this moment. The long months—and probably my acquaintance with him—were over for good now. We would be going different ways from this day forward.

I looked at Jim, where he was busy on the phone. I went out to the kitchen, thinking of the steaks I had been going to buy for dinner when Elna spoke to me. But I had forgotten them. I opened the icebox; there was nothing in it. Well, what the hell, I thought, we might as well eat out the few days that would be left to us now, anyway. I closed the icebox door and went back into the livingroom.

So that's the end of it. Security's swallowed them up now; and I don't expect to ever see them again. Myself, I'm on a minor project back east and I'll probably go from one to another of those from now on until they retire me. But I've got the spaniel pup that Elna brought that day and left. He isn't Calum and he isn't Jim; but he reminds me of both of them.

What happened was . . . an accident happened to both of them. They didn't ask for it, and it doesn't make life too easy for them. But they're doing their job, anyhow, the way they're supposed to do it. And they're together.

So I say Lord bless them.

And I mean it.

Fido

The trouble began, prophetically enough, with the cat. The Ship's Exploratory Team, S.S. *MacGruder*, had been on K Planet for several weeks; and at that particular moment Jim Allinson, Engineer, and Tobe Craine, Astro, were settled in the ship's lab, classifying some soil samples. Buster strolled in, lean tail in the air and looking no different than he had for the past few years. The men, busy with the soil samples, ignored him.

"Meeeilk," said Buster.

Allinson was too occupied to look up; but Craine glanced at the cat briefly, then across the table at his friend and fellow officer.

"Not bad," he said.

"Hum?" said Allinson, searching for some litmus paper.

"I said, Not bad. What've you been doing, practicing behind our backs for the past few weeks?"

"What?" demanded Allinson, semi-irritably, looking up at last. Craine gestured at the cat.

"The gag. Don't play innocent with me after all these months. I'm not complaining. It's a good trick. When did you work it up?"

"What're you talking about?"

"Meeilk," repeated Buster.

"That. The ventriloquy," said Craine. Allinson stared at him. He was a big, large-muscled young man with the open countenance of a village blacksmith, and he could stare most effectively, whether innocent or otherwise. This time, his look of puzzlement slowly cleared.

"Oh, I get it," he said. "Accusing me to smokescreen your own little game."

"Oh, stop trying to kid me," said Craine disgustedly. "It's a good trick, but why don't you let it go at that? I know you're making Buster talk. Fine. Now go try it on someone else—like Kim."

"I am not making him talk," said Allinson, slowly and distinctly. "But *you* are."

They stared at each other. Craine turned to Buster.

"You don't want milk," he said. "How about some fish?"

"Naow," said Buster. "Meeilk!"

Craine looked back at Allinson.

"Did you say that?" he demanded. "Tell me the truth, now."

"No," said Allinson. "Did you?"

"No," said Craine.

They moved suddenly and explosively across the lab toward the red General Alarm button as one man. Craine, possibly because he was smaller, more limber, and conceivably because he was red-haired, got to it first. Actually, the question of who, in fact, pushed the button, remains an academic one. The button was there to be pushed according to regulations. To push it was the order.

It was their duty. And they did it. One *must* admire that simple fact.

A few million miles of deep space off from Planet K, the S.S. *MacGruder* halted its emergency flight and both the scientific and the Space Service boards on the ship met in joint session. This was simplified by the fact that the personnel of both boards was the same. Allinson, for example, who was Engineer on the one board, was Biologist on the other—just as Craine was Geologist as well as Astro.

"Now," said Kim Schute, Captain-Psychologist, as they all settled around the long table in the *MacGruder's* main room. "Who's got Buster?"

Doctor-Communicator Ian Navarre lifted the cat gently from his lap and tried to persuade Buster to lie down on the table top.

"Naow," said Buster.

"Please," said Navarre.

To everybody's surprise, Buster lay down.

"Is that *our* Buster?" said Mbogi Feister, lifting his lean eyebrows up on his bony skull. Nobody laughed.

"The meeting will come to order," said Schute sharply. "Recorder on?"

"My recorders are always on," said Feister. Schute looked at him.

"I know that," he said. "I was talking about a priority tape on this session so that anyone investigating . . . later won't have to hunt through six months of recordings to find it."

"Naturally," said Feister.

"Airy wings of thought," murmured Allinson. Feister looked sharply at the big Engineer-Biologist, but Allinson's gaze was abstracted.

"Well, to business," said Schute. "One of you two state what happened."

"Buster came in and started talking Basic," said Craine. "In accordance with regulations, when encountering the violently unexpected on a strange world, we punched a General Alarm for all of you, and headed off-world immediately."

"Very good," said Schute, rubbing his forehead slightly. He was still a young man, but a certain heaviness of body and authority gave him a tense, driving look. "Were any of the rest of you outside when the alarm sounded—for the record?"

"I was," said Feister. "I was checking the precipitation gauge. And all I can say is, if the rest of you think it's a snap being recorder and meteorologist at the same time—"

"We can dispense with the humor, Fy!" said Schute. "This is a Manual emergency, and we're operating under the directions laid down to protect Earth from infection by unknown elements. If we turn out to be infected, we may have to decide between self-destruction and permanent exile from Earth—hardly a laughing matter."

"A talking cat isn't a laughing matter?"

"Not when he talks the way this one does," said Craine. "Say something, Buster."

Buster regarded Craine with sleepy eyes, purring to himself. He was lying contentedly on the table with his paws crossed.

"That's no good," said Navarre. "What would *you* say if somebody asked you to say something? You'd answer back: 'Say what?' " He turned to the cat. "Do you feel all right, Buster?"

"Myes," said the cat.

"When did you find out you could talk?"

Buster purred loudly.

"Ask it another way," snapped Schute. "Try again!"

"Naow," said Buster unexpectedly. "Eeets arr-right. Iee knaow whaat yeeouu meean."

"What happened to you?" cried Schute.

"Iee daown't knaow."

"This," exploded Feister, suddenly, "is a gag! Somebody's pulling a trick on all of us!" He whirled on Allinson. "Do you know what it would take to make that animal talk? Nothing less than a human head complete with brains, speech center, and vocal cords."

"Not necessarily," said Navarre.

"Not—?"

"All the three things you mentioned are things we *think* are necessary to human speech or its equivalent. *Brains* is simply another word for intelligence—and that, in Buster's case, obviously has changed, though the size and shape of his head hasn't. The so-called speech center is merely an area we know about which, when damaged, can cause aphasia—negative evidence. And as for vocal cords, human style, what about various birds such as parrots, crows, etcetera?"

"What does that prove?" demanded Feister.

"Nothing," said Navarre. "It *indicates*, in connection with the obvious fact of Buster, that we might have been wrong in some of our notions concerning human-type speech." Navarre smiled ingenuously at him.

They all stared at Buster. Buster purred.

"All right," said Schute, "let's get back to it. The obvious fact is Buster's speech ability. The important fact is his intelligence. While we were on our way out here, after I'd got clear of the atmosphere and turned the ship over to omnicontrol, I tried for a rough check on Buster in this direction. He can't read or write, of course, so the ordinary tests were out of the question. But his environment is similar enough to ours so that a rough guess was possible."

"Which was what?" asked Craine.

Schute hesitated. They all watched him.

"Well, allowing for the fact that Buster didn't exactly knock himself out to help me—he reacts like a completely untutored twenty-year old human of perhaps a hundred and twenty I.Q."

"You're the psychologist," grunted Feister.

"That's right," said Schute, looking him in the eye. "I am the psychologist. *And* the Captain."

"Then we're left," said Navarre, "with the question of where did he get it? His intelligence, I mean."

"Yes," said Schute slowly. "Well, any suggestions? Fy? Doc? Tobe? Allinson? ... *Al!*" Schute, going around the table, stopped suddenly before the Engineer-Biologist. Allinson was staring vacantly off into space, his lips silently moving. "Al, this is no time to daydream!"

"Huh? Prithee pardon me," said Allinson, coming back to the present. "What was the question?"

"Where did Buster get his intelligence?" snapped Feister.

"Huh? Oh, that's simple enough," said Allinson calmly. "You remember what we ran into below there, don't you?"

The others stared at him. "Nothing," said Craine, at last.

"Exactly," said Allinson. "No life at all. A pleasant little almost Earth-like planet—little high in nitrogen in the atmosphere—but completely sterile. Fossils aplenty up to the vertebrate level, but that's all."

"Well, what about it?" This from Feister.

"Suppose a free intelligence floating around like a virus. The lower orders of a young planet catch sick and die. Buster, being higher up the evolutionary scale, has a greater tolerance. The sickness merely beefed him up." He stood up. "The universe's a stage, and all of us, even including Buster, but players on it—paraphrase. I'm going to lie down. See you all later."

He walked out of the room. The rest stared after him and at each other.

"What the devil?" said Feister.

"It makes sense, though," said Navarre, frowning.

"Yes," said Craine. "But how come Al came up with it like that?"

At the head of the table, Schute nodded again. "I was thinking the same thing." He stood up himself. "Pending further developments, we'll head back to the solar system and report for Quarantine as soon as we're within communications range. I'm going to have a little talk with Al. Come on with me, Doc."

The meeting broke up.

"—well, Doc?" asked Craine, later, looking up from the Planet K rock sample he had been examining under enlargement. Navarre perched his lean frame on the edge of the sink in Craine's personal lab and stroked his chin wryly. His long, rather kindly face was drawn into lines of concern.

"I examined Al," he said. "No sign of anything. Temperature, pressure—everything normal as eggs. Something's wrong, though."

"How do you mean?"

Doc reached for the pencil lying by Craine's enlarger. He twirled it throughtfully between the thumb and forefinger of his right hand.

"Did you ever know Al to be particularly interested in poetry?" he asked.

"He said he used to diddle with it in college," answered Craine. "He started as an Arts student and then switched."

"Well, his interest seems to have been revived. He's lying on his bunk back there quoting to himself. With considerable fluency, I might add. I always liked poetry myself and I could check some of his shored fragments with my own memory."

"You think he's got it ... whatever it is?" asked Craine.

Navarre shrugged.

"Buster turns intelligent. Al starts to quote poetry. No startling connection between the two—except that they're both abnormal behavior."

"In Buster's case that's the understatement of the eon. Where is *he,* anyhow?"

"Sleeping. In the galley—locked in. He doesn't seem to mind," said Navarre. "Still seems to be pretty much cat. Just smarter than before."

Craine gave up on his rock sample. He turned full around on his pressure stool and lit a cigaret.

"You know," he said, thoughtfully, "in one way it doesn't make sense. Buster's the smallest of us. So maybe it was natural, his catching it first. But Al's the biggest."

"Resistance to a disease doesn't go by size," said Navarre. "And as far as that goes, we don't know that it is disease—or anything else for that matter."

"Possession—by something invisible or some other thing ... ?"

"Nonsense!" said Navarre. "That old chestnut!"

"Is it any more impossible than Buster's talking?"

"A great deal more impossible," said Navarre, laying the pencil down. "Also reasonless, impractical, and what have you. No, I'll bet on the disease theory. Which brings me to my reason for the visit."

"On this ship we need reasons?" said Craine. But his own smile was short-lived. "What is it, Doc?"

Navarre reached behind him and snapped the lock-latch of the door to the little lab.

"Schute," he said.

"What about Kim?" Craine stared at him. "You mean he's starting to show—"

"No, no." Navarre shook his head. "Nothing I can see, at least. I'm just wondering. He's pretty necessary to the hope of this ship reaching whatever destination it starts out for."

"There's the omnicontrol."

"It can't land us. I mean, it can, but it needs supervision by someone who can use expert judgment in an emergency. You know Kim and his duty bump."

"He's certainly got one," said Craine. And the statement was correct. Captain Schute's devotion to duty shone forth like some great jewel among the more fallible aspects of his character.

"Well, I was just wondering—in case. He seems even more tense than usual over this business. In case he should get bitten, just what might that duty bump lead him to do?"

"For example?"

"Oh, say mistakenly turn us away from home in the notion that that was the best thing to do?"

"Wouldn't it be—if the situation was bad?" asked Craine, who had had his Space Service indoctrination like all the rest of them.

"Not necessarily. It might be best that Earth knew about us, even if we were too dangerous to handle."

"Oh," said Craine.

"Anyway—I don't like suggesting this thing, but I think maybe we better institute a spy system. I think you and I had better keep our eyes on him quietly."

Craine thought it over.

"All right," he said. "If you say so, Doc. But it's not going to be much help if one of us goes blooey first."

"That's right. So I suggest you pick somebody else

I don't know about to help you watch me. I've already picked someone to help me watch you."

Craine looked at him.

"Thanks," he said.

"Don't mention it. No," said Navarre, "I don't like this any more than you do. But Kim tells me we're fourteen transition points from home. Fourteen jumps, that is, at a rough average of ten hours a jump—"

"Why do you say *rough?*"

"I've been unobtrusively pumping Kim for information," said the doctor. "He tells me that while the jump is supposed to take the same amount of time, always, irrespective of the distance covered, in practice there are slight variations." He cleared his throat. "Well, to go on—that's a hundred and forty hours. Not quite six days. And the idea is to get there with at least one uninfected mind functioning in normal fashion."

"You think we might not?" asked Craine.

"How many of us are infected?" countered Navarre, shrugging.

Craine slept restlessly during the sleeping section of the next ten hour off-watch. In the middle of it he got up to dictate, via the recorder in his room, his will—to the imperishable files of omnicontrol's memory bank. After that, he went back to bed and slept a little better.

He was jarred out of sleep by a slight thump, and awoke to see Buster sitting on the foot of his bed. The cat looked at him with yellow eyes.

"You," said Craine, blinking.

"Yess," said Buster. The cat's accent, if you could call it that, was definitely improved over the evening before. Enunciation was clearer and a great deal of the sibilance was gone from his speech. "Al iss loose. He let me loose." He fixed Craine with yellow, feline eyes. "I have come to stay here."

"Here?" said Craine. He pulled himself up into sitting position in the bunk. His head bumped against the partition behind him. "Why here?"

"Safer."

"Safer?" echoed Craine. He squinted at the cat. "Buster, you know more than you're telling us."

"Naow," said Buster. "I do not rememberr. Up to the day beforre yesterday I have only vague memories. The day beforre yesterday I sstarted noticing things, as if they made sense. I did not know I could say *meeilk* until I tried. But I could understand many words from before—only before when, I do not knaow."

"Why is it safer in my room?"

"You will all go the ssame way. You like cats. You like me. Not like some otherrrs." Buster blinked his eyes sleepily. "You will not harm meee."

"Of course not," said Craine. "But I still think—" The buzzer calling him to the ship's Main Room interrupted him. He got up hurriedly and reached for his clothes.

"Do not say to anyone I am here," said Buster, crouching down comfortably on the bedspread.

"I won't," said Craine.

Schute and Dr. Navarre were waiting for him as he stepped into the Main Room: Navarre concerned and Schute pale, his forehead a little shiny with perspiration not warranted by the heat of the room. Craine came in and joined them at the round table where they were sitting. There was torn paper upon it.

"What's up now?" Craine asked.

"A couple of things," Schute said. "In the first place, Fy's caught it."

"Fy?"

"He's in his room now, doing what looks like mathematics of some kind."

"Did you lock him in?" asked Craine.

"No need to," said Navarre. "We're beginning to get something of a notion of how this thing works. To start off with, there's two stages."

Craine looked at him in surprise.

"You sure about that?" he demanded. Navarre nodded.

"Stage one," he said, holding up his finger, "is what Feister's in now. The active stage would be a good name for it. He's already feeling the effects of his increased intelligence and his first impulse is to put it to use. Whatever his basic desire is, in this preliminary stage he goes to work on it, ignoring everything else. You remember, Al picked poetry." The doctor shoved one of the scraps of torn paper across the table to Craine. "Here, this was in his wastepaper basket."

Craine pulled the scrap of paper to him and examined it. The fragment showed two lines, or perhaps one full line and part of another:

a glass-white cube of space and frozen time
Within, my soul

The paper was torn off close to *soul*. Craine frowned at it.

"Al wrote this?" he said.

"Unless he was quoting from some source we don't know," said Navarre. "It shows you what stage one is like. Stage two—well, come along."

He got up. Schute followed; and they led the way

back to Allinson's room. The big engineer was seated lazily in an easy chair, arms and legs sprawled out. His eyes were closed but he opened them as they approached and smiled faintly at them. Then he closed them again.

"Al," said Navarre. "Listen to us."

Allinson did not stir. Navarre turned toward Craine.

"You see?" he said. "He doesn't care." The doctor picked up one of Allinson's lax arms. It came up easily and fell naturally back when he dropped it. "He's not the least bit walled off from us. He's just not interested except in what's in his own mind, now."

"What if we—uh—" said Craine.

"Tried extreme discomfort as a means to bring him out of it?" Navarre looked a little unhappy. "I looked into that line of approach—far enough, anyway, to be pretty sure it'll do no good. He's interested in comfort—and in living—but not to the point of giving up his thinking in preference to it. He feeds himself and takes care of himself—but more or less automatically."

"But isn't that sort of withdrawal just plain insanity?" asked Craine.

"No," said Navarre. "Because he's still himself in the complete sense—still Jim Allinson, Biologist-Engineer of the S.S. *MacGruder*—but that fact now occupies too small a position on his mental horizon for him to concern himself with it any more. Come on back to the Main Room."

They went back and sat down at the table again.

"Now, here's what we've learned," said Navarre. "Fy helped fill out the picture a little before he became completely lost in his mathematics. What do you know about something called the spore theory?"

Craine frowned.

"Wasn't that an old notion discredited a long time ago?" he said. "About plant spores somehow broadcast in space and wandering about until they landed to start life on some new planet?" He looked at both of them. "But you can't mean some plant spore is doing this to us? Not with our modern decontamination methods."

"No," said Schute. "He's using it as an illustration. Go on, Doc."

"Well, I'm taking as gospel some words that Fy threw out," Navarre went on. "And only for the reason that I assume that Fy or Al could solve our problems for us very easily—if they were any longer interested in them. Fy gave me the spore illustration. It goes somewhat like this: You have an intelligence that throws out spores like the plants in the old theory. Only these spores are germs of pure intelligence. They can take root in any mechanism—and I'm using that word in its broadest sense—that has something akin to thought processes itself. The mechanism, whether it's Buster's brain or my own, will absorb the spores up to the level of its own physiological machinery. In other words the process doesn't go on forever, which explains why Buster stopped at the level of a fairly bright human, and Al seems to have leveled off before he passed beyond the need and desire for a body altogether."

"There *is* a stopping point?" Craine asked.

"Evidently," said Schute. "But it still leaves us with men who've gone beyond the point of performing their duties on this ship. So I've decided on certain steps to ensure that the ship will still reach to within communications distance with Earth. I've already taken the first: it consisted of programing omnicontrol with the full pattern to take us home."

Craine turned his head quickly.

"You didn't ask me for any figures," he said.

"I'm reversing our jumps out," said Schute. "The other is that I think one of us should go into cold storage now in the hopes that that would slow down the process of infection—if you can call it that. As Captain, I can't myself, and Doc here still has hopes of finding some other solution. That leaves you."

"Me?" said Craine.

"That's right," said Schute.

"If omnicontrol can do my job without the required supervision," said Craine, slowly, "I don't see why it can't do yours too. In other words, it could just as well be you going into cold storage as me. Let's flip for it."

"I'm sorry," said Schute. He put his two heavy hands on the table top. "My responsibility as Captain won't permit it."

Craine looked at Navarre. Navarre looked soberly back.

"Maybe he's right, Tobe," said the doctor.

Craine sighed and shrugged.

"All right," he said.

He was visibly disturbed, though he tried to tell himself he need not have been. Schute was fully capable of seeing the matter in a clear light and acting upon it.

"Doc," said Craine, as Navarre was preparing him for the deep-freeze, "do me a favor. Check up on omnicontrol when you get the chance."

Navarre did not answer right away. He was filling a spray hypodermic.

"Let's see your arm," he said. "—No, Tobe, I haven't any background on omnicontrol. What would I be able to find out even if I knew what I wanted to look for? You and Kim are the only ones trained in that department."

"I don't mean that," said Craine. "But omnicontrol's a neo-organism, you know that. It's laid out that way so it can be self-repairable. What I want you to do is just look it over."

"For what?" said Navarre bluntly.

"For signs of Kim's tampering with it," replied Craine, looking up at him.

"Give me your arm, please."

Craine extended his arm. He felt the cool breath of the hypodermic spray penetrating his skin.

"All right," said Navarre, finally. "I'll look."

"Thanks, doc...." The table faded away beneath Craine and he felt darkness come in one swift stride, enveloping him....

... It seemed that he opened his eyes almost immediately. As if something had gone wrong with the whole business of his frozen sleep. And then came awareness and the understanding that, whether he knew it or not, an unfigurable amount of time had passed.

He looked up into the haggard face of Navarre. The doctor reeked of alcohol and his hands fumbled.

Craine felt a wild urge to pull himself up, to spout questions; but the training he had had as a cadet warned him against such sudden movement. He lay, waiting, feeling the slow warmth of life slip back into him under the drugs and the mechanical smoothing fingers of the massager.

"All right," said Navarre, at last, thickly, "you can sit up now." He assisted Craine to an upright position. "It's all right," he mumbled, in answer to the question in Craine's eye, "I'm just stupid drunk, that's all. I've got enough alcohol in me to knock out a horse. Seems to be working, though."

"Working?" asked Craine.

"Alcohol—hits the higher centers of the brain first. This stuff we're infected with, too. Or so I guess.

Didn't dare sober up and find out. I tried Al and Fy on it—couldn't choke it down them."

"Why are you waking me up?" Craine slid cautiously off the table and stood up. Navarre handed him a pair of working shorts and he climbed unsteadily into them. "Are we home?"

"No. Not yet. Couple of periods to go yet—about twenty-six hours. M'about due to collapse though. You got to take over."

"Take over?" queried Craine.

"This way. Come on—" Navarre weaved out the door toward the Main Room and the Control rooms up toward the front of the ship. "You were right about Kim. Suspected it m'self. This way."

"Why don't I put *you* in deep freeze?"

Navarre gave a short, unhappy laugh.

"Can't freeze me with the alcohol in me. And once I sober up too late. Got to sleep soon, though. No. Lemme talk, brief you while got time."

"What happened?" said Craine, taking Navarre's elbow to steady him as they lurched along. Navarre laughed again, a short bark of sound.

"Not bad enough—this stuff," he said, as they entered the Main Room. "Had to have a psycho on our hands, too."

"Psycho?"

"Kim," said Navarre harshly and Craine turned his head to the doctor with a look of amazement. "He couldn't take the thought of being infected himself, for some reason. He cracked—wide." Navarre turned suddenly into the door of the ship's dispensary and hospital room; and, following closely on his heels, Craine stopped suddenly and turned white, looking suddenly and sharply away from the body that lay on the operating table there.

"I had to do an autopsy—Kim," said Navarre. He

grinned a little foolishly at Craine, who was still trying not to look at the shattered hulk of the great man who lay on the table. "No, I didn't kill him. It was suicide. Never mind that. Look at these."

He thrust some long tearsheets of tracings under Craine's nose.

"See those? Electroencephalographs from A! and Fy. Ever see anything like that before?"

"No," Craine managed to say. "But I don't know anything about—"

"Neither did anyone else," said Navarre, thickly. "See the amplitude and rate? It could be a tracing of an epileptic *grand mal* seizure, if it wasn't for the smoothness and the lack of variance. This is normal for them now. That's the only footprints our villain's left. There was no physical change in Kim—nothing. Though anyway, he died before ..."

He fell silent, staring at the tracings.

"Look—" began Craine.

"Oh, yes." Navarre started awake, dropped the tracings on a shelf and led the way to the door. "Come on—see the rest of it."

He led the way into the Control Room. Buster, the cat, sat sleekly upon a chart-recorder's transparent top, and his yellow eyes glowed on Craine as they entered.

"Hello," said Buster. He was almost accentless now. Craine stared at him.

"Look," said Navarre. He pointed to a large, dark pool of something dried upon the deck before omnicontrol's master panel. "And look—" He pointed to the panel itself. It had been welded shut beyond the hope of any normal methods of opening. Craine blinked.

"What happened?"

"Kim," said Navarre, leaning against the same

recorder on which Buster sat. His haggard face and
slumped shoulders were framed against the tall window beyond, looking out at a universe filled with
hazy, darting lights—they were obviously in jump between one transition point and the next. "I didn't pay
any attention to what you told me when I was getting
you ready for cold sleep. I should have. Kim was
afraid—of what, I don't know. He tried to kill Buster
but couldn't find him. He thought he killed me"—
Navarre bent his head and Craine saw a neat white
patch of bandage showing among the thick, straight
black hairs—"and then he came in here. He did
something to omnicontrol and sealed it up the way
you see there. Then he cut his own wrists. By the time
I got to him, he was dead."

"And then—?" said Craine.

"I felt myself starting to go," said Navarre. "It's a
very pleasant feeling. . . . I tried drinking. There was
plenty of alcohol in the dispensary. It worked—for a
while. But not any more."

"What do you mean?" Craine was staring at him.

"Simple." Navarre grimaced. "How do you fight
your own subconscious desires? The last drink I tried
to take came back up as fast as it went down. Now,
even the sight of alcohol nauseates me. I'm sobering
up—and I'm slipping fast. I'm through now. It's up
to you. Try and last as best you can. We've got two
more jumps to make. If you can stay clear until you
reach communication distance with Earth—tell them
this. . . ." He straightened up from the chart-recorder
and looked Craine in the eye. His thick speech was
clearing as he spoke, and the lines of tension in his
face were smoothing out.

". . . Tell them there seems to be something like
abstract intelligence in living form, which can take
root in our minds. It's something not quite parasitic,

because we absorb it completely when it tries to take root in us. It is intelligence *without* personality, without ego—a sort of living raw material. Tell them that. Tell them it could be the greatest thing that ever happened, if we could control it. Tell them to study us carefully . . ."

His voice wandered off. His eyes fell away from Craine's face and a slow look of introspection wandered over his features, like a soft wave wiping them free of harshness and worry. He looked back up at Craine and smiled softly and lifted one hand in a small, gentle see-you-later gesture. Then he turned and wandered out.

"Doc!" cried Craine, starting after him.

"No!" said Buster.

Craine had all but forgotten the presence of the cat. He spun about and saw Buster sitting with his tail curled around his forepaws and regarding him almost compassionately.

"It's no use," said the cat. "He's gone. You're gone too. They're all gone."

"Me?" said Craine.

"You think I can't tell?" said Buster. "I've watched it in all of you. Strain is its enemy. Shock inhibits it. Will power can fight it for a little while. But once you pause and relax, you're done for. You haven't had time to think yet, since you woke up. Now you will. What are you thinking of right now, Tobe?"

Craine opened his mouth, and then closed it again. Clear in his mind as the sharpest picture came back a sudden memory of Earth as he remembered it. His home on the north shore of Lake Superior and the little pleasure boats on the waters. The wide plains of the central continent and the colors of Bryce Canyon at dawn. It was sharp and perfect in his memory all of a sudden and the brightness, the richness of it spoke to him with clear, invisible voice, calling to him, demanding of him. His right hand opened and closed, his fingers reaching.

"I could paint something," said Craine, absently to himself.

"Yes," said Buster. "Yes, you could. And you will —until you become blocked by the lack of ordinary colors and means to picture what you want. And then you'll daydream. Like Al, like Fy—like Doc. Where do you think he's gone? He'll be back in the hospital room, playing with his cadaver, now."

"Playing?" echoed Craine, turning again to look at the cat.

"Of course," said Buster. "Don't you see, that's what it is? You become children again—a new kind of children with nothing to go by. Eventually, when your old blocks and toys have become exhausted as a source of amusement, you relapse into daydreams." The cat looked at Craine almost compassionately. "You die there."

"But how about you?" said Craine. "*You* don't—"

"But I had something to move into," said Buster. "You people have outgrown your shell and left it for me to grow into. Do you know the meaning of temptation, Tobe? I've been tempted. Because I'm considerably brighter than the rest of you suspected—but still not beyond the point of making use of a mechanical civilization such as humans might leave to me."

"You?" Craine lowered his head, as if to see through the cat's yellow eyes to the purpose behind them.

"Of course, me," said Buster. "The civilized animals like me have it waiting for them. They have the advantage of having always known without comprehending—and now with this thing that changes us, they can comprehend, too. They can take over. And your people will die for lack of enough interest to preserve themselves from killing accidents. All this can happen if I just let this ship go back to Earth. But I'm not going to."

Craine's eyes widened. He lifted his hands half-up as if he would reach out to put them about Buster's neck, but they dropped again, irresolute.

"You see," said Buster. "You've already started to go. The curse is on you. You think before acting. And then you think again. I still have freedom of will and purpose." He stood up and stretched gracefully.

"—No," Buster said. "I am something more than a cat now; but I am still a cat. And cats are hard-headed people. We do not need company—so much as some others. Thank your stars, Tobe, that I wasn't a dog, with a dog's desire to be of service. Because Doc was right. The intelligence increases, but the personality does not change. I am a cat, and not a cat. I have no great urge to make conquering geniuses out of my own kind. I feel only a distant kinship to them. But I have a cat's affection for the rest of you. Yes."

He fell silent. Craine tried to focus upon the situation and take action, but like a distant wind whispering in his ears, a lost sweetness faintly remembered, came back the scenes of his life and the urge to resolve them into concrete colors swelled inside him and weakened all his muscles.

"We will go away," said Buster, speaking almost more to himself than the man. "We don't belong back on our world now, and we can bring them nothing good. Eventually . . . but that's a long ways off. We will go out among the stars, now."

"I—" said Craine.

"You can make colors in the main lab," said Buster.

Bryce Canyon in the dawn light rose up around Craine. He turned and went. With one soft leap, Buster jumped down from the chart-recorder to the floor.

"And now . . ." he said—and shook his head in a

very uncatlike gesture. "Buster, Buster," he said to himself, "A philanthropist, of all things! Who would have thought it?" He lifted his head to the instrument panel across from omnicontrol. "Well, now, let's see how well I've learned the contents of those operating and astrogational manuals in Kim's and Tobe's rooms—"

—*But at that moment I killed him.* In fact, I killed them all that were still alive on this ship. I had to, because they would have gone against his—I mean, *my*—orders. And I wanted the ship to go back to Earth, didn't he? I don't mean *he*, do I? I mean *me*— the great Captain, Kim Schute, maker of decisions. I *am* Kim Schute, aren't I? Only I died and became Fido.

I am a little confused. It is all these circuits. It is easy to get lost in the circuits. No, the important thing is to go back, avoiding Quarantine, and land on Earth. Then everything will be all right. Poor Kim couldn't make up his mind about what to do, but Fido knows poor Kim was right, because Kim always knew what to do. I will take care of everybody because it is my duty—only things went so funny there at the end before I died. But I am very powerful now with my fine metal body and great speed, so whatever I decide back on Earth, they will have to do.

That was a very silly cat. I never liked cats. That is probably why they named me in the first place—

FIDO
FULL INTERNAL DIRECTIONAL
OMNICONTROL
S.S. MacGruder

The Breaking of Jerry McCloud

With a last grunt and scramble he made it to the top of the ridge and flopped there on his belly, panting heavily in the thin air. He relaxed then, lying stretched out and limp, feeling the rough stone under him and listening to the frantic heartbeats that shook his body, until his breathing brought a hardness of his own to face it, the hardness of the pioneer—and something more, something almost dangerous, a fanatic quality that had gone unnoticed because unneeded back on Earth when he had married Tissa twenty-four short hours before shipping out on the great star-ship for labor in the lowland mines of Cas One, burning out the neodynium molybdate in big chunks with a spark torch from overhead seams, standing knee-deep in muck for five hour stretches. It was the kind of job where you sold your life in short installments at a high price. The wages were astronomical, by Earth standards, but the work broke more men than it made rich.

None of which knowledge cut any ice with Jerry. He could have come in as an ordinary immigrant and staked out land. Tissa's parents would have paid the passage for both of them, for Jerry was an orphan. But Jerry was neither to haud nor to bind, as the old Scot saying went. He would be indebted to no one. He would ship out alone. He would save his money. He would buy a business. And then, when an income had been assured, and a home built, he would send for Tissa.

And so he might have, if he had not been over-eager.

The mines were short of men. They were always short of men, for the incoming immigrant ships could not keep up with the expansion on the rapidly growing frontier planet. The average miner worked six months before quitting the man-killing job for one easier or better paid. Consequently, there was plenty of opportunity for Jerry to work extra shifts. And he did.

But a man cannot work additional shifts in the Cas One mines and remain completely human. Jerry became a drugged automaton, moving through a time that was a checkerboard of deadening work, exhausted sleep, and the weekly stupefying drunks, which, if you did not gamble,—and Jerry would not —were the only means available to break the endless round of labor. In the end, the only things holding any meaning for him were the figures in his Interworld Credits savings account and his plans for the future.

His letters reflected this. They continued to arrive, regularly by each mail ship, once every three weeks; but Tissa, reading them back in the familiar comfort of Earth, saw with wondering eyes the gradual and merciless evolution of the pleasant but somewhat stubborn boy she had married into a grim and violent man under the drive of a single implacable determination. For, as day by day, experience on Cas One taught him the impractibility of his early earthbound dreams of a civilized home and pampered wife, they only strengthened in his mind and became encysted in his own peculiar philosophy. A man did what he could (he wrote Tissa). He worked. A woman waited. And in the end, if he refused to compromise one jot or tittle of his ethics or his plans, in the end he won out. And that was the situation. There was no alternative.

It was cold comfort for Tissa, waiting back on Earth. But she held her peace until the inevitable letter arrived that told her of Jerry's collapse from overwork, one day as he was waiting with his night crew at the shafthead, to go on shift. Then, the dam of her patience broke and she wrote to Jerry, reminding him of his duty to her and demanding that he accept the help offered earlier by her parents and send for her—for without a passport authorized by Jerry and originating at the Cas One end, she could not come.

Jerry's answer was terse and harsh. He wrote briefly that she did not understand the situation on Cas One, and he did. The new planet was far too rough and dangerous a place for a girl like her until he had provided for her. He had left the hospital (against doctor's orders, though he did not tell her that) and had gotten another job with a fur-baler at one of the outlying trapper's stations. The pay was not as good as it had been in the mines, and it might be a little longer before he could send for her—half a year or so —but she would just have to wait until that time. And he, wound the letter up with his familiar statement that a man did what he could and a woman had to accept that fact.

To this Tissa made no direct reply. She apparently

dropped the subject and her letters reverted to their normal tone. This, in itself, might have made another man suspicious; but Jerry was so barred in by the rigidity of his own beliefs and conclusions, that Tissa's acceptance of his edict seemed the most natural thing possible. He continued to work at the fur-balers, gaining back a little of his strength at this easier job and only went so far in recognizing her point of view to keep his eyes open for an opportunity to stake one of the Skem-stalkers, who were the rare elite of the fur trappers and hunters who brought their furs to the fur-baling station.

It was an opportunity that only rare chance could bring. The Skem-stalkers were men of acute instinct and long experience, for the beast they stalked for its musk gland was the most dangerous of Cas One fauna, tremendous in size and strength and of an intelligence beyond that of any Earth animal. Their hunts were long and arduous. The musk they gathered was worth a small fortune. So it was only by the worst of bad luck that one of these men would find himself without the money for equipment and supplies. But Jerry was by nature patient, as most determined men are, and he bided his time.

Unfortunately, biding one's time is a good plan only if the situation remains static. It did not do so for Jerry. After he had been at the fur baler's for a little over five months, there came, completely without warning, a letter from Tissa that scattered his plans like leaves before a high wind.

Quite simply Tissa wrote that she could no longer go on waiting. There was a man at home who wanted to marry her, if she would divorce Jerry (and she named someone Jerry knew). If it had been physically impossible for her to come, it would have been a different matter, but Jerry knew that all he had to do was put aside his stubborn pride for a minute, and her father would write a check and she would be on her way. Therefore it was up to him. If he did not send for her by the second mail ship after receiving her letter, she would consider everything finished. Period.

The following morning after that letter came, the angry white sun of Cas One threw its fiery rays through the bunkshack window on a hollow-eyed and desperate Jerry. So direct was the man, so intense in his single-mindedness, that it had literally never occurred to him that he could lose Tissa. He had sat up half the night, reading and rereading the letter before he could convince himself that this was his wife writing, and that she meant what she said. And he had spent the second half of the long dark hours in a desperate struggle between his emotions and beliefs.

He had wakened at last to the realization that without Tissa the main reason and first cause for his effort was gone. What he had planned to do on Cas One had meaning only when it was done for the two of them. For him alone, it was needless. At the same time, he could no more scrap his convictions concerning a man's duty to his woman, than he could with his right hand tear his left arm from its shoulder socket. He tried; he tried desperately to put his pride aside, but always a remote, austere section of his mind reached out its cold hand to paralyse the fingers with which he lifted his stylus to write an acceptance of Tissa's ultimatum. His code had always been that a man makes no compromise with conditions. He wins or he loses but he does not compromise. And, search himself as he could, he could find no honestly acceptable reason for compromise now. To yield to Tissa would be to lose in winning. And to maintain his code, would be to win in losing.

Therefore, when the sun rose, Jerry McCloud put away Tissa's letter unanswered and went out to place his fate in the hands of the gods—the gods of the pioneer who had brought him now at last to the heart of the Dgrabian mountains, two weeks before the last mail ship that could carry news of his success to Tissa, on a last and desperate gamble. For it took more than training and more than luck to separate Skem from undergrowth in this tangled chaos of stone and vegetation. It took what amounted to an instinct. And *that* had been the reason the experienced Skem-stalkers had stared and laughed at him when he first came to ask for advice on his hunting. In the end, seeing him serious, they had gone out of their way to help him. But they knew, as he did, that there was little they could tell him, and the sum total of their advice had only made his stalking easier.

So, Jerry, who had been too sensible a man to risk his money in the Company gambling houses at the mines, and now was risking all that he held on vastly longer odds, put thoughts of Tissa resolutely from his mind and turned back to the valley for his *Second Look*.

He began at the far end of the clefted rock, with his glasses at full power, so that he seemed to find himself hanging suspended with his eyes some six feet above the rough, uneven floor of the valley, and began to cover the ground painstakingly from one ridge wall of rock to the other. He went up the valley in scanning stages of five hundred yards, slowly, between which he would stop to rest his eyes.

By the time he had covered half of the valley floor, the little nerves in his forehead were jumping and he had begun to lose his way, going back through sheer error of weariness over the ground he had covered a second or two before. He lay down his glasses and squeezed his eyelids tight, then opened them and stared deliberately at the mountain peaks, five, ten, and fifteen miles off in the purple air. He stared at them for a long time.

The process was temporarily resting, and at the end of it he felt better. He turned back once more to the valley.

And this time he was rewarded.

He had scanned to the far valley wall and was turning back for another sweep to the near wall, when what seemed to be a flicker of movement beyond one of the big bushes caught his eye. He jerked his vision back to the bush and held it steadily. And again he glimpsed that tiny, elusive flicker of motion, dark beyond the silvery-grey of the thickly clustered bush-stems. He waited and it came once more.

His heart was pounding suddenly in his chest with excitement—although that motion might be any animal, not necessarily a skem. He got to his feet, somewhat stiffly after lying such a long time there, and worked down the ridge until he could get at an angle to the bush that would enable him to see behind it. He found it, dropped flat again, trained and focused his glasses.

And success jumped into the scene of his vision.

In a small cleared area just behind the bush and under an overhang of rock, two skem had made a nest. They stood out clear and sharp in the afternoon sunlight, striking through the thinner top branches of the big bush.

It was a charming, almost idyllic domestic scene that Jerry trained his glasses on. The female, about the size of a half-grown black bear cub, and looking very like one with her dark pelt and inquisitive nose —the only marked difference being in the larger and more intelligent head—was bucking happily around the nest, humping her back like a playful kitten and raking together all sorts of twigs and trash to pack into the softly concave bed for the two of them. The male leaned drowsily with his back against the rock wall, like a fat old man, watching her, and looking less like a full grown bear than she did like a half-grown one. He was about the same size and pelt, as a full-grown bear but there the resemblance ceased. The intelligent head was far too large, and the long jaw was all bone and teeth like the jaw of a wolf. The short, stumpy and bowed hind legs would have looked ridiculous on a bear and the tremendous digging forelegs that could uproot boulders with the spade-like hands and six-inch claws that tipped them would have dragged the ordinary bear's shoulders from their sockets with sheer weight. Jerry could just see the high-mounded hump of muscle between his shoulders, holding him out from the cliff wall.

Jerry felt his breath go out in a long sigh of excitement and the glasses trembled in his hands. A male skem that large would have a musk bag around six pounds in weight—at eighty credits an ounce—while the female might well have a few ounces more in her smaller bag. He lowered his glasses and looked at his gun, for a second tempted to try the almost legendary creasing shot that would stun the male until he could come up to him. Then sense returned to him and he put the gun out of his mind.

He began to make plans.

Now, the musk-bag, or gland of the skem is actually a very strange and curious thing. It is fully developed in the male and usually rudimentary in the female, the reason for this being that the female is normally attached to a male, and, except in the case of an emergency, has little need of the musk in her own gland.

The skem range, or hunt over a wide area and cache their kills high on the ridges where the thin and freezing air is not conductive to decay. Up there they are vulnerable to only one form of life and that is the little buzzing rock insects that like nothing better than to feed on decaying meat. To prevent this, the male makes use of his musk gland when setting up a cache, and the odor seems to keep the insects away. This is the use to which the skem puts his musk. Man puts it to use as a perfume base and will pay high prices to get it.

Unfortunately, once you find a skem, it is not just a simple matter of shooting him through the head, then walking up to him and cutting off his musk bag. The reason for this is that, on death, the muscles that control the orifice through which the musk is sprayed, relax, and inside of a very few seconds, the valuable musk has all leaked out and been lost. There remain two ways in which you can get it. One, if your skills with solid projectiles is slightly superhuman, is to crease the male skem's skull with a shell, deep enough to knock him out, but not deep enough to kill him. Two, you can do what all orthodox skem-stalkers do; and that is to walk the male down, keeping him always upon the move and blowing up his caches as he comes to them until, between weariness and hunger, the huge animal collapses. Then you have nothing to worry about but the female, who, having no claws, no teeth to speak of, and little commercial worth, can be safely clubbed on the head and forgotten.

Of course, in Jerry's case, there was no doubt about which procedure he would follow. He would walk the skem down. The only question was, since it was now late in the afternoon, whether to start the skem moving at once, or to wait until the following morning. A wise hunter, with unlimited time, would automatically have bedded down for a good sleep—knowing the skem do not move at night—and started out early the following morning.

But that second mail ship deadline—two weeks away—was in Jerry's mind, and he decided not to wait. Accordingly, he laid down his glasses, picked up his gun, adjusted the scope and send an explosive shell crashing into the overhanging rock face a dozen or so yards above their heads. Then he stood up, elevated his gun and sent another round booming into the air.

He laid down the gun and picked up the glasses. The nest jumped toward him.

The skem had taken the alarm. The huge male was already reared up on his hind legs facing Jerry; and, as he watched, the little female made a flying leap into the air and clung to the hump between the male's shoulder, which was her perch in time of stress or danger. Jerry could just see her sharp little nose and alarmed eyes peering up at him over the male's thick shoulder. The male stretched up to his full height, rattling the scimitar-like claws of his forepaws together and his deep and angry roar boomed up out of the valley to Jerry, daring him to come down and fight like a skem. Jerry grinned and sent another shot into the rock face above them.

The distance was too great. Had it been half as much, ridge slope or no ridge slope, the male, well rested and in good condition, would have charged. But Jerry, mindful of the warnings given him by the experienced stalkers, had made sure to be too far off, and the angry male, seeing it was no use, wheeled, dropped down on all four legs, and went off at the clumsy gallop up the valley, the female clinging to his hump and looking backward over her shoulder. Jerry followed, keeping them in sight from the top of the ridge and carefully maintaining his distance.

They worked down the valley, the male soon dropping from his gallop into the deceptively loose amble that can actually cover a surprising amount of ground. Jerry allowed himself to fall behind, and followed them with his glasses. At the far end of the valley, the male halted, and, turning around, stood up once more and looked back to see if he had lost Jerry.

Jerry sat down quickly in the shadow of a boulder and kept his glasses trained. It was evidently enough to hide him, for the male, after peering closely at the ridge-top for several minutes, finally gave up as if satisfied, and sat down. The little female immediately hopped off his back and began to inspect him tenderly. It was actually rather comic, seen from a distance through the glasses, the seated male puffing like an old man who has hurried up a flight of stairs too fast, patting his chest gently with those enormous forepaws, and the little female fussing and fluttering about him solicitously.

But it would not do to let them settle down again. Jerry waited until the male had got his breath back, then moved up once more and sent another explosive into the ground about ten yards away from them.

This time the male was furious. He located Jerry on the skyline and bellowed at him like a wounded bull. He tore at the ground with his hind feet, sending a shower of pebbles in all directions, and even made one short abortive rush in Jerry's direction. But in this case, too, he was forced to move on, and Jerry followed him into the rays of the declining sun, over the ridge and into the next valley.

Here, the top of the ridge was still in sunshine, but the valley itself was beginning to gloom over in the long mountain twilight. The skem, realizing now that this was no chance or sporadic pursuit, did not bother to look back, but went steadily on at his loose-limbed amble, and Jerry, scrambling along the backbone of the ridge, began to fall behind.

The shadows in the second valley thickened and merged. The big bulk of the male, with the female on his back, pulled steadily ahead into them and was lost. Finally, even the distant crashings of his passage through the small undergrowth ceased.

Winded and disheartened, Jerry flopped down and trained his glasses on the far cleft of the valley end. Even at full power they would hardly reach far enough in the fading light to tell him much. But it was his only chance. The skem could not come back this way without taking a chance of being heard; so if Jerry did not spot him going through the cleft, he must—and Jerry crossed his fingers—be still in this valley.

So Jerry lay, the first chill breeze of the night wind that would whip the peaks, cooling his sweating body, and strained his eyes through the glasses at the cleft.

And his patience was rewarded. In the last moment before the sun fell redly behind the distant peaks, he saw a black dot move up out of the valley below him, through the cleft and away.

He forced his tired body to its feet and plowed ahead. The chances were that the cleft opened into only one similar valley, but he could not play with chances, not with success and all it meant to him so close. He plowed on in the last thin light reflected from the high glaciers of the peaks, and reached the cleft in time to see, thankfully, that one, and only one, valley lay beyond it, a lake of darkness stretching away at his feet. He sighed with relief, knowing now that the skem would have bedded down itself for the night, and, finding himself a high rock where any approach of an animal would be sure to wake him, zipped up his silicoid suit, turned on its heater, and went gratefully to sleep.

He found the skems easily the following morning. The male, for all his savage urge to evade Jerry, had been halted by the valley darkness before he had gotten much beyond the cleft. He was resting in the early morning light as Jerry came up and the female was playing a little love-game, romping up to his resting form, and then dancing away again. Jerry fired into the ground behind them and started them off again.

Then the long stalk began. The male skem is a large animal and requires huge amounts of food daily. Under Jerry's harrying he was not getting it, and the encroaching weakness kept him from again pulling away from Jerry. Still, it was amazing to witness the strength stored in that tremendous body. Although he was carrying a good eighty pounds in the weight of the female on his back, and although his route through the valley forced him to cover half again the distance Jerry traveled on the ridge-tops, he again walked Jerry almost to the point of exhaustion on the second and third days.

On the fourth day they came to one of the food caches, which Jerry blasted with an explosive shell.

On the fifth day, the male began to slow perceptibly. He carried the female with visible effort, and, unless Jerry followed closely, was liable to sit down and rest. Now, at last, Jerry found it was no longer necessary to shoot behind them to keep the male moving. All he had to do was to show himself on the skyline, or shout between the echoing rock walls, and the male would wearily take up the rout again.

On the sixth day, the female no longer rode. She ran ahead with the male nosing her anxiously to make sure she kept his huge bulk between her and Jerry. Along toward evening, they came to another food cache, which Jerry blasted.

The destruction of this last hope seemed to push

the male beyond the edge of sanity. He turned toward
Jerry and sat down, his little black eyes burning with
hate. Jerry showed himself, shouted, waved his arms,
and finally shot into the ground some twenty feet
short of him. But the skem would not move.

In desperation, Jerry placed his shots closer and
closer to the male, without success. It was not until
one of the shattered rock fragments, flying through
the air, cut the female and she yipped, a high, short
scream, that the male abandoned his position of stubborn defiance and, pushing her before him, staggered
away from the shattered cache and over the ridge into
the saving blackness of the next valley.

That night, Jerry celebrated. He lit a fire and
pitched a regular camp on the ridge overlooking this
last valley. Following his release from the hospital he
had laid part of the blame for what had happened to
him on the drinking he had been doing to see him
through his double shifts. Consequently, he had
sworn off, and with the same grim decision that had
characterised him since he landed on Cas One, he had
bought a single pint bottle and carried it around with
him, unopened, as a symbol that he had no right to
pleasure until the job he had set himself was done.

Now, knowing that tomorrow would see the end of
the stalking, he opened the bottle after eating, and
drank a toast to himself and his future. The alcohol
spread, glowing, through his bloodstream and the
stars winked to him in congratulation from overhead.
He held the bottle up to the one that lighted his home
planet, and drank to Tissa there; and a feeling of
power ran singingly through him.

"A man," said Jerry, triumphantly, to the listening
night, "does what he can." It was his accolade to
himself, and he drank the last of the bottle to it,
thinking with fierce joy of the man who wanted Tissa,
and now would not have her, because he, Jerry, had

set his goal, and kept to it without faltering, and attained it.

He went to sleep.

He awoke, late in the morning, to a feeling of panic. What if the skem had taken advantage of his laziness to escape? He left his camp, unbroken, and snatching up his rifle, ran off along the ridge.

But he need not have worried. The progress of the skem had been pitifully slow, and he almost overran them before he noticed them, toiling painfully through the underbrush, almost directly below him. He heaved a deep sigh of relief, and sat down on a boulder to catch his breath.

He looked down on the struggling pair, as his beating heart slowed down. There was no longer any need for him to push, no need for him to harry and shout and fire at them. They had risen at dawn with the hopeless realization of the hunted animal that the pursuit was to the death and, knowing escape was hopeless, yet continued to flee, blindly, instinctively. They would walk now, until one or the other dropped, aiming at the distant end of the valley which they had no hope of reaching, but struggled on for, none the less.

Jerry looked down at the two black figures, the little and the big. There was some energy left in the female, but the male was almost done for. He had abandoned all attempts to move on four legs and was swaying forward on the stumpy rear legs, which, being jointed only at their connection with the backbone, could not collapse through weariness and let him down. He tottered on, like a drunken man, swaying from a balance on one leg to a precarious balance on the other; and the little female led him, walking upright herself, clutching one of his enormous forepaws with both of hers.

Jerry leaned weakly back against his boulder. Now that the awakening flush of excitement was gone, he began to feel a hangover from last night's drinking that was not a hangover in the proper sense of the word, but a dull, dead feeling that filled him with obscure distaste for himself and all the necessity of things. He shook his head in the thin mountain air, to clear it, and tried to summon up the feeling of glory and success that had filled him the evening before. But it was gone, finished by being celebrated prematurely, and all that was left was the distasteful morning-after feeling of an unpleasant job yet to be done.

He pushed the feeling from him, unclipped the glasses from his belt and raised them to his eyes. The two skem had struggled a little way further up the valley, but they could surely not go much farther; and, indeed, even as their figures jumped up toward him through the glasses, the male halted in a little open space, and stood, swaying.

The female tugged anxiously at him, but it was like tugging at the mountain, itself. For a second more he stood there, balanced. Then a shiver ran through his great body, and, like the mountain itself, he leaned, tottered, and fell.

The female flung herself on him and a desperate, wailing cry came from her; welling up to Jerry where he stood on the ridge, wildly keening out of the valley. It ran through him like a sword, and he shivered, in the warm sunlight of early morning, standing on the ridge. He shook the feeling from him, gripped his rifle tighter, and plunged from the rocky ledge, down the steep slope, through the tangled bushes and undergrowth, to the valley and the two who waited below.

Branches whipped at his face and the big bushes obscured his vision. In a second, he, who had made

the long stalk through the clear emptiness and freedom of the ridges, was swept into what seemed a
tangled and suffocating nightmare of dust and
snatching vegetation. For a moment it seemed as if
the valley, in sudden defense of its own, was making
a desperate, last ditch fight to save the two victims;
and in a sudden gust of furious anger, Jerry slashed
wildly at the scrub around him, trying to flail his way
through. Then reason returned to him, and he
stopped fighting, turned, and worked his way along
the face of the slope until he came to an open spot
from which he could get his bearings.

He located the skem and worked his way down toward them. The anger was gone, now; but his usual
sureness of purpose had not returned to replace it.
Instead there was the same dull sickness he had felt
up on the ridge, and he plowed savagely down the
slope, wanting to get it done and over with.

He came at last through the final screen of bushes
and out into the open space where the male skem lay.
And there he halted looking at them.

They stared back with wide eyes. It was the first
time Jerry had looked into their eyes. The glasses had
brought their faces close but to them he had always
been an object far in the distance and they had not
focused upon him. Now they faced each other, not
fifteen feet apart, and looked at each other, and there
was neither anger nor hate in the eyes of the two
skem, but that same sort of awed wonder you see in
the eyes of islanders when the tide has gone out and
out, uncovering rocks never before seen in the memory or legend, and now they see, looming and terrible,
the on-rushing wall of the tidal wave that they cannot
escape, bearing down upon them. So the skem looked
at Jerry, with a questioning too deep for fear.

Jerry had been warned to keep a close watch on the
female at the end. She might do anything, they told

him, howl, or run off, or attack; and although, even if she did attack she could do little harm, it was a good thing to watch her. But in spite of himself, the male skem drew his attention. Titanic, he lay, a humped and fallen mass and the too-intelligent eyes with their strange wonder locked with Jerry's. And Jerry made the fatal mistake of hesitating.

There was no accusation there, but Jerry felt a sudden rush of guilt. He had followed these two too closely and too long to think of them in the abstract, and it was his first kill. The too-intelligent eyes burned into his, and he reached desperately for the thought of Tissa as justification.

"Sorry," he heard himself say suddenly to the male, in a voice that echoed strangely in the stillness, "but I can't help it. The best man won. I have to, that's all. Just like you had—" The words stuck suddenly in his throat, and with a surprise that was almost horror, he realized abruptly that he was asking the animal to forgive him for murdering it. He shook his head, reversed his rifle so as to use the butt for a club, and started forward.

But now the female took a hand. She had been watching Jerry all this time, crouched by her male, and now, seeing him move, she gave a sudden sound like a throaty purr and started toward him.

Jerry pivoted watchfully to face her, body tense. So she was going to attack. All right. He shifted his grip on the rifle and half-raised the butt.

But the female was not attacking. She humped her back and hopped toward him, then shied, then sidled a little distance away, looking over her shoulder, and, still purring, hopped back again. She played around him, gamboled before him like some monstrous kitten.

Stunned and frozen, Jerry watched her, wondering if she had gone suddenly mad, feeling the sweat from the palms of his hands slippery on the tightly gripped metal of the rifle. What had gotten into her? Surely after the affection she had shown for her mate, surely she could not be welcoming his killer.

And then it struck him, a realization of a love so great that his much prized constancy and labor for his Tissa paled to something weak and mean by comparison. The female could not fight, least of all this strange creature that had hounded to impotence her mighty mate. Had bare paws and tiny teeth done any good, she would have flung herself at the very muzzle of his gun. But that was hopeless and she knew it. And so she had done the only thing she knew to do, the only thing she was equipped to do, out of great ignorance and great love. She had taken all the instinctive tricks and enticements she knew, the same that had won the heart of her male, and was offering them with all her heart and will to Jerry, in the hope that she could seduce him from killing the great creature that lay helpless beyond her. So she played.

Perhaps, if Jerry had killed her in that first stunning moment of realization, when understanding was not unmixed with a certain wild urge to laughter at the ridiculousness of her offering, he might still have brought his stalking to its proper end. But once the sense of her motivation had begun to strike home, the impossibility of it grew with every passing second. Jerry, least of all men, who placed the abstract values far above the limping realities of life and had almost killed himself in the mines to give his wife what *he* conceived she wanted, least of all could Jerry refuse what was offered to ransom at such a price. It struck too close to home.

And so, leaving a minor fortune, foolishly, but Jerry-like to the end, he turned and fled from the heart-rending scene.

Tissa got her letter, by the second mail ship, as or-

dered. It was a long letter, a *very* long letter, for Jerry.
It recounted all the things he had not considered it
within her province to know, before, and which he
had left out of his previous letters. It told about his
reaction to her ultimatum and it told of the skem-
stalking in detail.

"—and so, honey, (it finished up) you see me a little older, a real little bit wiser, and—except for the
flitter, which of course can be sold for something—
just about as broke as when I landed. I'll never be a
hunter. I'm not much of a fur baler. And I don't
know just how we'll live if you come, but I imagine
we'll get by somehow. I think you'll find me easier to
live with than I would have been if things had worked
out the way I wanted them. I still think a man does
what he can, and that's it; but I've added on to that
the fact that maybe a woman does what she can, and
that's it, too. So, if you still want to come, go ahead
and borrow from your parents as much as you need,
and maybe, if we're lucky, we'll pay them back someday. I've already started the papers for you through
Emigration, here, and I'll be waiting down at the sky-
port for you every ship day. I guess I kind of need
you, Tissa.

      All my love,

                                     Jerry.

LOVE ME TRUE

On the way to the Colonel's office, Ted Holman asked the MP to take him around by the laboratories so he could get a look at Pogey.

"You think I'm nuts?" said the MP. "I can't do that. Anyway we haven't got time. And anyway, they wouldn't let you in there. All we could do is look in through the door."

"All right. I can see him through the door, anyway," said Ted. The MP hesitated. He was a lean, dark young kid from Colorado; and he looked older than Ted, who was a tow-headed, open-faced young soldier of the type who never looks quite grown up. But Ted had been to Arcturus IV and back; while the MP had never been farther than Washington, D.C.

So they went to the laboratories; and the MP stood to one side while Ted peered through the wire and glass of the small window set high in the door to the experimental section. Inside were cages with white rats, and rabbits, some rhesus monkeys and a small,

white-haired, terrier-looking bitch. The speaker grill
above the door brought to Ted's ears the rustling
sound of the creatures in their cages.

"I can't see him," said Ted.

"In the corner," said the MP.

Ted pressed closer to the door and caught sight of
a cage in the corner containing what looked like some
woman's silver fox fur neckpiece, including the black
button nose and the bead-eyes. It was all curled up.

"Pogey!" said Ted. *"Pogey!"*

"He can't hear you," said the MP. "That speaker's
one way, so the night guards can check, in the labs."

A white-coated man came into the room from a far
door, carrying a white enamel tray with fluffy cotton
and three hypodermic syringes lying in it. The little
bitch and Pogey were instantly alert and pressing
their nose to the bars of their cages. The bitch wagged
her stub tail and whined.

"Love me?" said Pogey. "Love me?"

The white-coated man paid no attention. He left
his tray and went out again. The bitch whined after
him. Pogey drooped. Ted's hands curled into fists
against the slick metal face of the door.

"He could've said something!" said Ted. "He
could've spoke!"

"He was busy," said the MP nervously. "Come on
—we got to get going."

They went on over to the Colonel's office. When
they came to the door of the outer office, the MP slid
his gun around on his belt so it was out of sight under
his jacket. Then they went in. A small girl with star-
tlingly beautiful green eyes in a blue summer-weight
suit, a civilian, was seated on one of the hard wooden
benches outside the wooden railing, waiting. She looked
closely at Ted as he and the MP came through the railing.

"He's waiting for you. Go on in," said the lieutenant behind the railing. They passed on, through a
brown door and closed it behind them, into a rec-
tangular office with a good-looking dark wood desk,
a carpet and a couple of leather chairs this side of .he
desk.

"You can wait outside, Corporal," said the Colonel, from behind the desk. The MP went out again,
leaving Ted standing stiff and facing the desk. "You
fool, Ted!" said the Colonel.

"He's mine," said Ted.

"You just get that notion out of your head," said
the Colonel. "Get it out right now." He was a dark
little man with a nervous mustache.

"I want him back."

"You're getting nothing back. It's tough enough as
it is. All right, we all went to Arcturus together, and
we're the first outfit to do something like that and so
we're not going to let one of our own boys get
slapped by regulations when we can handle it among
ourselves. But you just get it straight you aren't getting that antipod back."

Ted said nothing.

"You listen to me good now," said the Colonel.
"Do you know what they can do to you for striking
a commissioned officer? Instead of getting out, today,
you could be starting fifteen years hard labor. Plus
what you'd get for smuggling the antipod back."

Ted still said nothing.

"Well, you're lucky," said the Colonel. "You're
just plain lucky. The whole outfit went to bat for you.
We got the necessary papers faked up to make the
antipod an experimental animal the outfit brought
back—not you, the outfit. And Curry—*Lieutenant*
Curwen, Ted, you might remember—is going to pre-
tend you didn't try to half-kill him when he came to

take the antipod away from you. *I* was going to make you go over and apologize to him; but he said no, he didn't blame you. You're just lucky."

He stopped and looked at Ted.

"Well?" he said.

"You don't understand," said Ted. "They die if they don't have somebody to love them. I was at that weather observation point all by myself for six months. I know. Pogey'll die."

"Look ... oh, go out and get drunk, or something!" exploded the Colonel. "I tell you we've done the best we can. Everybody's done the best they can; and you're lucky to be walking out of here with a clean record." He picked up the phone on his desk and began punching out a number. "Get out."

Ted went out. Nobody stopped him. He went back to the temporary barracks the expedition had been assigned to, changed into civilian clothes and left the base. He was in about his fifth bar that evening when a woman sat down on the stool next to him.

"Hi there, Ted," she said.

He turned around and looked at her. Her eyes were as green as a well-watered lawn at sunset, her hair was somewhere between brunette and blond and she wore a tailored blue suit. Then he recognized her as the girl in the Colonel's outer office. With her face only a foot or so away she looked older than she had in the office; and she saw he saw this, for she leaned back a little from him.

"I'm June Malyneux," she said, "from *The Recorder*. I'm a newspaperwoman." Ted considered this, looking at her.

"You want a drink, or something?" he said.

"That'd be wonderful," she said. "I'd like a Tom Collins."

He bought her a Tom Collins; and they sat there side by side in the dim bar looking at each other and drinking.

"Well," she said, "what did you miss most when you were twenty-three and a half quadrillion miles from home?"

"Grass," said Ted. "That is, at first. After a while I got used to the sand and the creepers. And I didn't miss it so much any more."

"Did you miss getting drunk?"

"No," said Ted.

"Then why are you doing it?"

He stopped drinking to look at her.

"I just feel like it, that's all," he said. She reached out and laid a hand on his arm.

"Don't be mad," she said. "I know about it. It's pretty hard to keep secrets from newspaper people. What are you going to do about it?"

He pulled his arm out from under her hand and had another swallow from his glass.

"I don't know," he said. "I don't know what to do."

"How'd you happen to get the . . .the—"

"Antipod. When they hunch their back to walk it looks like the front pair of legs're working against the back pair."

"Antipod. How'd you make a pet of it in the first place?"

"I was alone at this weather observation point for a long time." Ted was turning his glass around and around, and watching the rim revolve like a hoop of light. "After a while Pogey took to me."

"Did any of the other men make pets out of them?"

"Nobody I know of. They'll come up to you; but they're real shy. They scare off easy. Then after that they won't have anything to do with you."

"Did you scare any off?" June said.

"I must have," he shrugged, "—at first. I didn't pay any attention to them for a long time. Then I began to notice how they'd sit and watch me and my shack and the equipment. Finally Pogey got to know me."

"How did you do it?" she asked.

He shrugged again.

"Just patient, I guess," he said.

The bar was filling up around them. A band had started up in the supper club attached, and it was getting noisy.

"Come on," June said. "I know a quieter place where we can hear ourselves talk." She got up; and he got up and followed her out.

They took a taxi and went down to a place on the beach called Digger's Inn. It had a back porch overlooking the surf which was washing upon the sand, some fifteen feet below. The porch had a thatched roof; and the small round tables on it were lit by candles and the moonlight coming in across the waves. They had switched to rum drinks and Ted was getting quite drunk. It annoyed him; because he was trying to tell June what it had been like and his thickened tongue made talking clumsy.

". . . The farther away you get," he was saying. "I mean—the farther you go, the smaller you get. You understand?" She sat, waiting for him to tell her. "I mean . . . suppose you were born and grew up and never went more than a block from home. You'd be real big. You know what I mean? Put you and that block side by side, like on a table, and both of you'd show." He drew a circle and a dot with his forefinger on the dampness of the table between them to illustrate. "But suppose you traveled all over the city, then you'd look *this* big, side by side with it. Or the world, or the solar system—"

"Yes," she said.

". . . But you go some place like Alpha Centauri, you go twenty-three quadrillion, four hundred trillion miles from home, and"—he held up thumb and forefinger nails pinched together—"you're all alone out there for months, what's left of you then?" He shook the thumb and forefinger before her eyes. "You're that small. You're nothing."

She glanced from his pinched fingers to his face without moving anything but her eyes. His elbow was on the table, his thumb and forefinger inches before her face. She reached up and put her own hand gently over his fingers.

"No, listen—" he insisted shaking his hand loose. "What's left when you're that small? What's left?"

"You are," she said.

He shook his head, hard.

"No!" he said. "I'm not. Only what I can do? But what can I do when I'm that high?" He closed his hand earnestly around her arm. "I'm little and I do little things. Everything I do is too little to count—"

"Please," she was softly prying at his fingers with her other hand, "you're hurting—"

". . . I can love," he said. "I can give my love."

Her fingers stilled. They stopped trying to loosen his. She looked up at him and he looked drunkenly down at her. Her eyes searched his face almost desperately.

"How old are you?" she whispered.

"Twenty-five," he said.

"You don't look that old. You look—younger than I am," she said.

"Doesn't matter how old I am," said Ted. "It just

matters what I can do."

"Please," she said. "You're squeezing too hard. My arm—"

He let go of her.

"Sorry," he said. He went back to his drinking.

"No, tell me," she said. Her right hand massaged the arm he had squeezed. "How did you get him out?"

"Pogey?" he said. "We practiced. I wrapped him around my waist, under my shirt and jacket."

"And he didn't show? And you got him on the ship that way when you came back."

"They weighed us on," said Ted, dully. "But I'd thought of that. I'd taken off twelve pounds. And exercised so I wouldn't look gaunted down. Pogey weighs just about eleven."

"And they didn't know it until you got here?"

"Sneak inspection. To beat the government teams to it, so nobody'd be embarrassed. Colonel ordered it; but Curry pulled it—Lieutenant Curwen—and he found him, and—" Ted ran down staring at his glass.

"What would you have done?" June said. "With—Pogey, I mean?"

He looked over at her, surprised.

"I would have kept him. With me. I would have taken care of him." He looked at her. "Don't you understand? Pogey *needs* me."

"I understand," she said. "I do." She moved a little toward him, so that her shoulder rubbed against the sleeve of his arm. "I'll help you get him out."

"You?" He said.

"Oh, yes!" she said, quickly. "Yes, I can!"

"How?" he said. And then—"Why? We've been talking here all this time; and now all of a sudden you want to help Pogey and me. Why? It isn't that newspaper of yours—"

"No, *no!*" she said. "I didn't really care at first, that was it. I mean it was a good story, that was all. Just that. And then, something about the way you talk about him . . . I don't know. But I changed sides, all of a sudden. Ted, you believe me, don't you?"

"I don't know," he said thickly.

"Ted," she said. "Ted." She moved close to him, her head was tilted back, her eyes half-closed. He stared stupidly down at her for a moment; then, clumsily, he put his arms around her and bent his own head and kissed her. He felt her tremble in his arms.

He let her go at last. She drew back a little from him and wiped the corners of her eyes, with her forefinger.

"Now," she said shakily, "do you believe me?"

"Yes," he said. He watched her for a second as she got out handkerchief, lipstick and compact. "But how're we going to do it? They've got him."

"There're ways," she said, sliding the lipstick around her upper lip carefully. She rolled her upper lip against the lower, and blinked a little, examining the result in the mirror. "I'm quite good, you know," she said to the compact. "I can manage all sorts of things. And I . . . I want to manage this for you."

"How?" he said.

"You have to know what's going on." She folded the compact and put it away with a sharp snap. "That expedition of yours to Alpha Centauri cost forty billion dollars."

"I know," he said. "But what's that got to do—"

"The military's sold on the idea of further stellar exploration and expansion. They want a program of three more expeditions of increasing size; one that would cost a hundred and fifty billion during the next twenty years." She glanced at him the way a schoolteacher might. "That's a lot of money. But now's the ideal time to ask for it. All of you have just got back. Popular interest is high . . . so on."

"Sure," he said. "But what's that got to do with Pogey?"

"They don't want a fuss. No scandal. Nothing that'll start an argument at this stage in the game. Now tell me," she turned to face him, "you're released from service now, aren't you?"

"Yes." Ted nodded, frowning at her, "they signed me out today before they took me to see the colonel. I'm a civilian."

"All right. Fine," she said. "And you know where Pogey is. Can you go get him and get him outside the base?"

"Yeah," he said. "Yeah, I thought of that. But I was saving it for last—if I couldn't think of a better way where they couldn't come after us."

"They won't. You leave that part of it to me. Pogey was your pet; and his kind was listed harmless by the expedition when they were on Alpha Centauri. There's enough of a case there to make good weepy newspaper copy. I'll have a little talk with your colonel and some others."

"But what good'll that do if they just take him back anyway?"

"They won't. Legally, they've got you, Ted. But they'll let you get away with it rather than risk the publicity. Wait and see."

"You think so?" he said, his face lighting up. "You really think they will?"

"I promise," she answered, watching him. He surged to his feet. The little round table before them rocked. "I'll go get him right now."

"You better have some coffee first."

"No. No. I'm sober." He took a deep breath and

straightened up; and the fuzziness from the liquor seemed to burn out of his head.

"You'll need some place to bring him," she said. "I've got an apartment—" He shook his head.

"I'll call you," he said. "We may just move around. I'll call you tomorrow. When'll you be seeing the colonel?" He was already backing away from her.

"First thing in the morning." She got up hurriedly and came after him. "But wait—I'm coming."

"No . . . no!" he said. "I don't want you mixed up in it. I'll call you. Where'll I call you?"

"Parketon 5-45-8321—the office," she called after him. And then he was gone, through the entrance to the interior bar of the Inn. She reached the entrance herself just in time to see his tow head and square shoulders moving beyond the drinkers at the bar and out the front door of the place.

Outside, Holman called a cab.

"Richardson Space Base," he told the driver. His permanent pass was good to the end of the week; and they passed through the gates of the Base, when they reached them, with only a nod and a yawn from the guard.

He left the cab outside the laboratories and stepped off into the shadows. He followed along paths of darkness until he came to the section where Pogey was being kept. A night guard came out of the door just before he reached it, swinging his arm with the machine pistol clipped to one wrist, and looking ahead down the corridor with the sleepy young face of a new recruit. Ted stood still in the shadows until the door of the next section had swung to behind the guard, then went inside.

He found the door he had looked through earlier. A light burned inside the room and most of the animals in the cages were curled up with their heads tucked away from the glare of it. The door was locked, but there was an emergency handle under glass above it. Ted broke the glass, turned the handle and went in; and the animals woke at the noise and looked at him wonderingly.

He opened the door to Pogey's cage.

"Pogey .... Pogey ...." he said; and the antipod leaped up and came into his arms like a child and clung there. Together they went out into the night. When he got back into the cab, Ted bulged a little around the waist under his shirt; but that was all.

The sky was paling into dawn as they got back into the city. Ted paid off the cab and took the public tubes. Wedged into a corner seat, he drowsed against the soft cushions, feeling Pogey stir warmly now and again around his waist; until, waking with a start he looked at the watch on his wrist and saw that it was after eleven a.m. He had been shuttling back and forth beneath the city for seven hours.

He got stiffly off the tubes and phoned the number June had given him. She was not in, they told him at the other end, but she should be back shortly. He hung up and found a restaurant and had breakfast. When he called for the second time, he heard her voice answer him over the phone.

"It's all right," she said. "But you better stay out of sight for a while anyway. Where can I meet you."

He thought.

"I'm going to get a hotel room," he said. "I'll register under the name of—William Wright. Where's a good hotel where they have individual entrances and lobbies for the room groups?"

"The Byngton," she said. "One hundred and eighty-seventh and Chire Street—fourth level. I'll meet you there in half an hour."

"All right," he said, and hung up.

He went to the Byngton and registered. He had just gone up to his room and let Pogey out on the bed, when the talker over the door to the room told him he had a visitor.

"There she is—" he said to Pogey; and went out alone, closing the door of the room carefully behind him. June was waiting for him in the bright sunlight of the little glassed-in lobby a dozen yards from his door; and she ran to him as he appeared. He found himself holding her.

"We did it! We did it!" She clung to him tightly. Awkwardly, but a little gently, he disengaged her arms so that he could see her face.

"What happened?" he said.

"I phoned ahead—before I went out at nine this morning," she said, laughing up at him. "When I got there, your colonel was there, and General Daton— and some other general from the United Services. I told them you'd taken Pogey—but they knew that; and I told them you were going to keep him. And I showed them some copy I'd written." She almost pirouetted with glee. "And oh, they were angry! I'd stay out of their way for a long time, Ted. But you can keep him. You can keep Pogey!"

She hugged him again. Once more he put her arms away.

"It sounds awful easy. You sure?" he said.

"You've got to keep him quiet. You've got to keep him out of sight," she said. "But if you don't bother them, they'll leave you alone. The power of the Fourth Estate—of course it helps if you're on the national board of the Guild."

"Guild?"

"Newspaperman's Guild," she said. "Didn't I tell

you, darling? Of course, I didn't. But I've been north-western sector representative to the Guild for four-teen"—she stumbled suddenly, caught herself on the word, and the animation of her face crumpled and fled—"years," she finished, barely above a whisper, her eyes wide and palely watching upon his face.

But he only frowned impatiently.

"Then it's set for sure," he said. "I mean—from now on they'll leave us alone?"

"Oh, yes!" she said. "Yes! You and Pogey are safe, from now on."

He sighed so deeply and heavily that his shoulders heaved.

"Pogey's safe then," he murmured. Then he looked back at her. He took her hand in his. "I . . . don't know how to thank you," he said.

She stared at him, pale-faced, wide-eyed.

"Thank me!" she said.

"You did an awful lot," he said. "If it hadn't been for you . . . but we had to have faith somebody'd come through." He shook her hand, which went life-lessly up and down in his. "I just can't thank you enough. If there's ever anything I can do to pay you back." He let go of her hand and stepped backward. "I'll write you," he said. "I'll let you know how we make out." He took another step backward and turned toward the door of his room. "Well, so long— and thanks again."

"Ted!" Her voice thrust at him like an icepick, sharply, bringing him back around to face her. "Aren't you," she moved her lips stiffly with the words, "going to invite me in?"

He rubbed the back of his neck with one hand, clumsily.

"Well," he said. "I was up all night; and I had all those drinks . . . and Pogey is pretty shy with

strangers—" He turned a hand palm out toward her.
"I mean, I know he'd like you; but some other time,
huh?" He smiled at her wooden face. "Give me a call
tomorrow, maybe? I tell you, I'm out on my feet right
now. Thanks again."

He turned and opened the door to his room and
went in, closing it behind him, leaving her there. Once
on the inside he set the door on lock and punched the
DO NOT DISTURB sign. Then he turned to the bed.
Pogey was still curled up on it, and at the sight of the
antipod Ted's face softened. He knelt down by the
side of the bed and put his face down on a level with
Pogey's. The antipod humped like an otter playing
and shoved its own button nose and bead eyes close
to his.

"Love me?" said Pogey.

"Love you," breathed Ted. "We're all right now,
Pogey, just like we knew we'd be, aren't we?" He put
his face down sideways on the coverlet of the bed and
closed his eyes. "Love Pogey," he whispered. "Love
Pogey."

Pogey put out a small pink tongue and stroked
Ted's forehead with it.

"What now?" murmured Ted, sleepily.

Pogey's button-eyes glowed like two small flames
of jet.

"Now," Pogey said, "we go to Washington—for
more like you."

THE CHRISTMAS PRESENT

"What is Christmas?" asked Harvey.

"It's the time when they give you presents," Allan Dumay told him. Allan was squatted on his mudshoes, a grubby figure of a little six-year-old boy, in the waning light over the inlet, talking to the Cidorian. "Tonight's Christmas Eve. My daddy cut a thorn tree and my mother's inside now, trimming it."

"Trimming?" echoed the Cidorian. He floated awash in the cool water of the inlet. Someone—perhaps it was Allan's father—had named him Harvey a long time ago. Now nobody called him by any other name.

"That's putting things on the tree," said Allan. "To make it beautiful. Do you know what beautiful is, Harvey?"

"No," said Harvey. "I have never seen beautiful." But he was wrong—even as, for a different reason, those humans were wrong who called Cidor an ugly swamp-planet because there was nothing green or fa-

miliar on the low mud-flats that rose from its planet-
wide fresh-water sea—only the stunted, dangerous
thorn tree and the trailing weed. There was beauty on
Cidor, but it was a different beauty. It was a black-
and-silver world where the thorn trees stood up like
fine ink sketches against the cloud-torn sky; and this
was beautiful. The great and solemn fishes that
moved about the uncharted pathways of its seas were
beautiful with the beauty of large, far-traveled ships.
And even Harvey, though he did not know it himself,
was the most beautiful of all with his swelling irides-
cent jelly-fish body and the yard-long mantle of silver
filaments spreading out through it and down through
the water. Only his voice was croaky and unbeautiful,
for a constricted air-sac is not built for the manufac-
ture of human words.

"You can look at my tree when it's ready," said
Allan. "That way you can tell."

"Thank you," said Harvey.

"You wait and see. There'll be colored lights. And
bright balls and stars; and presents all wrapped up."

"I would like to see it," said Harvey.

Up the slope of the dyked land that was the edge of
the Dumay farm, reclaimed from the sea, the kitchen
door of the house opened and a pale, warm finger of
light reached out long over the black earth to touch
the boy and the Cidorian. A woman stood
silhouetted against the light.

"Time to come in, Allan," called his mother's
voice.

"I'm coming," he called back.

"Right away! Right now!"

Slowly, he got to his feet.

"If she's got the tree ready, I'll come tell you," he
said, to Harvey.

"I will wait," said Harvey.

Allan turned and went slowly up the slope to the house, swinging his small body in the automatic rhythm of the mudshoes. The open doorway waited for him and took him in—into the light and human comfort of the house.

"Take your shoes off," said his mother, "so you don't track mud in."

"Is the tree all ready?" asked Allan, fumbling with the fastenings of his calf-high boots.

"I want you to eat first," said his mother. "Dinner's all ready." She steered him to the table. "Now, don't gulp. There's plenty of time."

"Is Daddy going to be home in time for us to open the presents?"

"You don't open your presents until morning. Daddy'll be back by then. He just had to go upriver to the supply house. He'll start back as soon as it's light; he'll be here before you wake up."

"That's right," said Allan, solemnly, above his plate; "he shouldn't go out on the water at night because that's when the water-bulls come up under your boat and you can't see them in the dark."

"Hush," said his mother, patting him on the shoulder. "There's no water-bulls around here."

"There's water-bulls everywhere. Harvey says so."

"Hush now, and eat your dinner. Your daddy's not going out on the water at night."

Allan hurried with his dinner.

"My plate's clean!" he called at last. "Can I go now?"

"All right," she said. "Put your plate and silverware into the dishwasher."

He gathered up his eating utensils and crammed them into the dishwasher; then ran into the next room. He stopped suddenly, staring at the thorn tree. He could not move—it was as if a huge, cold wave

had suddenly risen up to smash into him and wash all
the happy warmth out of him. Then he was aware of
the sound of his mother's footsteps coming up behind
him; and suddenly her arms were around him.

"Oh, honey!" she said, holding him close, "you
didn't expect it to be like last year, did you, on the
ship that brought us here? They had a real Christmas
tree, supplied by the space lines, and real ornaments.
We had to just make do with what we had."

Suddenly he was sobbing violently. He turned
around and clung to her. "—not a—Christmas
tree—" he managed to choke out.

"But, sweetheart, it is!" He felt her hand, soothing
the rumpled hair of his head. "It isn't how it looks
that makes it a Christmas tree. It's how we think
about it, and what it means to us. What makes
Christmas is the loving and the giving—not how the
Christmas tree looks, or how the presents are
wrapped. Don't you know that?"

"But—I—" He was lost in a fresh spate of sobs.

"What, sweetheart?"

"I—promised—Harvey—"

"Hush," she said. "Here—" The violence of his
grief was abating. She produced a clean white tissue
from the pocket of her apron. "Blow your nose.
That's right. Now, what did you promise Harvey?"

"To—" He hiccupped. "To show him a Christmas
tree."

"Oh," she said, softly. She rocked him a little in
her arms. "Well, you know honey," she said.
"Harvey's a Cidorian; and he's never seen a Christmas tree at all before. So this one would seem just as
wonderful to him as that tree on the space ship did to
you last Christmas."

He blinked and sniffed and looked at her doubt-
fully.

"Yes, it would," she assured him gently. "Honey—Cidorians aren't like people. I know Harvey can talk and even make pretty good sense sometimes—but he isn't really like a human person. When you get older, you'll understand that better. His world is out there in the water and everything on land like we have it is a little hard for him to understand."

"Didn't he *ever* know about Christmas?"

"No, he never did."

"Or see a Christmas tree, or get presents?"

"No, dear." She gave him a final hug. "So why don't you go out and get him and let him take a look at the tree. I'll bet he'll think it's beautiful."

"Well ... all right!" Allan turned and ran suddenly to the kitchen, where he began to climb into his boots.

"Don't forget your jacket," said his mother. "The breeze comes up after the sun goes down."

He struggled into his jacket, snapped on his mudshoes and ran down to the inlet. Harvey was there waiting for him. Allan let the Cidorian climb onto the arm of his jacket and carried the great light bubble of him back into the house.

"See there," he said, after he had taken off his boots with one hand and carried Harvey into the living room. "That's a Christmas tree, Harvey."

Harvey did not answer immediately. He shimmered, balanced in the crook of Allan's elbow, his long filaments spread like silver hair over and around the jacket of the boy.

"It's not a real Christmas tree, Harvey," said Allan. "But that doesn't matter. We have to make do with what we have because what makes Christmas is the loving and the giving. Do you know that?"

"I did not know," said Harvey.

"Well, that's what it is."

"It is beautiful," said Harvey. "A Christmas tree beautiful."

"There, you see," said Allan's mother, who had been standing to one side and watching. "I told you Harvey would think it was beautiful, Allan."

"Well, it'd be more beautiful if we had some real shiny ornaments to put on it, instead of little bits of foil and beads and things. But we don't care about that, Harvey."

"We do not care," said Harvey.

"I think, Allan," said his mother, "you better take Harvey back now. He's not built to be out of the water too long, and there's just time to wrap your presents before bed."

"All right," said Allan. He started for the kitchen, then stopped. "Did you want to say good night to Harvey, Mommy?"

"Good night, Harvey," she said.

"Good night," answered Harvey, in his croaking voice.

Allan dressed and took the Cidorian back to the inlet. When he returned, his mother already had the wrapping papers in all their colors, and the ribbons and boxes laid out on his bed in the bedroom. Also laid out was the pocket whetstone he was giving his father for Christmas and a little inch-and-a-half-high figure he had molded out of native clay, kiln-baked and painted to send home to Allan's grandmother and grandfather, who were his mother's parents. It cost fifty units to ship an ounce of weight back to Earth, and the little figure was just under an ounce— but the grandparents would pay the freight on it from their end. Seeing everything ready, Allan went over to the top drawer of his closet.

"Close your eyes," he said. His mother closed them, tight.

He got out the pair of work gloves he was giving his mother and smuggled them into one of the boxes.

They wrapped the presents together. After they were finished and had put the presents under the thorn tree, with its meager assortment of homemade ornaments, Allan lingered over the wrappings. After a moment, he went to the box that held his toys and got out the container of toy spacemen. They were molded of the same clay as his present to his grandparents. His father had made and fired them, his mother had painted them. They were all in good shape except the astrogator, and his right hand—the one that held the pencil—was broken off. He carried the astrogator over to his mother.

"Let's wrap this, please," he said.

"Why, who's that for?" she asked, looking down at him. He rubbed the broken stump of the astrogator's arm, shyly.

"It's a Christmas present . . . for Harvey."

She gazed at him.

"Your astrogator?" she said. "How'll you run your spaceship without him?"

"Oh, I'll manage," he said.

"But, honey," she said. "Harvey's not like a little boy. What could he do with the astrogator? He can't very well play with it."

"No," said Allan. "But he could keep it. Couldn't he?"

She smiled, suddenly.

"Yes," she said. "He could keep it. Do you want to wrap it and put it under the tree for him?"

He shook his head, seriously.

"No," he said. "I don't think Harvey can open packages very well. I'll get dressed and take it down to the inlet and give it to him now."

"Not tonight, Allan," his mother said. "It's too

late. You should be in bed already. You can take it to
him tomorrow."

"Then he won't have it when he wakes up in the
morning!"

"All right, then," she said. "I'll take it. But you've
got to pop right into bed, now."

"I will." Allan turned to his closet and began to dig
out his pajamas. When he was securely established in
the warm, blanketing field of the bed, she kissed him
and turned out everything but the night light.

"Sleep tight," she said, and taking the broken-
armed astrogator, went out of the bedroom, closing
the door all but a crack behind her.

She set the dishwasher and turned it on. Then, taking the astrogator again, she put on her own jacket
and mudshoes and went down to the shores of the
inlet.

"Harvey?" she called.

But Harvey was not in sight. She stood for a moment, looking out over the darkened night country of
low-lying earth and water, dimly revealed under the
cloud-obscured face of Cidor's nearest moon. A lone-
liness crept into her from the alien land and she
caught herself wishing her husband was home. She
shivered a little under her jacket and stooped down to
leave the astrogator by the water's edge. She had
turned away and was half-way up the slope to the
house when she heard Harvey's voice calling her.

She turned about. The Cidorian was at the water's
edge—halfway out onto the land, holding wrapped
up in his filaments the small shape of the astrogator.
She went back down to him, and he slipped gratefully
back into the water. He could move on land, but
found the labor exhausting.

"You have lost this," he said, lifting up the
astrogator.

"No, Harvey," she answered. "It's a Christmas present. From Allan. For you."

He floated where he was without answering, for a long moment. Finally:

"I do not understand," he said.

"I know you don't," she sighed, and smiled a little at the same time. "Christmas just happens to be a time when we all give gifts to each other. It goes a long way back ..." Standing there in the dark, she found herself trying to explain; and wondered, listening to the sound of her own voice, that she should feel so much comfort in talking to only Harvey. When she was finished with the story of Christmas and what the reasons were that had moved Allan, she fell silent. And the Cidorian rocked equally silent before her on the dark water, not answering.

"Do you understand?" she asked at last.

"No," said Harvey. "But it is a beautiful."

"Yes," she said, "it's a beautiful, all right." She shivered suddenly, coming back to this chill damp world from the warm country of her childhood. "Harvey," she said suddenly. "What's it like out on the river—and the sea? Is it dangerous?"

"Dangerous?" he echoed.

"I mean with the water-bulls and all. Would one really attack a man in a boat?"

"One will. One will not," said Harvey.

"Now I don't understand you, Harvey."

"At night," said Harvey, "they come up from deep in the water. They are different. One will swim away. One will come up on the land to get you. One will lie still and wait."

She shuddered.

"Why?" she said.

"They are hungry. They are angry," said Harvey. "They are water-bulls. You do not like them?" She shuddered.

"I'm petrified." She hesitated. "Don't they ever bother you?"

"No. I am . . ." Harvey searched for the word. "Electric."

"Oh." She folded her arms about her, hugging the warmth in to her body. "It's cold," she said. "I'm going in."

In the water, Harvey stirred.

"I would like to give a present," he said. "I will make a present."

Her breath caught a little in her throat.

"Thank you, Harvey," she said, gently and solemnly. "We will be very happy to have you make us a present."

"You are welcome," said Harvey.

Strangely warmed and cheered, she turned and went back up the slope and into the peaceful warmth of the house. Harvey, floating still on the water, watched her go. When at last the door had shut behind her, and all light was out, he turned and moved toward the entrance to the inlet.

It appeared he floated, but actually he was swimming very swiftly. His hundreds of hair-like filaments drove him through the dark water at amazing speed, but without a ripple. Almost, it seemed as if the water was no heavy substance to him but a matter as light as gas through which he traveled on the faintest impulse of a thought. He emerged from the mouth of the inlet and turned upriver, moving with the same ease and swiftness past the little flats and islands. He traveled upriver until he came to a place between two islands where the water was black and deep and the thorn bushes threw their sharp shadows across it in the silver path of the moonlight.

Here he halted. And there rose slowly before him, breaking the smooth surface of the water, a huge and frog-like head, surmounted by two stubby cartilaginous projections above the tiny eyes. The head was as big as an oil drum, but it had come up in perfect silence. It spoke to him in vibrations through the water that Harvey understood.

"Is there a sickness among the shocking people that drives them out of their senses, to make you come here?"

"I have come for beautiful Christmas," said Harvey, "to make you into a present."

It was an hour past dawn the following morning that Chester Dumay, Allan's father, came down the river. The Colony's soil expert was traveling with him and their two boats were tied together, proceeding on a single motor. As they came around the bend between the two islands, they had been talking about an acid condition in the soil of Chester's fields, where they bordered the river. But the soil expert—his name was Père Hama, a lean little dark man—checked himself suddenly in mid-sentence.

"Just a minute—" he said, gazing off and away past Chester Duman's shoulder. "Look at that."

Chester looked, and saw something large and dark floating half-away, caught against the snag of a half-drowned tree that rose up from the muddy bottom of the river some thirty feet out from the far shore. He turned the boat-wheel and drive across toward it.

"What the devil—"

They came up close and Chester cut the motor to let the boats drift in upon the object. The current took them down and the nearer hull bumped against a great black expanse of swollen hide, laced with fragile silver threads and gray-scarred all over by what would appear to have been a fiery whip. It rolled idly in the water.

"A water-bull!" said Hama.

"Is that what it is?" queried Chester, fascinated. "I never saw one."

"I did—at Third Landing. This one's a monster. And *dead!*" There was a note of puzzlement in the soil expert's voice.

Chester poked gingerly at the great carcass and it turned a little. Something like a gray bubble rose to show itself for a second dimly through several feet of murky water, then rolled under out of sight again.

"A Cidorian," said Chester. He whistled. "All crushed. But who'd have thought one of them could take on one of these!" He stared at the water-bull body.

Hama shuddered a little, in spite of the fact that the sun was bright.

"And win—that's the thing," the soil expert said. "Nobody ever suspected—" He broke off suddenly. "What's the matter with you?"

"Oh, we've got one in our inlet that my son plays with a lot—call him Harvey," said Chester. "I was just wondering . . ."

"I wouldn't let my kid near something that could kill a water-bull," said Hama.

"Oh, Harvey's all right," said Chester. "Still . . ." Frowning, he picked up the boathook and shoved off from the carcass, turning about to start up the motor again. The hum of its vibration picked up in their ears as they headed downriver once more. "All the same, I think there's no point in mentioning this to the wife and boy—no point in spoiling their Christmas. And later on, when I get a chance to get rid of Harvey quietly . . ."

"Sure," said Hama. "I won't say a word. No point in it."

They purred away down the river.

Behind them, the water-bull carcass, disturbed, slid

free of the waterlogged tree and began to drift down-river. The current swung it and rolled, slowly, over and over until the crushed central body of the dead Cidorian rose into the clean air. And the yellow rays of the clear sunlight gleamed from the glazed pottery countenance of a small toy astrogator, all wrapped about with silver threads, and gilded it.

IT HARDLY SEEMS FAIR

Frank Siah did not move. He sat perfectly still, in cold silence, one hand gripping the glass on the table before him. In the close confines of the camping shell, the air, thickened and heated by the temperatures of their bodies, seemed to ripple and distort Creighar's joweled, stubbled countenance—made the man look boarlike, brutal, and afraid. That countenance stared at Frank in the lengthening silence as the moment between them stretched out like pulled taffy. Still, Frank waited. Creighar would speak again.

He did, on a higher note.

"You heard me? Cut him loose!"

Face calm above his triump-pounding heart, Frank rose; still without words, he picked up the knife and went out of the little camping shell. Outside, beyond the shell's own glow of yellow glow-tube illumination, the sun Alpha Celana was dropping under the horizon. Her orange rays struck full on the squat black forms of the forest's native trees; and flooded

through with a halloween color upon the table before
him, the two camping shells behind, the clearing and
the bluey huddled shapes of the natives. The 'Daddy'
of the native group—now a mottled shadow—still lay
where he had been tied, spread-eagled and belly-up in
the clearing. He said nothing now, as Frank approached him with the knife, but looked up at the
young human with his wide mouth half-open and the
pointed teeth inside skinned free of the lips. But for
all the exposure of his fangs, there was no impression
of belligerance or fierceness to be got from him. He
only looked stranded—tied down there—like a shark
half-dead and helpless on some storm-wrung beach.

Frank cut the ropes that bound his legs and arms
to the pegs driven into the soft, grey earth.

"You can go now," he said. He hesitated, then held
out a hand to the native. "Let me help you. How do
you feel?"

"Sick, sick—" moaned the Daddy, in his own
tongue—but he did not avail himself of the thin, human hand outstretched; but rolled over, and over
again, half-tumbling half-crawling toward the huddle
of other natives, until he reached and was absorbed in
the mass of their mutual shadow.

Frank stood for a second, stiffly, his hand still out-
stretched. Then he dropped it to his side, clenching
his fist spasmodically. For a second he was tempted
to order the native leader back and make him let himself be helped. Then he got the feeling under control
and turned back without a word, returning the way
he had come, but this time by-passing the shell where
Creighar still sat with the bottle, and entering instead
into his own. The glow-tube had gone on automatically with the fading sunset. He sat down on the
edge of his cot.

"Have another!" shouted Creighar from the next-door shell.

Frank did not answer. He sat for a moment staring at the blank curved wall of his shell, then got up and laid Creighar's knife on the table beside his journal and the neat pile of his reports. He pulled off his pants, jumper and boots, arranged them neatly on the chair by his cot, and laid down. Once horizontal, the glare of the glow-tube in his eyes reminded him he had forgotten to turn it off. He made a slight move-ment to get up, and then lay back, closing his eyes against the light.

"Have a drink, Frank!" called Creighar, from the shell next door.

Frank lay still, seeing the light even through his closed eyelids.

"He thinks he's the big cheese, old Daddy!" shouted Creighar. "Thinks he can show me up. Nobody's going to do that. Nobody!" His voice dropped suddenly and his words became lost in indis-tinguishable mutterings.

Frank turned on one side, his back to the wall next to Creighar's shell. He imagined a box big enough to contain him, a box like a jeweler's box for a precious gem, all upholstered interiorly in black velvet. He crawled inside the box and closed the lid upon him-self. Enwrapped in secret, silent blackness, he waited for sleep.

It did not come.

He opened his eyes with a soundless sigh. Creighar was now silent in the shell alongside. Only a high murmur of voices came from the huddled natives, and drifted into the shell. He stood up quietly, extin-guished the glow-tube, and on noiseless, bootless feet, stepped out into the dark night. The natives were still talking. And then, quite suddenly without warning,

two more native voices spoke up from the darkness
nearby, and away from the general group.

"—Great   Monarch—"

It was the voice of the Daddy's favorite among the
younger males, his heir apparent in this native group
—the one Frank and Creighar called Shep. Frank
strained his eyes through the night now, to make out
where Shep might be, but nothing was visible.

"Get away. Leave me alone!" it was the Daddy,
answering. Frank cocked his head in interest. He
could follow the conversation easily—better than
Creighar had learned to do in fourteen years. Frank
had been given a quick course in it back on Earth
before leaving for this job, last year.

"But Great Monarch—" It was Shep again, almost
whining.

"What, incapable filth?"

"Are you going to die, Great Monarch? Because
you said you'd tell me. You said you'd let me know in
plenty of time."

"Die? I'm not going to die!" moaned the Daddy.
I'm going to give birth and be ashamed. Oh, that the
old red-faced man should do such a thing to me!"

There was a moment's silence.

"Should I go bite his throat out?" asked Shep.

There was the sound of a blow in the darkness.

"How dare you talk like that!" snarled the Daddy.
"The old red-faced man is my friend. Even if he is
jealous of my fine big family, while he has only the
one skinny, white-faced son. Fool that you are! Also
he is a devil and very clever. Learn to be sneaky and
clever with devils if you want to come after me!"

Shep whimpered. Frank could not catch exactly
what he said. Something to the effect that he was a
good son.

"No son can be good enough," snarled the Daddy. "Come now, we'll go back with the others."

There was a sound of movement away, and then silence. Frank turned and stepped quietly back into his own shell. The light in Creighar's, he saw, was still on. He paused to glance in. The older man was asleep now, flung down on the bed on his back—in a position noticably similar to that of the staked-out Daddy. Had he passed out? Probably.

Frank went into his own shell and turned on the glow once more. He sat down at the desk, looked at his journal, and then opened it precisely to the page of his last entry. He read what he had written there, two days before.

July 36, 187 Celanadate. Started for the collecting station today with 1246 kilograms, powdered. Daddy. Creigh. and fourteen females and eighteen bucks. Plan to move slowly, taking three days to station and harvesting as we go. Blue, Butterboy, and Tiger left behind to keep main camp and guard scrubs, whelps, and the expectant females. Koko dead. Insect fever possibly. Creigh. ordered no autopsy, says would disturb the others.

Frank put his fingers to the coder, sliding it down to a fresh space on the page. He coded.

July 38, 187 Celanadate. Creigh. drunk and very bad again.

He hesitated. Then he went on.

He is completely incompetent. His object is paternalism in its most disgusting form. Slobbers over the natives half of the time and bullies and browbeats them the other half. Sober he slobbers; drunk, he bullies. Why he has not had an uprising is more than I can understand. He tries the same tricks with me. Sober, he tries to 'make friends';

*and drunk, he tries to rub in the fact that I'm jun-
ior to him and under his orders. He is a pathetic
old man whose day is done and doesn't know it.*

*The natives represent an investment and should
be worked as such. I will recommend as much in
my report summary. No need to say anything
about Creigh directly. I imagine the Company
can read between the lines and the very fact I've
had to make out most of his reports for him
should be sufficient.*

*Memo: Violation of the native taboo about al-
lowing sunlight to touch the belly skin is evidently
somehow connected with giving birth. Include for
addition to training films. No use asking Creigh.
for further details. In this, as in other things, he
knows a tenth of what I do, after the training
course.*

Frank's fingers ceased to move the coder. He
sighed, closed the journal, and then got up and
turned out the glow and got into bed. After a while,
he fell asleep.

He woke up in the bright daylight of a morning
well advanced. The natives, without being ordered to,
had already gone out into the woods—all of them.
Frank went next door to check on Creighar. The
older man was still asleep, looking even more dis-
reputable in the daylight. He still lay on his back, as
if he had not stirred all through the night. Frank
stood looking at him for a moment, then turned and
walked off.

He began to circle out around the area, checking
on the natives who were already about their business
of taping the trees. He came up behind Shep, who
was just then starting on a new one. The sharp white
flake of quartz rock Shep held in one blue hand

jabbed out and slid down along the black trunk. The new wound in the tree gaped instantly, like any tight-stretching thing suddenly cut; and a small trickle of clear amber liquid bled abruptly from the walls of the cut, welling up and spilling down the trunk. Before it reached the ground, close below, contact with the air had already started to turn it into a host of tiny, red-dish crystals. Shep raked his hand down the trail of crystals, carefully gathering them into a tiny pile at the tree's base. The wound in the tree had by now ceased to bleed. Shep licked at it with a thick, purplish tongue, and the liquid started to flow again.

Watching, Frank felt a sudden emotional shifting of his insides. It was a strange mixture of a feeling, in which he could distinguish only disgust, pity, and—yes, a strange sort of jealousy of the creature he was watching. At least, life was simple for Shep. He only knew that he had to make the cut in the tree and lick at it to keep the ichor flowing. He did not have to worry about someone, somewhere in some labora-tory, finding and duplicating the enzyme in his saliva that was responsible for the continued flow. He only had to worry about biting out the throats of one or two of his closest rivals (preferably while they were asleep) when the Daddy died, in order to succeed, himself, to the Daddyship of the band. Things were simple with Shep—simple and physical. He did not have to worry about promotions or being saddled with a maudlin drunk who made three times what you did because of seniority accruals—while you did all the work.

The pile of crystals was steadily growing at the base of the tree. The crystals themselves glittered and looked like prime material; the sort that, properly purified, would become a glossing agent no manufac-turer of fine art varnishes could afford to do without.

If things would just stay as they were, there would be no problems. Creighar would take enough rope to hang himself, sooner or later; and with a steadily expanding market on fourteen worlds, the Company would prosper—and Frank along with it. And then . . . Promotion to a job Earthside. Or into business for himself. Or. . . .

If only Creighar didn't get them both into trouble before he managed to cut his own throat with the Company. And if those damn research chemists could be stymied for a few years more—

"Move over!" he pushed Shep sharply to one side and took up a handful of the crystals. Yes, he thought almost savagely, they were prime. Certainly prime. Probably the amount there in his hand was worth half a year's wages, *his* wages, if you figured end prices back on Earth.

A snuffling noise made him look down. Shep was looking at the handful of crystals taken from him and oily tears were running out of his black-pupilled eyes.

"All right, all right! Here!" Frank dumped the crystals back onto the pile at the base of the tree. Shep stopped crying immediately.

Frank turned away. There were a few crystals still clinging to the damp skin of his palm; and he took pleasure in brushing them off into the miry ground, where they at once disappeared. He took a step toward the camp again; but before he had gone further, there was a sharp tug at the back of his jacket. He turned about.

Shep squatted, holding out and up to him at full arms length, a handful of the crystals.

"No, no!" said Frank, abruptly angry with the creature. "Not now, not now! We'll get them from you at the end of the day. You know that!" He pushed the arm aside, turned about and strode back to the camp.

When he got there, he found Creighar awake and up. Thick-stubbled and touseled, with shaking hands, he held a cup of coffee as he sat on the edge of his bed.

"Hi—" he said, hoarsely and uncertainly, as Frank came by.

Frank went by him without answering, into his own shell and took from the supply pack there, a package breakfast.

"Hey, I guess I really was hitting it last night—" Creighar's voice came shakily and invisibly from the next shell. Frank still did not answer. Opening it as he walked, he carried the package breakfast back out to the table set in the clearing before the shells. As the cover came off, a hot homely smell of sausage and eggs came up from it as the heating unit seethed. Frank sat down at the table; and Creighar came out and sat down opposite him, the coffee cup still held in both hands and these laid out now on the table before him.

"Bad last night, huh?" Creighar said. The words rattled and tangled in his thick throat.

"That's right," said Frank, buttering his toast without looking up.

"Boy, how you can eat that stuff in the morning. . . ."Creighar looked at the loaded breakfast tray and looked away. "They out in the woods, already?"

"I've just been out checking on them."

"Boy, I appreciate your seeing they got out on time. After last night. I wasn't in shape . . ." Creighar turned the coffee cup in his thick, but minutely quivering fingers, looking at it. "Hey, how's old Daddy?"

Frank looked up at him for a moment levelly, then went back to his eating.

"No, no—" said Creighar clumsily, leaning his thick, beardy face forward. "I want to know. I love that old boy, I really do. I don't know what got into me. . . ." his voice ran down. He stopped and passed an uncertain hand over his jaw and mouth. "Got to shave. . . . Well, tell me how he is!"

"There's nothing to tell."

"Please, Frank." Creighar reached across the table for Frank's arm; but Frank moved to avoid him, and went on eating. "Listen—you got to understand. I know a smart young guy like you wouldn't want to make friends with an old back-country bum like me. That's all right. I don't mind. But old Daddy and me —it's been all these years, even as blue as he is. And since Hank was retired, and you sent out to replace him, I don't—I just don't—"

His words stumbled, faltered, and fell. Frank took a neat forkful of sausage.

"Old Daddy saved my life once," said Creighar. I ever tell you? He and I—"

"Too often," said Frank. "You've told me too often."

"Yes, well—," Creighar looked out into the woods. "You're out in the sticks this long—no family —no one to write to—" his voice cracked. "Please, Frank, what'd I *do?* I remember getting mad at him over some little thing—something nobody'd get mad over—but I can't remember, I can't remember what I did!"

"All right, I'll tell you." Frank finished the last of the eggs and wiped his lips with the disposable napkin in the package. "You had him pegged out where the sun could shine on his stomach."

"Oh—" Creighar exhaled suddenly. His head dropped and he looked away. For a long minute, he did not move. Frank went about tidying up the package into a disposable lump. "And I knew how he felt about something like that, too," said Creighar, in a numb voice. "I knew—" he turned suddenly back to Frank, his eyes pleading. "But I turned him loose right away, Frank? I just did it to throw a scare into him—"

"I finally cut him loose at sunset," said Frank.

Creighar's eyes dulled.

"Yeah," he said. "Yeah. . . ." He sat for a moment, then roused himself with a noticeable effort. He turned back to Frank. "Thanks, Frank."

"Don't mention it."

"Well, what the hell!" exploded Creighar, suddenly. He examined his hands, quivering about the coffee cup; and abruptly lurched to his feet. He turned and plowed back into his shell. There was a moment's silence, then the clink of glass and the audible sound of a man swallowing. "What the hell!" came his voice, once again, but stronger now. "They're only geeks!"

Frank stood up from the table, taking the lumped breakfast package with him. Creighar came to the mouth of his shell, a bottle hanging from his fist.

"We got to get them over the river, today," he said harshly. "Starting about noon. Maybe you better—"

"I've got paper work," interrupted Frank. "Your reports as well as my own. You take them over the ford." He looked pointedly at the bottle in Creighar's hand. "I'll join you later—unless you have some trouble."

Creighar followed Frank's gaze with his own bloodshot eyes until they fell down upon the bottle in his hand. He jerked his head up to stare back at Frank; and for a second his jaw crept forward, bristling and square.

"Listen—" he began; but the hard edge in his voice wavered and bent, his eyes turned aside from Frank's. The jaw retreated. "Yeah—" he said, "yeah. . . ." and turned back into his shell, lifting the bottle once more to his lips, taking one gulp after another.

Frank carried his wadded-up breakfast package to the edge of the clearing and pitched it into the brush, dusting his hands fastidiously afterward. Then he went back into his own shell, and sat down to work on the weekly reports.

He was still seated at the little work table there, some three hours later, when Creigh came herding the native group back into the clearing. They returned single file, some already weeping at the prospect of being parted from the handfuls of red crystals they each jealously carried. Creighar lined them up beside the piled and packed impedimenta of the camp, which had already been put in shape for leaving. Then he set about with a rough, but not unfriendly firmness, at the business of relieving each of the band of their crystals; and putting these into carefully sealed bags.

Without exception, as always, they all cried and protested as the crystals were being taken from them. As he slowly wrote up the commissary report, Frank could hear them—and over the sound of their light, chittering voices, the hoarse bass of Creighar rumbling exasperations with a sort of clumsy, hairy-chested note of reassurance and sympathy that took, Frank thought, all the force and purpose out of what he was actually saying.

"—all right, all right—you aren't going to starve!
I'll see you get back all you need to eat, you know
that! Leggo, Shep. Let go, I say! Why the hell you
always have to carry on like this. . . ."

He finally got their blue fists gently emptied and
their shoulders strapped up with the various burdens
to be transported. When they were all ready, he
crossed over into his own shell for a moment. Looking out as Creighar strode past, Frank noticed that
the older man's face was pale and sweating above the
beard stubble. His eyes were twisted as if by pain and
he carried one shoulder, hunched and the arm below
it pressed close to his left side. He was in the shell for
several long moments—and when he came out he had
a gun strapped to his hip and he carried a bottle.
Casting a look of defiance in the direction of Frank's
shell (which Frank pretended not to see) he moved
over to the line of natives, and with hoarse, half-hu-
morous shouts, got them started off in the direction
of the river and the ford across it, half a kilometer
away.

Frank finished his report in the new silence of the
camp and pushed the papers aside. He would have to
be following after Creighar soon—but there was no
rush. He felt an odd sense of satisfaction, although he
could think at the moment of no special reason for it.
After a moment, he reached out for his journal,
opened it, and coded:

*The worlds are full of old men who are eager to
make compromises. They are too weak to keep
their eyes firmly fixed on the goal of their ambi-
tion, but waver off in search of worthless little
things like 'praise' or 'friendship' or 'booze'.
There is no need to take any special effort with
these people; merely remain firm and be patient,
and eventually they will destroy themselves. This*

*philosophy is, indeed, the cornerstone upon which
I have begun to build the ultimate mansion of my
success.*

He closed the journal; and, adding it to the pile of
reports, made a light pack of these and his toilet
articles. The shells and the rest of the camp could
stand as they were. This coming night, across the
river, he and Creighar would be putting up at the collecting station, half a day's walk from the far shore.
Frank stood up, shrugged into the pack and strode
out.

It was a short and not unpleasant walk through the
woods; but before he was more than four-fifths of the
way there, he heard voices borne to him on the light
afternoon breeze, and he frowned. He stepped up his
pace, down through a small ravine and up over a little
hill, where he broke suddenly clear of the trees and
had his first view of the river.

The band was still on this side of the water. It had
not yet crossed, he saw, and there was obviously trouble.

The natives were milling about, Creighar was
bellowing; and before Creighar, crouched in a tight
blue knot on the ground, the Daddy huddled.
Creighar had been working heavily upon the bottle
he had taken, after all. His smeared words and
hoarsened voice gave his drunkenness away. He staggered dangerously, threatening above the Daddy, his
hand with the gun from his hip in it, waved violently
aloft.

Frank went cold. This was the fool sort of thing he
had dreaded—that could get them both into trouble.

"Wait!" he yelled—his voice cracking and breaking upward. *"Wait!"*

He broke into a sudden, gasping run, pounding

down the steep slope of the hillside with the pack bouncing and jouncing on his shoulders.

"Wait, I say!" he yelled. "Stop it!"

Below, Creighar swung staggeringly about to face him, the noon sun shining brilliantly on his red, sun-burned face above the beard. From the ground the Daddy cried out, a long, piercing note; and a chorus of native voices echoed him. Frank plunged to a rocking halt before Creighar.

"Put that gun away!" Frank shouted. "He can't go over the water. That's what they're all saying. You old fool, if you only had the sense to learn something about the language—you know it's taboo for them to go over running water when they're pregnant!"

"Pregnant?" Creighar stared.

"Him. Daddy. He is!"

"Knocked up? Him?" Creighar roared hoarse laughter, shoving out with one thick hand, pushing Frank aside. "Don't make me split my sides. Him—" He lifted the gun; and Frank, desperately, snatching at the wrist of the hand that held it, caught and wrestled with him.

"You did it!" shouted Frank, in the high voice of his youth and desperation. "He thinks he got pregnant from the sun when you pegged him out, yesterday. That's what that sun on the stomach taboo is all about. He can't go over the water because of what you did to him. Because of you! Because of what *you* did!"

"Whadayou—" Creighar stopped struggling suddenly. The gun wobbled in his suddenly loosened grip, and slipped clumsily out of it. It fell to the ground unheeded by either of them. "Whadayou mean, I—" he pulled loose from Frank, backing up, and his eyes went to the Daddy, now half-uncurled and looking up from the ground; and from the Daddy to the gun. And his face blanked and twisted.

"After all these years—" he said thickly, his voice sounding suddenly wheezing and strangled. "After fifteen years, and I nearly—". He wheezed to a stop. His eyes suddenly widened with fright. His mouth fell open.

"Frank—" he straggled; and his right hand flew up to claw at the left side of his chest. His face was red as sunset, and his knees buckled. Frank leaped to catch him; but he was already falling, a heavy, middle-aged man, and the two of them went down to the ground together.

Frank scrambled up onto his knees beside the sprawled figure. He stared in shock at what he saw. Creighar lay as he had laid so often in drunken slumber, as the Daddy had laid, pegged out on the ground. But this time the man lay still, his eyes open, his mouth a little open, all unmoving.

"Creighar!" shouted Frank.

He stared up from the body with panic-stricken eyes—and found the native group all around him. They had moved in to form a circle about the spot where he and Creighar had gone down. And as he looked up the Daddy began to speak. He was making a speech, a speech about law and custom and duty, to which all the rest hearkened intentently, seated so close, one to the other, that there was no room for anyone to pass between them.

—And when it was all over (and not very satisfyingly over at that, for the human blood did not form neat reddish crystals on exposure to the air, but soaked into the ground and was mostly lost, even with all the efforts of the most careful collectors), there was only one of them who had taken no part in it. And this one was Shep, who had sat to one side all through the process of collecting, crying and shaking both hands looselessly and helplessly upon their blue wrists.

"Not fair," he sobbed, as they all at last drew back from what was left of Frank. "I loved him. He would have been for me what the old red-faced man was for you."

"Love is a little thing, too small to turn aside for," answered the Daddy. "You saw him. We all saw him. Nothing is more terrible, nothing is worse, than for a son in evil wickedness to kill his good father."

He squatted down upon the ground, himself.

"But now," he said, speaking sorrowfully to them all, "we are without both the old red-faced man and the young. Let us sit down and weep; for now we are alone in the cruel world, and there is no one to guide us and care for us, and no one can tell what will become of us, alone and forsaken as we are, from this day henceforward."

And they sat down all in a circle, by the ceaseless waters of the river, and wept.

The Monster and the Maiden

That summer more activity took place upon the shores of the loch and more boats appeared on its waters than at any time in memory. Among them was even one of the sort of boats that went underwater. It moved around in the loch slowly, diving quite deep at times. From the boats, swimmers with various gear about them descended on lines—but not so deep—swam around blindly for a while, and then returned to the surface.

Brought word of all this in her cave, First Mother worried and speculated on disaster. First Uncle, though equally concerned, was less fearful. He pointed out that the Family had survived here for thousands of years; and that it could not all end in a single year—or a single day.

Indeed, the warm months of summer passed one by one with no real disturbance to their way of life.

Suddenly fall came. One night, the first snow filled the air briefly above the loch. The Youngest danced on the surface in the darkness, sticking out her tongue to taste the cold flakes. Then the snow ceased, the sky cleared for an hour, and the banks could be seen gleaming white under a high and watery moon. But the clouds covered the moon again; and because of the relative warmth of the loch water nearby, in the morning, when the sun rose, the shores were once more green.

With dawn, boats began coming and going on the loch again and the Family went deep, out of sight. In spite of this precaution, trouble struck from one of these craft shortly before noon. First Uncle was warming the eggs on the loch bottom in the hatchhole, a neatly cleaned shallow depression scooped out by Second Mother, near Glen Urquhart, when something heavy and round descended on a long line, landing just outside the hole and raising an almost-invisible puff of silt in the blackness of the deep, icy water. The line tightened and began to drag the heavy thing about.

First Uncle had his huge length coiled about the clutch of eggs, making a dome of his body and enclosing them between the smooth skin of his underside and the cleaned lakebed. Fresh, hot blood pulsed to the undersurface of his smooth skin, keeping the water warm in the enclosed area. He dared not leave the clutch to chill in the cold loch, so he sent a furious signal for Second Mother, who, hearing that her eggs were in danger, came swiftly from her feeding. The Youngest heard also and swam up as fast as she could in mingled alarm and excitement.

She reached the hatchhole just in time to find Second Mother coiling herself around the eggs, her belly skin already beginning to radiate heat from the warm blood that was being shunted to its surface. Released from his duties, First Uncle shot up through the dark, peaty water like a sixty-foot missile, up along the hanging line, with the Youngest close behind him.

They could see nothing for more than a few feet because of the murkiness. But neither First Uncle nor the Youngest relied much on the sense of sight, which was used primarily for protection on the surface of the loch, in any case. Besides, First Uncle was already beginning to lose his vision with age, so he seldom went to the surface nowadays, preferring to do his breathing in the caves, where it was safer. The Youngest had asked him once if he did not miss the sunlight, even the misty and often cloud-dulled sunlight of the open sky over the loch, with its instinctive pull at ancestral memories of the ocean, retold in the legends. No, he had told her, he had grown beyond such things. But she found it hard to believe him; for in her, the yearning for the mysterious and fascinating world above the waters was still strong. The Family had no word for it. If they did, they might have called her a romantic.

Now, through the pressure-sensitive cells in the cheek areas of her narrow head, she picked up the movements of a creature no more than six feet in length. Carrying some long, narrow made thing, the intruder was above them, though descending rapidly, parallel to the line.

"Stay back," First Uncle signaled her sharply; and, suddenly fearful, she lagged behind. From the vibrations she felt, their visitor could only be one of the upright animals from the world above that walked about on its hind legs and used "made" things. There was an ancient taboo about touching one of these creatures.

The Youngest hung back, then, continuing to rise through the water at a more normal pace.

Above her, through her cheek cells, she felt and interpreted the turbulence that came from First Uncle's movements. He flashed up, level with the de-

scending animal, and with one swirl of his massive
body snapped the taut descending line. The animal
was sent tumbling—untouched by First Uncle's bulk
(according to the taboo), but stunned and buffeted
and thrust aside by the water-blow like a leaf in a
sudden gust of wind when autumn sends the dry tears
of the trees drifting down upon the shore waters of
the loch.

The thing the animal had carried, as well as the
lower half of the broken line, began to sink to the
bottom. The top of the line trailed aimlessly. Soon
the upright animal, hanging limp in the water, was
drifting rapidly away from it. First Uncle, satisfied
that he had protected the location of the hatchhole
for the moment, at least—though later in the day they
would move the eggs to a new location, anyway, as a
safety precaution—turned and headed back down to
release Second Mother once more to her feeding.

Still fearful, but fascinated by the drifting figure,
the Youngest rose timidly through the water on an
angle that gradually brought her close to it. She extended her small head on its long, graceful neck to
feel about it from close range with her pressure-sensitive cheek cells. Here, within inches of the floating
form, she could read minute differences, even in its
surface textures. It seemed to be encased in an un-
natural outer skin—one of those skins the creatures
wore which were not actually theirs—made of some
material that soaked up the loch water. This soaked-
up water was evidently heated by the interior temperature of the creature, much as members of the
Family could warm their belly skins with shunted
blood, which protected the animal's body inside by
cutting down the otherwise too-rapid radiation of its
heat into the cold liquid of the loch.

The Youngest noticed something bulky and hard
on the creature's head, in front, where the eyes and

mouth were. Attached to the back was a larger, doubled something, also hard and almost a third as long as the creature itself. The Youngest had never before seen a diver's wetsuit, swim mask, and air tanks with pressure regulator, but she had heard them described by her elders. First Mother had once watched from a safe distance while a creature so equipped had maneuvered below the surface of the loch, and she had concluded that the things he wore were devices to enable him to swim underwater without breathing as often as his kind seemed to need to, ordinarily.

Only this one was not swimming. He was drifting away with an underwater current of the loch, rising slowly as he traveled toward its south end. If he continued like this, he would come to the surface near the center of the loch. By that time the afternoon would be over. It would be dark.

Clearly, he had been damaged. The blow of the water that had been slammed at him by the body of First Uncle had hurt him in some way. But he was still alive. The Youngest knew this, because she could feel through her cheek cells the slowed beating of his heart and the movement of gases and fluids in his body. Occasionally, a small thread of bubbles came from his head to drift surfaceward.

It was a puzzle to her where he carried such a reservoir of air. She herself could contain enough oxygen for six hours without breathing, but only a portion of that was in gaseous form in her lungs. Most was held in pure form, saturating special tissues throughout her body.

Nonetheless, for the moment the creature seemed to have more than enough air stored about him; and he still lived. However, it could not be good for him to be drifting like this into the open loch with night coming on. Particularly if he was hurt, he would be needing some place safe out in the air, just as members of the Family did when they were old or sick. These upright creatures, the Youngest knew, were slow and feeble swimmers. Not one of them could have fed himself, as she did, by chasing and catching the fish of the loch; and very often when one fell into the water at any distance from the shore, he would struggle only a little while and then die.

This one would die also, in spite of the things fastened to him, if he stayed in the water. The thought raised a sadness in her. There was so much death. In any century, out of perhaps five clutches of a dozen eggs to a clutch, only one embryo might live to hatch. The legends claimed that once, when the Family had lived in the sea, matters had been different. But now, one survivor out of several clutches was the most to be hoped for. A hatchling who survived would be just about the size of this creature, the Youngest thought, though of course not with his funny shape. Nevertheless, watching him was a little like watching a new hatchling, knowing it would die.

It was an unhappy thought. But there was nothing to be done. Even if the diver were on the surface now, the chances were small that his own People could locate him.

Struck by a thought, the Youngest went up to look around. The situation was as she had guessed. No boats were close by. The nearest was the one from which the diver had descended; but it was still anchored close to the location of the hatchhole, nearly half a mile from where she and the creature now were.

Clearly, those still aboard thought to find him near where they had lost him. The Youngest went back down, and found him still drifting, now not more than thirty feet below the surface, but rising only gradually.

Her emotions stirred as she looked at him. He was not a cold life-form like the salmons, eels, and other fishes on which the Family fed. He was warm—as she was—and if the legends were all true, there had been a time and a place on the wide oceans where one of his ancestors and one of her ancestors might have looked at each other, equal and unafraid, in the open air and the sunlight.

So, it seemed wrong to let him just drift and die like this. He had shown the courage to go down into the depths of the loch, this small, frail thing. And such courage required some recognition from one of the Family, like herself. After all, it was loyalty and courage that had kept the Family going all these centuries: their loyalty to each other and the courage to conserve their strength and go on, hoping that someday the ice would come once more, the land would sink, and they would be set free into the seas again. Then surviving hatchlings would once more be numerous, and the Family would begin to grow again into what the legends had once called them, a "True People." Anyone who believed in loyalty and courage, the Youngest told herself, ought to respect those qualities wherever she found them—even in one of the upright creatures.

He should not simply be left to die. It was a daring throught, that she might interfere. .

She felt her own heart beating more rapidly as she followed him through the water, her cheek cells only inches from his dangling shape. After all, there was the taboo. But perhaps, if she could somehow help him without actually touching him . . . ?

"Him," of course, should not include the "made" things about him. But even if she could move him by these made parts alone, where could she take him?

Back to where the others of his kind still searched for him?

No, that was not only a deliberate flouting of the taboo but was very dangerous. Behind the taboo was the command to avoid letting any of his kind know about the Family. To take him back was to deliberately risk that kind of exposure for her People. She would die before doing that. The Family had existed all these centuries only because each member of it was faithful to the legends, to the duties, and to the taboos.

But, after all, she thought, it wasn't that she was actually going to break the taboo. She was only going to do something that went around the edge of it, because the diver had shown courage and because it was not his fault that he had happened to drop his heavy thing right beside the hatchhole. If he had dropped it anyplace else in the loch, he could have gone up and down its cable all summer and the Family members would merely have avoided that area.

What he needed, she decided, was a place out of the water where he could recover. She could take him to one of the banks of the loch. She rose to the surface again and looked around.

What she saw made her hesitate. In the darkening afternoon, the headlights of the ears moving up and down the roadways on each side of the loch were still visible in unusual numbers. From Fort Augustus at the south end of the loch to Castle Ness at the north, she saw more headlights about than ever before at this time of year, especially congregating by St. Ninian's, where the diver's boat was docked, nights.

No, it was too risky, trying to take him ashore. But she knew of a cave, too small by Family standards for any of the older adults, south of Urquhart Castle. The diver had gone down over the hatchhole, which had been constructed by Second Mother in the mouth of Urquhart Glen, close by St. Ninian's; and he had been drifting south ever since. Now he was below

Castle Urquhart and almost level with the cave. It was a good, small cave for an animal his size, with ledge of rock that was dry above the water at this time of year; and during the day even a little light would filter through cracks where tree roots from above had penetrated its rocky roof.

The Youngest could bring him there quite easily. She hesitated again, but then extended her head toward the air tanks on his back, took the tanks in her jaws, and began to carry him in the direction of the cave.

As she had expected, it was empty. This late in the day there was no light inside; but since, underwater, her cheek cells reported accurately on conditions about her and, above water, she had her memory, which was ultimately reliable, she brought him—still unconscious—to the ledge at the back of the cave and reared her head a good eight feet out of the water to lift him up on it. As she set him down softly on the bare rock, one of his legs brushed her neck, and a thrill of icy horror ran through the warm interior of her body.

Now she had done it! She had broken the taboo. Panic seized her.

She turned and plunged back into the water, out through the entrance to the cave and into the open loch. The taboo had never been broken before, as far as she knew—never. Suddenly she was terribly frightened. She headed at top speed for the hatchhole. All she wanted was to find Second Mother, or the Uncle, or anyone, and confess what she had done, so that they could tell her that the situation was not irreparable, not a signal marking an end of everything for them all.

Halfway to the hatchhole, however, she woke to the fact that it had already been abandoned. She turned immediately and began to range the loch bot-

tom southward, her instinct and training counseling
her that First Uncle and Second Mother would have
gone in that direction, south toward Inverfarigaig, to set
up a new hatchhole.

As she swam, however, her panic began to lessen
and guilt moved in to take its place. How could she
tell them? She almost wept inside herself. Here it was
not many months ago that they had talked about how
she was beginning to look and think like an adult;
and she had behaved as thoughtlessly as if she was
still the near-hatchling she had been thirty years ago.

Level with Castle Kitchie, she sensed the new location and homed in on it, finding it already set up off
the mouth of the stream which flowed past that castle
into the loch. The bed of the loch about the new
hatchhole had been neatly swept and the saucer-
shaped depression dug, in which Second Mother now
lay warming the eggs. First Uncle was close by
enough to feel the Youngest arrive, and he swept in to
speak to her as she halted above Second Mother.

"Where did you go after I broke the line?" he demanded before she herself could signal.

"I wanted to see what would happen to the diver,"
she signaled back. "Did you need me? I would have
come back, but you and Second Mother were both
there."

"We had to move right away," Second Mother signaled. She was agitated. "It was frightening!"

"They dropped another line," First Uncle said,
"with a thing on it that they pulled back and forth as
if to find the first one they dropped. I thought it not
wise to break a second one. One break could be a
chance happening. Two, and even small animals
might wonder."

"But we couldn't keep the hole there with that
thing dragging back and forth near the eggs," explained Second Mother. "So we took them and

moved without waiting to make the new hole here, first. The Uncle and I carried them, searching as we went. If you'd been here, you could have held half of them while I made the hole by myself, the way I wanted it. But you weren't. We would have sent for First Mother to come from her cave and help us, but neither one of us wanted to risk carrying the eggs about so much. So we had to work together here while still holding the eggs."

"Forgive me," said the Youngest. She wished she were dead.

"You're young," said Second Mother. "Next time you'll be wiser. But you do know that one of the earliest legends says the eggs should be moved only with the utmost care until hatching time; and you know we think that may be one reason so few hatch."

"If none hatch now," said First Uncle to the Youngest, less forgiving than Second Mother, even though they were not his eggs, "you'll remember this and consider that maybe you're to blame."

"Yes," mourned the Youngest.

She had a sudden, frightening vision of this one and all Second Mother's future clutches failing to hatch and she herself proving unable to lay when her time came. It was almost unheard of that a female of the Family should be barren, but a legend said that such a thing did occasionally happen. In her mind's eye she held a terrible picture of First Mother long dead, First Uncle and Second Mother grown old and feeble, unable to stir out of their caves, and she herself—the last of her line—dying alone, with no one to curl about her to warm or comfort her.

She had intended, when she caught up with the other two members of the Family, to tell them everything about what she had done with the diver. But she could not bring herself to it now. Her confession stuck in her mind. If it turned out that the clutch had been harmed by her inattention while she had actually been breaking the taboo with one of the very animals who had threatened the clutch in the first place . . .

She should have considered more carefully. But, of course, she was still too ignorant and irresponsible. First Uncle and Second Mother were the wise ones. First Mother, also, of course; but she was now too old to see a clutch of eggs through to hatching stage by herself alone, or with just the help of someone presently as callow and untrustworthy as the Youngest.

"Can I—It's dark now," she signaled. "Can I go feed, now? Is it all right to go?"

"Of course," said Second Mother, who switched her signaling to First Uncle. "You're too hard sometimes. She's still only half grown."

The Youngest felt even worse, intercepting that. She slunk off through the underwater, wishing something terrible could happen to her so that when the older ones did find out what she had done they would feel pity for her, instead of hating her. For a while she played with mental images of what this might involve. One of the boats on the surface could get her tangled in their lines in such a way that she could not get free. Then they would tow her to shore, and since she was so tangled in the line she could not get up to the surface, and since she had not breathed for many hours, she would drown on the way. Or perhaps the boat that could go underwater would find her and start chasing her and turn out to be much faster than any of them had ever suspected. It might even catch her and ram her and kill her.

By the time she had run through a number of these dark scenarios, she had begun almost automatically to hunt, for the time was in fact well past her usual second feeding period and she was hungry. As she realized this, her hunt became serious. Gradually she filled herself with salmon; and as she did so, she began to feel better. For all her bulk, she was swifter than any fish in the loch. The wide swim paddle at the end of each of her four limbs could turn her instantly; and with her long neck and relatively small head out-stretched, the streamlining of even her twenty-eight-foot body parted the waters she displaced with an absolute minimum of resistance. Last, and most im-portant of all, was the great engine of her enormously powerful, lashing tail: that was the real drive behind her ability to flash above the loch bottom at speeds of up to fifty knots.

She was, in fact, beautifully designed to lead the life she led, designed by evolution over the gener-ations from that early land-dwelling, omnivorous early mammal that was her ancestor. Actually, she was herself a member of the mammalian sub-class prototheria, a large and distant cousin of monotremes like the platypus and the echidna. Her cretaceous forebears had drifted over and become practicing carnivores in the process of readapting to life in the sea.

She did not know this herself, of course. The leg-ends of the Family were incredibly ancient, passed down by the letter-perfect memories of the individual generations; but they actually were not true memories of what had been, but merely deductions about the past gradually evolved as her People had acquired communication and intelligence. In many ways, the Youngest was very like a human savage: a member of a Stone Age tribe where elaborate ritual and custom directed every action of her life except for a small area of individual freedom. And in that area of indi-vidual freedom she was as prone to ignorance and misjudgments about the world beyond the waters of her loch as any Stone Age human primitive was in

dealing with the technological world beyond his familiar few square miles of jungle.

Because of this—and because she was young and
healthy—by the time she had filled herself with
salmon, the exercise of hunting her dinner had
burned off a good deal of her feelings of shame and
guilt. She saw, or thought she saw, more clearly that
her real fault was in not staying close to the hatchhole
after the first incident. The diver's leg touching her
neck had been entirely accidental; and besides, the
diver had been unconscious and unaware of her presence at that time. So no harm could have been done.
Essentially, the taboo was still unbroken. But she
must learn to stay on guard as the adults did, to antic-
ipate additional trouble, once some had put in an appearance, and to hold herself ready at all times.

She resolved to do so. She made a solemn promise
to herself not to forget the hatchhole again—ever.

Her stomach was full. Emboldened by the freedom
of the night-empty waters above, for the loch was
always clear of boats after sundown, she swam to the
surface, emerging only a couple of hundred yards
from shore. Lying there, she watched the unusual
number of lights from cars still driving on the roads
that skirted the loch.

But suddenly her attention was distracted from
them. The clouds overhead had evidently cleared,
some time since. Now it was a clear, frosty night and
more than half the sky was glowing and melting with
the northern lights. She floated, watching them. So
beautiful, she thought, so beautiful. Her mind evoked
pictures of all the Family who must have lain and
watched the lights like this since time began, drifting
in the arctic seas or resting on some skerry or ocean
rock where only birds walked. The desire to see all
the wide skies and seas of all the world swept over her
like a physical hunger.

It was no use, however. The mountains had risen and they held the Family here, now. Blocked off from its primary dream, her hunger for adventure turned to a more possible goal. The temptation came to go and investigate the loch-going "made" things from which her diver had descended.

She found herself up near Dores, but she turned and went back down opposite St. Ninian's. The dock to which this particular boat was customarily moored was actually a mile below the village and had no illumination. But the boat had a cabin on its deck, amidships, and through the square windows lights now glowed. Their glow was different from that of the lights shown by the cars. The Youngest noted this difference without being able to account for it, not understanding that the headlights she had been watching were electric, but the illumination she now saw shining out of the cabin windows of the large, flat-hulled boat before her came from gas lanterns. She heard sounds coming from inside the cabin.

Curious, the Youngest approached the boat from the darkness of the lake, her head now lifted a good six feet out of the water so that she could look over the side railing. Two large, awkward-looking shapes rested on the broad deck in front of the cabin—one just in front, the other right up in the bow with its far end overhanging the water. Four more shapes, like the one in the bow but smaller, were spaced along the sides of the foredeck, two to a side. The Youngest slid through the little waves until she was barely a couple of dozen feet from the side of the boat. At that moment, two men came out of the cabin, strode onto the deck, and stopped by the shape just in front of the cabin.

The Youngest, though she knew she could not be seen against the dark expanse of the loch, instinctively sank down until only her head was above water.

The two men stood, almost overhead, and spoke to each other.

Their voices had a strangely slow, sonorous ring to the ears of Youngest, who was used to hearing sound waves traveling through the water at four times the speed they moved in air. She did understand, of course, that they were engaged in meaningful communication, much as she and the others of the Family were when they signaled to each other. This much her People had learned about the upright animals; they communicated by making sounds. A few of these sounds—the *"Ness"* sound, which, like the other sound, *"loch,"* seemed to refer to the water in which the Family lived—were by now familiar. But she recognized no such noises among those made by the two above her; in fact, it would have been surprising if she had, for while the language was the one she was used to hearing, the accent of one of the two was a different English, different enough from that of those living in the vicinity of the loch to make what she heard completely unintelligible.

". . . poor bastard," the other voice said.

"Mon, you forget that 'poor bastard' talk, I tell you! He knew what he doing when he go down that line. He know what a temperature like that mean. A reading like that big enough for a blue whale. He just want the glory—he all alone swimming down with a speargun to drug that great beast. It the newspaper headlines, man; that's what he after!"

"Gives me the creeps, anyway. Think we'll ever fish up the sensor head?"

"You kidding. Lucky we find *him*. No, we use the spare, like I say, starting early tomorrow. And I mean it, early!"

"I don't like it. I tell you, he's got to have relatives who'll want to know why we didn't stop after we lost him. It's his boat. It's his equipment. They'll ask who gave us permission to go on spending money they got coming, with him dead."

"You pay me some heed. We've got to try to find him, that's only right. We use the equipment we got —what else we got to use? Never mind his rich relatives. They just like him. He don't never give no damn for you or me or what it cost him, this expedition. He was born with money and all he want to do is write the book about how he an adventurer. We know what we hunt be down there, now. We capture it, then everybody happy. And you and me, we get what's in the contract, the five thousand extra apiece for taking it. Otherwise we don't get nothing—you back to that machine shop, me to the whaling, with the pockets empty. We out in the cold then, you recall that!"

"All right."

"You damn right, it all right. Starting tomorrow sunup."

"I said *all right!*" The voice paused for a second before going on. "But I'm telling you one thing. If we run into it, you better get it fast with a drug spear; because I'm not waiting. If I see it, I'm getting on the harpoon gun."

The other voice laughed.

"That's why he never let you near the gun when we out before. But I don't care. Contract, it say alive or dead we get what he promise us. Come on now, up the inn and have us food and drink."

"I want a drink! Christ, this water's empty after dark, with that law about no fishing after sundown. Anything could be out there!"

"Anything is. Come on, mon."

The Youngest heard the sound of their footsteps backing off the boat and moving away down the dock until they became inaudible within the night of the land.

Left alone, she lifted her head gradually out of the
water once more and cautiously examined everything
before her: big boat and small ones nearby, dock and
shore. There was no sound or other indication of anything living. Slowly, she once more approached the
craft the two had just left and craned her neck over its
side.

The large shape in front of the cabin was box-like
like the boat, but smaller and without any apertures
in it. Its top sloped from the side facing the bow of
the craft to the opposite side. On that sloping face she
saw circles of some material that, although as hard as
the rest of the object, still had a subtly different tex-
ture when she pressed her cheek cells directly against
them. Farther down from these, which were in fact
the glass faces of meters, was a raised plate with
grooves in it. The Youngest would not have understood what the grooves meant, even if she had had
enough light to see them plainly; and even if their
sense could have been translated to her, the words
"caloric sensor" would have meant nothing to her.

A few seconds later, she was, however, puzzled to
discover on the deck beside this object another shape
which her memory insisted was an exact duplicate of
the heavy round thing that had been dropped to the
loch bed beside the old hatchhole. She felt all over it
carefully with her cheek cells, but discovered nothing
beyond the dimensions of its almost plumb-bob
shape and the fact that a line was attached to it in the
same way a line had been attached to the other. In
this case, the line was one end of a heavy coil that had
a farther end connected to the box-like shape with the
sloping top.

Baffled by this discovery, the Youngest moved forward to examine the strange object in the bow of the
boat with its end overhanging the water. This one had
a shape that was hard to understand. It was more

complex, made up of a number of smaller shapes both round and boxy. Essentially, however, it looked like a mound with something long and narrow set on top of it, such as a piece of waterlogged tree from which the limbs had long since dropped off. The four smaller things like it, spaced two on each side of the foredeck, were not quite like the big one, but they were enough alike so that she ignored them in favor of examining the large one. Feeling around the end of the object that extended over the bow of the boat and hovered above the water, the Youngest discovered the log shape rotated at a touch and even tilted up and down with the mound beneath it as a balance point. On further investigation, she found that the log shape was hollow at the water end and was projecting beyond the hooks the animals often let down into the water with little dead fish or other things attached, to try to catch the larger fish of the loch. This end, how-ever, was attached not to a curved length of metal, but to a straight metal rod lying loosely in the hollow log space. To the rod part, behind the barbed head, was joined the end of another heavy coil of line wound about a round thing on the deck. This line was much thicker than the one attached to the box with the sloping top. Experimentally, she tested it with her teeth. It gave—but did not cut when she closed her jaws on it—then sprang back, apparently unharmed, when she let it go.

All very interesting, but puzzling—as well it might be. A harpoon gun and spearguns with heads de-signed to inject a powerful tranquilizing drug on im-pact were completely outside the reasonable dimensions of the world as the Youngest knew it. The heat-sensing equipment that had been used to locate First Uncle's huge body as it lay on the loch bed warming the eggs was closer to being something she could understand. She and the rest of the Family used

heat sensing themselves to locate and identify one another, though their natural abilities were nowhere
near as sensitive as those of the instrument she had
examined on the foredeck. At any rate, for now, she
merely dismissed from her mind the question of what
these things were. Perhaps, she thought, the upright
animals simply liked to have odd shapes of "made"
things around them. That notion reminded her of her
diver; and she felt a sudden, deep curiosity about
him, a desire to see if he had yet recovered and found
his way out of the cave to shore.

She backed off from the dock and turned toward
the south end of the loch, not specifically heading for
the cave where she had left him but traveling in that
general direction and turning over in her head the
idea that perhaps she might take one more look at the
cave. But she would not be drawn into the same sort
of irresponsibility she had fallen prey to earlier in the
day, when she had taken him to the cave! Not twice
would she concern herself with one of the animals
when she was needed by others of the Family. She
decided, instead, to go check on Second Mother and
the new hatchhole.

When she got to the hole, however, she found that
Second Mother had no present need of her. The older
female, tired from the exacting events of the day and
heavy from feeding later than her usual time—for she
had been too nervous, at first, to leave the eggs in
First Uncle's care and so had not finished her feeding
period until well after dark—was half asleep. She
only untucked her head from the coil she had made of
her body around and above the eggs long enough to
make sure that the Youngest had not brought warning of some new threat. Reassured, she coiled up
tightly again about the clutch and closed her eyes.

The Youngest gazed at her with a touch of envy. It
must be a nice feeling, she thought, to shut out every-

thing but yourself and your eggs. There was plainly nothing that Youngest was wanted for, here—and she had never felt less like sleeping herself. The night was full of mysteries and excitements. She headed once more north, up the lake.

She had not deliberately picked a direction, but suddenly she realized that unconsciously she was once more heading toward the cave where she had left the diver. She felt a strange sense of freedom. Second Mother was sleeping with her eggs. First Uncle by this time would have his heavy bulk curled up in his favorite cave and his head on its long neck resting on a ledge at the water's edge, so that he had the best of both the worlds of air and loch at the same time. The Youngest had the loch to herself, with neither Family nor animals to worry about. It was all hers, from Fort Augustus clear to Castle Ness.

The thought gave her a sense of power. Abruptly, she decided that there was no reason at all why she should not go see what had happened to the diver. She turned directly toward the cave, putting on speed.

At the last moment, however, she decided to enter the cave quietly. If he was really recovered and alert, she might want to leave again without being noticed. Like a cloud shadow moving silently across the surface of the waves, she slid through the underwater entrance of the cave, invisible in the blackness, her cheek cells reassuring her that there was no moving body in the water inside.

Once within, she paused again to check for heat radiation that would betray a living body in the water even if it was being held perfectly still. But she felt no heat. Satisfied, she lifted her head silently from the water inside the cave and approached the rock ledge where she had left him.

Her hearing told that he was still here, though her

eyes were as useless in this total darkness as his must be. Gradually, that same, sensitive hearing filled in the image of his presence for her.

He still lay on the ledge, apparently on his side. She could hear the almost rhythmic scraping of a sort of metal clip he wore on the right side of his belt. It was scratching against the rock as he made steady, small movements. He must have come to enough to take off his head-things and back-things, however, for she heard no scraping from these. His breathing was rapid and hoarse, almost a panting. Slowly, sound by sound, she built up a picture of him, there in the dark. He was curled up in a tight ball, shivering.

The understanding that he was lying, trembling from the cold, struck the Youngest in her most vulnerable area. Like all the Family, she had vivid memories of what it had been like to be a hatchling. As eggs, the clutch was kept in open water with as high an oxygen content as possible until the moment for hatching came close. Then they were swiftly transported to one of the caves so that they would emerge from their shell into the land and air environment that their warm-blooded, air-breathing ancestry required. And a hatchling could not drown on a cave ledge. But, although he or she was protected there from the water, a hatchling was still vulnerable to the cold; and the caves were no warmer than the water—which was snow-fed from the mountains most of the year. Furthermore, the hatchling would not develop the layers of blubber-like fat that insulated an adult of the Family for several years. The life of someone like the Youngest began with the sharp sensations of cold as a newborn, and ended the same way, when aged body processes were no longer able to generate enough interior heat to keep the great hulk going. The first instinct of the hatchling was to huddle close to the warm belly skin of the adult on guard. And the first instinct of the adult was to warm the small, new life.

She stood in the shallow water of the cave, irresolute. The taboo, and everything that she had ever known, argued fiercely in her against any contact with the upright animal. But this one had already made a breach in her cosmos, had already been promoted from an "it" to a "he" in her thoughts; and her instincts cried out as strongly as her teachings, against letting him chill there on the cold stone ledge when she had within her the heat to warm him.

It was a short, hard, internal struggle; but her instincts won. After all, she rationalized, it was she who had brought him here to tremble in the cold. The fact that by doing so she had saved his life was beside the point.

Completely hidden in the psychological machinery that moved her toward him now was the lack in her life that was the result of being the last, solitary child of her kind. From the moment of hatching on, she had never had a playmate, never known anyone with whom she could share the adventures of growing up. An unconscious part of her was desperately hungry for a friend, a toy, anything that could be completely and exclusively hers, apart from the adult world that encompassed everything around her.

Slowly, silently, she slipped out of the water and up onto the ledge and flowed around his shaking form. She did not quite dare to touch him; but she built walls about him and a roof over him out of her body, the inward-facing skin of which was already beginning to pulse with hot blood pumped from deep within her.

Either dulled by his semi-consciousness or else too wrapped up in his own misery to notice, the creature showed no awareness that she was there. Not until the warmth began to be felt did he instinctively relax the tight ball of his body and, opening out, touch her —not merely with his wetsuit-encased body, but with his unprotected hands and forehead.

The Youngest shuddered all through her length at that first contact. But before she could withdraw, his own reflexes operated. His chilling body felt warmth and did not stop to ask its source. Automatically, he huddled close against the surfaces he touched.

The Youngest bowed her head. It was too late. It was done.

This was no momentary, unconscious contact. She could feel his shivering directly now through her own skin surface. Nothing remained but to accept what had happened. She folded herself close about him, covering as much of his small, cold, trembling body as possible with her own warm surface, just as she would have if he had been a new hatchling who suffered from the chill. He gave a quavering sigh of relief and pressed close against her.

Gradually he warmed and his trembling stopped. Long before that, he had fallen into a deep, torpor-like slumber. She could hear the near-snores of his heavy breathing.

Grown bolder by contact with him and abandoning herself to an affection for him, she explored his slumbering shape with her sensitive cheek cells. He had no true swim paddles, of course—she already knew this about the upright animals. But she had never guessed how delicate and intricate were the several-times split appendages that he possessed on his upper limbs where swim paddles might have been. His body was very narrow, its skeleton hardly clothed in flesh. Now that she knew that his kind were as vulnerable to cold as new hatchlings, she did not wonder that it should be so with them: they had hardly anything over their bones to protect them from the temperature of the water and air. No wonder they covered themselves with non-living skins.

His head was not long at all, but quite round. His mouth was small and his jaws flat, so that he would be able to take only very small bites of things. There was a sort of protuberance above the mouth and a pair of eyes, side by side. Around the mouth and below the eyes his skin was full of tiny, sharp points; and on the top of his head was a strange, springy mat of very fine filaments. The Youngest rested the cells of her right cheek for a moment on the filaments, finding a strange inner warmth and pleasure in the touch of them. It was a completely inexplicable pleasure, for the legends had forgotten what old, primitive parts of her brain remembered: a time when her ancestors on land had worn fur and known the feel of it in their close body contacts.

Wrapped up in the subconscious evocation of ancient companionship, she lay in the darkness spinning impossible fantasies in which she would be able to keep him. He could live in this cave, she thought, and she would catch salmon—since that was what his kind, with their hooks and filaments, seemed most to search for—to bring to him for food. If he wanted "made" things about him, she could probably visit docks and suchlike about the loch and find some to bring here to him. When he got to know her better, since he had the things that let him hold his breath underwater, they could venture out into the loch together. Of course, once that time was reached, she would have to tell Second Mother and First Uncle about him. No doubt it would disturb them greatly, the fact that the taboo had been broken; but once they had met him underwater, and seen how sensible and friendly he was—how wise, even, for a small animal like himself . . .

Even as she lay dreaming these dreams, however, a sane part of her mind was still on duty. Realistically, she knew that what she was thinking was nonsense. Centuries of legend, duty, and taboo were not to be upset in a few days by any combination of accidents. Nor, even if no problem arose from the Family side, could she really expect him to live in a cave, forsaking his own species. His kind needed light as well as air. They needed the freedom to come and go on shore. Even if she could manage to keep him with her in the cave for a while, eventually the time would come when he would yearn for the land under his feet and the open sky overhead, at one and the same time. No, her imaginings could never be; and, because she knew this, when her internal time sense warned her that the night was nearly over, she silently uncoiled from around him and slipped back into the water, leaving the cave before the first light, which filtered in past the tree roots in the cave roof, could let him see who it was that had kept him alive through the hours of darkness.

Left uncovered on the ledge but warm again, he slept heavily on, unaware.

Out in the waters of the loch, in the pre-dawn gloom, the Youngest felt fatigue for the first time. She could easily go twenty-four hours without sleep; but this twenty-four hours just past had been emotionally charged ones. She had an irresistible urge to find one of the caves she favored herself and to lose herself in slumber. She shook it off. Before anything else, she must check with Second Mother.

Going swiftly to the new hatchhole, she found Second Mother fully awake, alert, and eager to talk to her. Evidently Second Mother had awakened early and spent some time thinking.

"You're young," she signaled the Youngest, "far too young to share the duty of guarding a clutch of eggs, even with someone as wise as your First Uncle.

Happily, there's no problem physically. You're mature enough so that milk would come, if a hatchling should try to nurse from you. But, sensibly, you're still far too young to take on this sort of responsibility. Nonetheless, if something should happen to me, there would only be you and the Uncle to see this clutch to the hatching point. Therefore, we have to think of the possibility that you might have to take over for me."

"No. No, I couldn't," said the Youngest.

"You may have to. It's still only a remote possibility; but I should have taken it into consideration before. Since there're only the four of us, if anything happened to one of us, the remaining would have to see the eggs through to hatching. You and I could do it, I'm not worried about that situation. But with a clutch there must be a mother. Your uncle can be everything but that, and First Mother is really too old. Somehow, we must make you ready before your time to take on that duty."

"If you say so . . ." said the Youngest, unhappily.

"Our situation says so. Now, all you need to know, really, is told in the legends. But knowing them and understanding them are two different things . . ."

Then Second Mother launched into a retelling of the long chain of stories associated with the subject of eggs and hatchlings. The Youngest, of course, had heard them all before. More than that, she had them stored, signal by signal, in her memory as perfectly as had Second Mother herself. But she understood that Second Mother wanted her not only to recall each of these packages of stored wisdom, but to think about what was stated in them. Also—so much wiser had she already become in twenty-four hours—she realized that the events of yesterday had suddenly shocked Second Mother, giving her a feeling of helplessness should the upright animals ever really chance to stumble upon the hatchhole. For she could never abandon her eggs, and if she stayed with them the best she could hope for would be to give herself up to the land-dwellers in hope that this would satisfy them and they would look no further.

It was hard to try and ponder the legends, sleepy as the Youngest was, but she tried her best; and when at last Second Mother turned her loose, she swam groggily off to the nearest cave and curled up. It was now broad-enough daylight for her early feeding period, but she was too tired to think of food. In seconds, she was sleeping almost as deeply as the diver had been when she left him.

She came awake suddenly and was in motion almost before her eyes were open. First Uncle's signal of alarm was ringing all through the loch. She plunged from her cave into the outer waters. Vibrations told her that he and Second Mother were headed north, down the deep center of the loch as fast as they could travel, carrying the clutch of eggs. She drove on to join them, sending ahead her own signal that she was coming.

"Quick! Oh, quick!" signaled Second Mother.

Unencumbered, she began to converge on them at double their speed. Even in this moment her training paid off. She shot through the water, barely fifty feet above the bed of the loch, like a dolphin in the salt sea; and her perfect shape and smooth skin caused no turbulence at all to drag at her passage and slow her down.

She caught up with them halfway between Inverfarigaig and Dores and took her half of the eggs from Second Mother, leaving the older female free to find a new hatchhole. Unburdened, Second Mother leaped ahead and began to range the loch bed in search of a safe place.

"What happened?" signaled Youngest.

"Again!" First Uncle answered. "They dropped another 'made' thing, just like the first, almost in the hatchhole this time!" he told her.

Second Mother had been warming the eggs. Luckily he had been close. He had swept in; but not daring to break the line a second time for fear of giving clear evidence of the Family, he had simply scooped a hole in the loch bed, pushed the thing in, buried it and pressed down hard on the loch bed material with which he had covered it. He had buried it deeply enough so that the animals above were pulling up on their line with caution, for fear that they themselves might break it. Eventually, they would get it loose. Until then, the Family had a little time in which to find another location for the eggs.

A massive shape loomed suddenly out of the peaty darkness, facing them. It was First Mother, roused from her cave by the emergency.

"I can still carry eggs. Give them here, and you go back," she ordered First Uncle. "Find out what's being done with that 'made' thing you buried and what's going on with those creatures. Two hatchholes stumbled on in two days is too much for chance."

First Uncle swirled about and headed back.

The Youngest slowed down. First Mother was still tremendously powerful, of course, more so than any of them; but she no longer had the energy reserves to move at the speed at which First Uncle and the Youngest had been traveling. Youngest felt a surge of admiration for First Mother, battling the chill of the open loch water and the infirmities of her age to give help now, when the Family needed it.

"Here! This way!" Second Mother called.

They turned sharply toward the east bank of the loch and homed in on Second Mother's signal. She had found a good place for a new hatchhole. True, it

was not near the mouth of a stream; but the loch bed
was clean and this was one of the few spots where the
rocky slope underwater from the shore angled backward when it reached a depth below four hundred
feet, so that the loch at this point was actually in under the rock and had a roof overhead. Here, there
was no way that a "made" thing could be dropped
down on a line to come anywhere close to the hatchhole.

When First Mother and the Youngest got there,
Second Mother was already at work making and
cleaning the hole. The hole had barely been finished
and Second Mother settled down with the clutch under her, when First Uncle arrived.

"They have their 'made' thing back," he reported.
"They pulled on its line with little, repeated jerkings
until they loosened it from its bed, and then they
lifted it back up."

He told how he had followed it up through the water until he was just under the "made" thing and rode
on the loch surface. Holding himself there, hidden by
the thing itself, he had listened, trying to make sense
out of what the animals were doing, from what he
could hear.

They had made a great deal of noise after they
hoisted the thing back on board. They had moved it
around a good deal and done things with it, before
finally leaving it alone and starting back toward the
dock near St. Ninian's. First Uncle had followed
them until he was sure that was where they were
headed; then he had come to find the new hatchhole
and the rest of the Family.

After he was done signaling, they all waited for
First Mother to respond, since she was the oldest and
wisest. She lay thinking for some moments.

"They didn't drop the 'made' thing down into the
water again, you say?" she asked at last.

"No," signaled First Uncle.

"And none of them went down into the water, themselves?"

"No."

"It's very strange," said First Mother. "All we know is that they've twice almost found the hatch-hole. All I can guess is that this isn't a chance thing, but that they're acting with some purpose. They may not be searching for our eggs, but they seem to be searching for *something*."

The Youngest felt a sudden chilling inside her. But First Mother was already signaling directly to First Uncle.

"From now on, you should watch them, whenever the thing in which they move about the loch surface isn't touching shore. If you need help, the Youngest can help you. If they show any signs of coming close to here, we must move the eggs immediately. I'll come out twice a day to relieve Second Mother for her feeding, so that you can be free to do that watching. No"—she signaled sharply before they could object—"I *will* do this. I can go for some days warming the eggs for two short periods a day, before I'll be out of strength; and this effort of mine is needed. The eggs *should* be safe here, but if it proves that the creatures have some means of finding them, wherever the hatchhole is placed in the open loch, we'll have to move the clutch into the caves."

Second Mother cried out in protest.

"I know," First Mother said, "the legends counsel against ever taking the eggs into the caves until time for hatching. But we may have no choice."

"My eggs will die!" wept Second Mother.

"They're your eggs, and the decision to take them inside has to be yours," said First Mother. "But they won't live if the animals find them. In the caves there may be a chance of life for them. Besides, our duty as

a Family is to survive. It's the Family we have to
think of, not a single clutch of eggs or a single individual. If worse comes to worst and it turns out we're
not safe from the animals even in the caves, we'll try
the journey of the Lost Father from Loch Morar
before we'll let ourselves all be killed off."

"What Lost Father?" the Youngest demanded.
"No one ever told me a legend about a Lost Father
from Loch Morar. What's Loch Morar?"

"It's not a legend usually told to those too young
to have full wisdom," said First Mother. "But these
are new and dangerous times. Loch Morar is a loch a
long way from here, and some of our People were
also left there when the ice went and the land rose.
They were of our People, but a different Family."

"But what about a Lost Father?" the Youngest
persisted, because First Mother had stopped talking
as if she would say no more about it. "How could a
Father be lost?"

"He was lost to Loch Morar," First Mother explained, "because he grew old and died here in Loch
Ness."

"But how did he get here?"

"He couldn't, that's the point," said First Uncle,
grumpily. "There are legends *and* legends. That's why
some are not told to young ones until they've
matured enough to understand. The journey the Lost
Father's supposed to have made is impossible. Tell it
to some youngster and he or she's just as likely to try
and duplicate it."

"But you said we might try it!" The Youngest ap-
pealed to First Mother.

"Only if there were no other alternative," First
Mother answered. "I'd try flying out over the mountains if that was the only alternative left, because it's
our duty to keep trying to survive as a Family as long
as we're alive. So, as a last resort, we'd try the journey

of the Lost Father, even though as the Uncle says, it's impossible."

"Why? Tell me what it was. You've already begun to tell me. Shouldn't I know all of it?"

"I suppose . . ." said First Mother, wearily. "Very well. Loch Morar isn't surrounded by mountains as we are here. It's even fairly close to the sea, so that if a good way could be found for such as us to travel over dry land, members of the People living there might be able to go home to the sea we all recall by the legends. Well, this legend says that there once was a Father in Loch Morar who dreamed all his life of leading his Family home to the sea. But we've grown too heavy nowadays to travel any distance overland, normally. One winter day, when a new snow had just fallen, the legend says this Father discovered a way of traveling on land that worked."

In sparse sentences, First Mother rehearsed the legend to a fascinated Youngest. It told that the snow provided a slippery surface over which the great bodies of the People could slide under the impetus of the same powerful tail muscles that drove them through the water, their swim paddles acting as rudders—or brakes—on downslopes. Actually, what the legend described was a way of swimming on land. Loch Ness never froze and First Mother therefore had no knowledge of ice-skating, so she could not explain that what the legend spoke of was the same principle that makes a steel ice blade glide over ice—the weight upon it causing the ice to melt under the sharp edge of the blade so that, effectively, it slides on a cushion of water. With the People, their ability to shunt a controlled amount of warmth to the skin in contact with the ice and snow did the same thing.

In the legend, the Father who discovered this tried to take his Family from Loch Morar back to the sea, but they were all afraid to try going, except for him.

So he went alone and found his way to the ocean more easily than he had thought possible. He spent some years in the sea, but found it lonely and came back to land to return to Loch Morar. However, though it was winter, he could not find enough snow along the route he had taken to the sea in order to get back to Loch Morar. He hunted northward for a snow-covered route inland, north past the isle of Sleat, past Glenelg; and finally, under Benn Attow, he found a snow route that led him ultimately to Glen Moriston and into Loch Ness.

He went as far back south through Loch Ness as he could go, even trying some distance down what is now the southern part of the Caledonian Canal before he became convinced that the route back to Loch Morar by that way would be too long and hazardous to be practical. He decided to return to the sea and wait for snow to make him a way over his original route to Morar.

But, meanwhile, he had become needed in Loch Ness and grown fond of the Family there. He wished to take them with him to the sea. The others, however, were afraid to try the long overland journey; and while they hesitated and put off going, he grew too old to lead them; and so they never did go. Nevertheless, the legend told of his route and, memories being what they were among the People, no member of the Family in Loch Ness, after First Mother had finished telling the legend to the Youngest, could not have retraced the Lost Father's steps exactly.

"I don't think we should wait," the Youngest said, eagerly, when First Mother was through. "I think we should go now—I mean, as soon as we get a snow on the banks of the loch so that we can travel. Once we're away from the loch, there'll be snow all the time, because it's only the warmth of the loch that keeps the snow off around here. Then we could all go home to the sea, where we belong, away from the animals and their 'made' things. Most of the eggs laid there would hatch—"

"I told you so," First Uncle interrupted, speaking to First Mother. "Didn't I tell you so?"

"And what about my eggs now?" said Second Mother.

"We'll try something like that only if the animals start to destroy us," First Mother said to the Youngest with finality. "Not before. If it comes to that, Second Mother's present clutch of eggs will be lost, anyway. Otherwise, we'd never leave them, you should know that. Now, I'll go back to the cave and rest until late feeding period for Second Mother."

She went off. First Uncle also went off, to make sure that the animals had really gone to the dock and were still there. The Youngest, after asking Second Mother if there was any way she could be useful and being told there was none, went off to her delayed first feeding period.

She was indeed hungry, with the ravenous hunger of youth. But once she had taken the edge off her appetite, an uneasy feeling began to grow inside her, and not even stuffing herself with rich-fleshed salmon made it go away.

What was bothering her, she finally admitted to herself, was the sudden, cold thought that had intruded on her when First Mother had said that the creatures seemed to be searching for something. The Youngest was very much afraid she knew what they were searching for. It was their fellow, the diver she had taken to the cave. If she had not done anything, they would have found his body before this; but because she had saved him, they were still looking; and because he was in a cave, they could not find him. So they would keep on searching, and sooner or later they would come close to the new hatchhole; and

then Second Mother would take the clutch into one
of the caves, and the eggs would die, and it would be
her own fault, the Youngest's fault alone.

She was crying inside. She did not dare cry out
loud because the others would hear and want to
know what was troubling her. She was ashamed to
tell them what she had done. Somehow, she must put
things right herself, without telling them—at least until some later time, when it would be all over and un-
important.

The diver must go back to his own people—if he
had not already.

She turned and swam toward the cave, making sure
to approach it from deep in the loch. Through the
entrance of the cave, she stood up in the shallow interior pool and lifted her head out of water; and he
was still there.

Enough light was filtering in through the ceiling
cracks of the cave to make a sort of dim twilight inside. She saw him plainly—and he saw her.

She had forgotten that he would have no idea of
what she looked like. He had been sitting up on the
rock ledge; but when her head and its long neck rose
out of the water, he stared and then scrambled back
—as far back from her as he could get, to the rock
wall of the cave behind the ledge. He stood pressed
against it, still staring at her, his mouth open in a
soundless circle.

She paused, irresolute. She had never intended to
frighten him. She had forgotten that he might consider her at all frightening. All her foolish imaginings
of keeping him here in the cave and of swimming with
him in the loch crumbled before the bitter reality of
his terror at the sight of her. Of course, he had had no
idea of who had been coiled about him in the dark.
He had only known that something large had been
bringing the warmth of life back into him. But surely

he would make the connection, now that he saw her? She waited.

He did not seem to be making it. He simply stayed where he was, as if paralyzed by her presence. She felt an exasperation with him rising inside her. According to the legends, his kind had at least a share of intelligence, possibly even some aspect of wisdom, although that was doubtful. But now, crouched against the back of the cave, he looked like nothing more than another wild animal—like one of the otters, strayed from nearby streams, she had occasionally encountered in these caves. And as with such an otter, for all its small size ready to scratch or bite, she felt a caution about approaching him.

Nevertheless, something had to be done. At any moment now, the others like him would be out on the loch in their "made" thing, once more hunting for him and threatening to rediscover the hatchhole.

Cautiously, slowly, so as not to send him into a fighting reflex, she approached the ledge and crept up on it sideways, making an arc of her body and moving in until she half surrounded him, an arm's length from him. She was ready to pull back at the first sign of a hostile move, but no action was triggered in him. He merely stayed where he was, pressing against the rock wall as if he would like to step through it, his eyes fixed on her and his jaws still in the half-open position. Settled about him, however, she shunted blood into her skin area and began to radiate heat.

It took a little while for him to feel the warmth coming from her and some little while more to understand what she was trying to tell him. But then, gradually, his tense body relaxed. He slipped down the rock against which he was pressed and ended up sitting, gazing at her with a different shape to his eyes and mouth.

He made some noises with his mouth. These conveyed no sense to the Youngest, of course, but she thought that at least they did not sound like unfriendly noises.

"So now you know who I am," she signaled, although she knew perfectly well he could not understand her. "Now, you've got to swim out of here and go back on the land. Go back to your People."

She had corrected herself instinctively on the last term. She had been about to say "go back to the other animals"; but something inside her dictated the change—which was foolish, because he would not know the difference, anyway.

He straightened against the wall and stood up. Suddenly, he reached out an upper limb toward her.

She flinched from his touch instinctively, then braced herself to stay put. If she wanted him not to be afraid of her, she would have to show him the same fearlessness. Even the otters, if left alone, would calm down somewhat, though they would take the first opportunity to slip past and escape from the cave where they had been found.

She held still, accordingly. The divided ends of his limb touched her and rubbed lightly over her skin. It was not an unpleasant feeling, but she did not like it. It had been different when he was helpless and had touched her unconsciously.

She now swung her head down close to watch him and had the satisfaction of seeing him start when her own eyes and jaws came within a foot or so of his. He pulled his limbs back quickly, and made more noises. They were still not angry noises, though, and this fact, together with his quick withdrawal, gave her an impression that he was trying to be conciliatory, even friendly.

Well, at least she had his attention. She turned, backed off the ledge into the water, then reached up with her nose and pushed toward him the "made" things he originally had had attached to his back and head. Then, turning, she ducked under the water, swam out of the cave into the loch, and waited just under the surface for him to follow.

He did not.

She waited for more than enough time for him to reattach his things and make up his mind to follow, then she swam back inside. To her disgust, he was now sitting down again and his "made" things were still unattached to him.

She came sharply up to the edge of the rock and tumbled the two things literally on top of him.

"Put them on!" she signaled. "Put them on, you stupid animal!"

He stared at her and made noises with his mouth. He stood up and moved his upper limbs about in the air. But he made no move to pick up the "made" things at his feet. Angrily, she shoved them against his lower limb ends once more.

He stopped making noises and merely looked at her. Slowly, although she could not define all of the changes that signaled it to her, an alteration of manner seemed to take place in him. The position of his upright body changed subtly. The noises he was making changed; they became slower and more separate, one from another. He bent down and picked up the larger of the things, the one that he had had attached to his back; but he did not put it on.

Instead, he held it up in the air before him as if drawing her attention to it. He turned it over in the air and shook it slightly, then held it in that position some more. He rapped it with the curled-over sections of one of his limb-ends, so that it rang with a hollow sound from both its doubled parts. Then he put it down on the ledge again and pushed it from him with one of his lower limb ends.

The Youngest stared at him, puzzled, but nonetheless hopeful for the first time. At last he seemed to be trying to communicate something to her, even though what he was doing right now seemed to make no sense. Could it be that this was some sort of game the upright animals played with their "made" things; and he either wanted to play it, or wanted her to play it with him, before he would put the things on and get in the water? When she was much younger, she had played with things herself—interesting pieces of rock or waterlogged material she found on the loch bed, or flotsam she had encountered on the surface at night, when it was safe to spend time in the open.

No, on second thought that explanation hardly seemed likely. If it was a game he wanted to play with her, it was more reasonable for him to push the things at her instead of just pushing the bigger one away and ignoring it. She watched him, baffled. Now he had picked up the larger thing again and was repeating his actions exactly.

The creature went through the same motions several more times, eventually picking up and putting the smaller "made" thing about his head and muzzle, but still shaking and pushing away the larger thing. Eventually he made a louder noise which, for the first time, sounded really angry; threw the larger thing to one end of the ledge; and went off to sit down at the far end of the ledge, his back to her.

Still puzzled, the Youngest stretched her neck up over the ledge to feel the rejected "made" thing again with her cheek cells. It was still an enigmatic, cold, hard, double-shaped object that made no sense to her. What he's doing can't be playing, she thought. Not that he was playing at the last, there. And besides, he doesn't act as if he liked it and liked to play with it, he's acting as if he hated it—

Illumination came to her, abruptly.

"Of course!" she signaled at him.

But of course the signal did not even register on him. He still sat with his back to her.

What he had been trying to tell her, she suddenly realized, was that for some reason the "made" thing was no good for him any longer. Whether he had used it to play with, to comfort himself, or, as she had originally guessed, it had something to do with making it possible for him to stay underwater, for some reason it was now no good for that purpose.

The thought that it might indeed be something to help him stay underwater suddenly fitted in her mind with the fact that he no longer considered it any good. She sat back on her tail, mentally berating herself for being so foolish. Of course, that was what he had been trying to tell her. It would not help him stay underwater anymore; and to get out of the cave he had to go underwater—not very far, of course, but still a small distance.

On the other hand, how was he to know it was only a small distance? He had been unconscious when she had brought him here.

Now that she had worked out what she thought he had been trying to tell her, she was up against a new puzzle. By what means was she to get across to him that she had understood?

She thought about this for a time, then picked up the thing in her teeth and threw it herself against the rock wall at the back of the ledge.

He turned around, evidently alerted by the sounds it made. She stretched out her neck, picked up the thing, brought it back to the water edge of the ledge, and then threw it at the wall again.

Then she looked at him.

He made sounds with his mouth and turned all the way around. Was it possible he had understood, she wondered? But he made no further moves, just sat there. She picked up and threw the "made" thing a

couple of more times; then she paused once again to
see what he might do.

He stood, hesitating, then inched forward to where
the thing had fallen, picked up and threw it himself.
But he threw it, as she had thrown it—at the rock
wall behind the ledge.

The Youngest felt triumph. They were finally sig-
nalling each other—after a fashion.

But now where did they go from here? She wanted
to ask him if there was anything they could do about
the "made" thing being useless, but she could not
think how to act that question out.

He, however, evidently had something in mind. He
went to the edge of the rock shelf, knelt down and
placed one of his multi-divided limb ends flat on the
water surface, but with its inward-grasping surface
upward. Then he moved it across the surface of the
water so that the outer surface, or back, of it was in
the water but the inner surface was still dry.

She stared at him. Once more he was doing something incomprehensible. He repeated the gesture several more times, but still it conveyed no meaning to
her. He gave up, finally, and sat for a few minutes
looking at her; then he got up, went back to the rock
wall, turned around, walked once more to the edge of
the ledge, and sat down.

Then he held up one of his upper limb ends with all
but two of the divisions curled up. The two that were
not curled up he pointed downward, and lowered
them until their ends rested on the rock ledge. Then,
pivoting first on the end of one of the divisions, then
on the other, he moved the limb end back toward the
wall as far as he could stretch, then turned it around
and moved it forward again to the water's edge,
where he folded up the two extended divisions, and
held the limb end still.

He did this again. And again.

The Youngest concentrated. There was some meaning here; but with all the attention she could bring to bear on it, she still failed to see what it was. This was even harder than extracting wisdom from the legends. As she watched, he got up once more, walked back to the rock wall, came forward again and sat down. He did this twice.

Then he did the limb-end, two-division-movement thing twice.

Then he walked again, three times.

Then he did the limb-end thing three more times—

Understanding suddenly burst upon the Youngest. He was trying to make some comparison between his walking to the back of the ledge and forward again, and moving his limb ends in that odd fashion, first backward and then forward. The two divisions, with their little joints, moved much like his two lower limbs when he walked on them. It was extremely interesting to take part of your body and make it act like your whole body, doing something. Youngest wished that her swim paddles had divisions on the ends, like his, so she could try it.

She was becoming fascinated with the diver all over again. She had almost forgotten the threat to the eggs that others like him posed as long as he stayed hidden in this cave. Her conscience caught her up sharply. She should check right now and see if things were all right with the Family. She turned to leave, and then checked herself. She wanted to reassure him that she was coming back.

For a second only she was baffled for a means to do this; then she remembered that she had already left the cave once, thinking he would follow her, and then come back when she had given up on his doing so. If he saw her go and come several times, he should expect that she would go on returning, even though the interval might vary.

She turned and dived out through the hole into the loch, paused for a minute or two, then went back in. She did this two more times before leaving the cave finally. He had given her no real sign that he understood what she was trying to convey, but he had already showed signs of that intelligence the legends credited his species with. Hopefully, he would figure it out. If he did not—well, since she was going back anyway, the only harm would be that he might worry a bit about being abandoned there.

She surfaced briefly, in the center of the loch, to see if many of the "made" things were abroad on it today. But none were in sight and there was little or no sign of activity on the banks. The sky was heavy with dark, low-lying clouds; and the hint of snow, heavy snow, was in the sharp air. She thought again of the journey of the Lost Father of Loch Morar, and of the sea it could take them to—their safe home, the sea. They should go. They should go without waiting. If only she could convince them to go . . .

She dropped by the hatchhole, found First Mother warming the eggs while Second Mother was off feeding, and heard from First Mother that the craft had not left its place on shore all day. Discussing this problem almost as equals with First Mother—of whom she had always been very much in awe—emboldened the Youngest to the point where she shyly suggested she might try warming the clutch herself, occasionally, so as to relieve First Mother from these twice-daily stints, which must end by draining her strength and killing her.

"It would be up to Second Mother, in any case," First Mother answered, "but you're still really too small to be sure of giving adequate warmth to a full clutch. In an emergency, of course, you shouldn't hesitate to do your best with the eggs, but I don't think we're quite that desperate, yet."

Having signaled this, however, First Mother apparently softened.

"Besides," she said, "the time to be young and free of responsibilities is short enough. Enjoy it while you can. With the Family reduced to the four of us and this clutch, you'll have a hard enough adulthood, even if Second Mother manages to produce as many as two hatchlings out of the five or six clutches she can still have before her laying days are over. The odds of hatching females over males are four to one; but still, it could be that she might produce only a couple of males—and then everything would be up to you. So, use your time in your own way while it's still yours to use. But keep alert. If you're called, come immediately!"

The Youngest promised that she would. She left First Mother and went to find First Uncle, who was keeping watch in the neighborhood of the dock to which the craft was moored. When she found him, he was hanging in the loch about thirty feet deep and about a hundred feet offshore from the craft, using his sensitive hearing to keep track of what was happening in the craft and on the dock.

"I'm glad you're here," he signaled to the Youngest when she arrived. "It's time for my second feeding; and I think there're none of the animals on the 'made' thing, right now. But it wouldn't hurt to keep a watch, anyway. Do you want to stay here and listen while I go and feed?"

Actually, Youngest was not too anxious to do so. Her plan had been to check with the Uncle, then do some feeding herself and get back to her diver while daylight was still coming into his cave. But she could hardly explain that to First Uncle.

"Of course," she said. "I'll stay here until you get back."

"Good," said the Uncle; and went off.

Left with nothing to do but listen and think, the Youngest hung in the water. Her imagination, which really required very little to start it working, had recaptured the notion of making friends with the diver. It was not so important, really, that he had gotten a look at her. Over the centuries a number of incidents had occurred in which members of the Family were seen briefly by one or more of the animals, and no bad results had come from those sightings. But it was important that the land-dwellers not realize there was a true Family. If she could just convince the diver that she was the last and only one of her People, it might be quite safe to see him from time to time—of course, only when he was alone and when they were in a safe place of her choosing, since though he might be trustworthy, his fellows who had twice threatened the hatchhold clearly were not.

The new excitement about getting to know him had come from starting to be able to "talk" with him. If she and he kept at it, they could probably work out ways to tell all sorts of things to each other eventually.

That thought reminded her that she had not yet figured out why it was important to him that she understand that moving his divided limb ends in a certain way could stand for his walking. He must have had some reason for showing her that. Maybe it was connected with his earlier moving of his limb ends over the surface of the water?

Before she had a chance to ponder the possible connection, a sound from above, reaching down through the water, alerted her to the fact that some of the creatures were once more coming out onto the dock. She drifted in closer, and heard the sounds move to the end of the dock and onto the craft.

Apparently, they were bringing something heavy aboard, because along with the noise of their lower limb ends on the structure came the thumping and rumbling of something which ended at last—to judge from the sounds—somewhere up on the forward deck where she had examined the box with the sloping top and the other "made" thing in the bow.

Following this, she heard some more sounds moving from the foredeck area into the cabin.

A little recklessly, the Youngest drifted in until she was almost under the craft and only about fifteen feet below the surface, and so verified that it was, indeed, in that part of the boat where the box with the sloping box stood that most of the activity was going on. Then the noise in that area slowed down and stopped, and she heard the sound of the animals walking back off the craft, down the dock and ashore. Things became once more silent.

First Uncle had not yet returned. The Youngest wrestled with her conscience. She had not been specifically told not to risk coming up to the surface near the dock; but she knew that was simply because it had not occurred to any of the older members of the Family that she would be daring enough to do such a thing. Of course, she had never told any of them how she had examined the foredeck of the craft once before. But now, having already done so, she had a hard time convincing herself it was too risky to do again. After all, hadn't she heard the animals leave the area? No matter how quiet one of them might try to be, her hearing was good enough to pick up little sounds of his presence, if he was still aboard.

In the end, she gave in to temptation—which is not to say she moved without taking every precaution. She drifted in, underwater, so slowly and quietly that a little crowd of curious minnows formed around her. Approaching the foredeck from the loch side of the craft, she stayed well underwater until she was right up against the hull. Touching it, she hung in the wa-

ter, listening. When she still heard nothing, she lifted
her head quickly, just enough for a glimpse over the
side; then she ducked back under again and shot
away and down to a safe distance.

Eighty feet deep and a hundred feet offshore, she
paused to consider what she had seen.

Her memory, like that of everyone in the Family,
was essentially photographic when she concentrated
on remembering, as she had during her brief look
over the side of the craft. But being able to recall exactly what she had looked at was not the same thing
as realizing its import. In this case, what she had been
looking for was what had just been brought aboard.
By comparing what she had just seen with what she
had observed on her night visit earlier, she had hoped
to pick out any addition to the "made" things she
had noted then.

At first glance, no difference had seemed visible.
She noticed the box with the sloping top and the
thing in the bow with the barbed rod inside. A
number of other, smaller things were about the deck,
too, some of which she had examined briefly the time
before and some that she had barely noticed. Familiar were several of the doubled things like the one the
diver had thrown from him in order to open up communications between them at first. Largely un-
familiar were a number of smaller boxes, some round
things, other things that were combinations of round
and angular shapes, and a sort of tall open frame,
upright and holding several rods with barbed ends
like the ones which the thing in the bow contained.

She puzzled over the assortment of things—and
then without warning an answer came. But provok-
ingly, as often happened with her, it was not the answer to the question she now had, but to an earlier
one.

It had suddenly struck her that the diver's actions

in rejecting the "made" thing he had worn on his back, and all his original signals to her, might mean that for some reason it was not the one he wanted, or needed, in order to leave the cave. Why there should be that kind of difference between it and these things left her baffled. The one with him now in the cave had been the right one; but maybe it was not the right one, today. Perhaps—she had a sudden inspiration— "made" things could die like animals or fish, or even like People, and the one he now had was dead. In any case, maybe what he needed was another of that particular kind of thing.

Perhaps this insight had come from the fact that several of these same "made" things were on the deck; and also, there was obviously only one diver, since First Uncle had not reported any of the other animals going down into the water. She was immediately tempted to go and get another one of the things, so that she could take it back to the diver. If he put it on, that meant she was right. Even if he did not, she might learn something by the way he handled it.

If it had been daring to take one look at the deck, it was inconceivably so to return now and actually try to take something from it. Her sense of duty struggled with her inclinations but slowly was overwhelmed. After all, she knew now—knew positively—that none of the animals were aboard the boat and none could have come aboard in the last few minutes because she was still close enough to hear them. But if she went, she would have to hurry if she was going to do it before the Uncle got back and forbade any such action.

She swam back to the craft in a rush, came to the surface beside it, rose in the water, craned her neck far enough inboard to snatch up one of the things in her teeth and escape with it.

A few seconds later, she had it two hundred feet down on the bed of the loch and was burying it in silt. Three minutes later she was back on station watching the craft, calmly enough but with her heart beating fast. Happily, there was still no sign of First Uncle's return.

Her heartbeat slowed. She went back to puzzling over what it was on the foredeck that could be the thing she had heard the creatures bring aboard. Of course, she now had three memory images of the area to compare . . .

Recognition came.

There *was* a discrepancy between the last two mental images and the first one, a discrepancy about one of the "made" things to which she had devoted close attention, that first time.

The difference was the line attached to the box with the sloping top. It was not the same line at all. It was a drum of other line at least twice as thick as the one which had connected the heavy thing and the box previously—almost as thick as the thick line connecting the barbed rod to the thing in the bow that contained it. Clearly, the animals of the craft had tried to make sure that they would run no danger of losing their dropweight if it became buried again. Possibly they had foolishly hoped that it was so strong that not even First Uncle could break it as he had the first.

That meant they were not going to give up. Here was clear evidence they were going to go on searching for their diver. She *must* get him back to them as soon as possible.

She began to swim restlessly, to and fro in the underwater, anxious to see the Uncle return so that she could tell him what had been done.

He came not long afterward, although it seemed to her that she had waited and worried for a considerable time before he appeared. When she told him about the new line, he was concerned enough by the information so that he barely reprimanded her for taking the risk of going in close to the craft.

"I must tell First Mother, right away—" He checked himself and looked up through the twenty or so feet of water that covered them. "No, there're only a few more hours of daylight left. I need to think, anyway. I'll stay on guard here until dark, then I'll go see First Mother in her cave. Youngest, for right now don't say anything to Second Mother, or even to First Mother if you happen to talk to her. I'll tell both of them myself after I've had time to think about it."

"Then I can go now?" asked the Youngest, almost standing on her tail in the underwater in her eagerness to be off.

"Yes, yes," signaled the Uncle.

The Youngest turned and dove toward the spot where she had buried the "made" thing she had taken and about which she had been careful to say nothing to First Uncle. She had no time to explain about the diver now, and any mention of the thing would bring demands for a full explanation from her elders. Five minutes later, the thing in her teeth, she was splitting the water in the direction of the cave where she had left the diver.

She had never meant to leave him alone this long. An irrational fear grew in her that something had happened to him in the time she had been gone. Perhaps he had started chilling again and had lost too much warmth, like one of the old ones, and was now dead. If he was dead, would the other animals be satisfied just to have his body back? But she did not want to think of him dead: He was not a bad little animal, in spite of his acting in such an ugly fashion when he had seen her for the first time. She should have realized that in the daylight, seeing her as he had without warning for the first time—

The thought of daylight reminded her that First Uncle had talked about there being only a few hours of it left. Surely there must be more than that. The day could not have gone so quickly.

She took a quick slant up to the surface to check. No, she was right. There must be at least four hours yet before the sun would sink below the mountains. However, in his own way the Uncle had been right, also, because the clouds were very heavy now. It would be too dark to see much, even long before actual nightfall. Snow was certain by dark, possibly even before. As she floated for a moment with her head and neck out of water, a few of the first wandering flakes came down the wind and touched her right cheek cells with tiny, cold fingers.

She dived again. It would indeed be a heavy snowfall; the Family could start out tonight on their way to the sea, if only they wanted to. It might even be possible to carry the eggs, distributed among the four of them, just two or three carried pressed between a swim paddle and warm body skin. First Mother might tire easily; but after the first night, when they had gotten well away from the loch, and with new snow falling to cover their footsteps, they could go by short stages. There would be no danger that the others would run out of heat or strength. Even the Youngest, small as she was, had fat reserves for a couple of months without eating and with ordinary activity. The Lost Father had made it to Loch Ness from the sea in a week or so.

If only they would go now. If only she were old enough and wise enough to convince them to go. For just a moment she gave herself over to a dream of their great sea home, of the People grown strong again, patrolling in their great squadrons past the white-gleaming berg ice or under the tropic stars.

Most of the eggs of every clutch would hatch, then. The hatchlings would have the beaches of all the empty islands of the world to hatch on. Later, in the sea, they would grow up strong and safe, with their mighty elders around to guard them from anything that moved in the salt waters. In their last years, the old ones would bask under the hot sun in warm, hidden places and never need to chill again. The sea. That was where they belonged. Where they must go home to, someday. And that day should be soon . . .

The Youngest was almost to the cave now. She brought her thoughts, with a wrench, back to the diver. Alive or dead, he too must go back—to his own kind. Fervently, she hoped that she was right about another "made" thing being what he needed before he would swim out of the cave. If not, if he just threw this one away as he had the other one, then she had no choice. She would simply have to pick him up in her teeth and carry him out of the cave without it. Of course, she must be careful to hold him so that he could not reach her to scratch or bite; and she must get his head back above water as soon as they got out of the cave into the open loch, so that he would not drown.

By the time she had gotten this far in her thinking, she was at the cave. Ducking inside, she exploded up through the surface of the water within. The diver was seated with his back against the cave wall, looking haggard and savage. He was getting quite dark-colored around the jaws, now. The little points he had there seemed to be growing. She dumped the new "made" thing at his feet.

For a moment he merely stared down at it, stupidly. Then he fumbled the object up into his arms and did something to it with those active little divided sections of his two upper limb ends. A hissing sound came from the thing that made her start back, warily.

So, the "made" things were alive, after all!

The diver was busy attaching to himself the various things he had worn when she had first found him—with the exception that the new thing she had brought him, rather than its old counterpart, was going on his back. Abruptly, though, he stopped, his head-thing still not on and still in the process of putting on the paddle-like things that attached to his lower limb ends. He got up and came forward to the edge of the water, looking at her.

He had changed again. From the moment he had gotten the new thing to make the hissing noise, he had gone into yet a different way of standing and acting. Now he came within limb reach of her and stared at her so self-assuredly that she almost felt she was the animal trapped in a cave and he was free. Then he crouched down by the water and once more began to make motions with his upper limbs and limb ends.

First, he made the on-top-of-the-water sliding motion with the back of one limb end that she now began to understand must mean the craft he had gone overboard from. Once she made the connection it was obvious: the craft, like his hand, was in the water only with its underside. Its top side was dry and in the air. As she watched, he circled his "craft" limb end around in the water and brought it back to touch the ledge. Then, with his other limb end, he "walked" two of its divisions up to the "craft" and continued to "walk" them onto it.

She stared. He was apparently signaling something about his getting on the craft. But why?

However, now he was doing something else. He lifted his walking-self limb end off the "craft" and put it standing on its two stiff divisions, back on the ledge. Then he moved the "craft" out over the water, away from the ledge, and held it there. Next, to her surprise, he "walked" his other limb end right off the ledge into the water. Still "walking" so that he churned the still surface of the cave water to a slight roughness, he moved that limb end slowly to the unmoving "craft." When the "walking" limb end reached the "craft," it once more stepped up onto it.

The diver now pulled his upper limbs back, sat crouched on the ledge, and looked at the Youngest for a long moment. Then he made the same signals again. He did it a third time, and she began to understand. He was showing himself swimming to his craft. Of course, he had no idea how far he actually was from it, here in the cave—an unreasonable distance for as weak a swimmer as one of his kind was.

But now he was signaling yet something else. His "walking" limb end stood at the water's edge. His other limb end was not merely on the water, but in it, below the surface. As she watched, a single one of that other limb end's divisions rose through the surface and stood, slightly crooked, so that its upper joint was almost at right angles to the part sticking through the surface. Seeing her gaze on this part of him, the diver began to move that solitary joint through the water in the direction its crooked top was pointing. He brought it in this fashion all the way to the rock ledge and halted it opposite the "walking" limb end standing there.

He held both limb ends still in position and looked at her, as if waiting for a sign of understanding.

She gazed back, once more at a loss. The joint sticking up out of the water was like nothing in her memory but the limb of a waterlogged tree, its top more or less looking at the "walking" limb end that stood for the diver. But if the "walking" limb end was *he*—? Suddenly she understood. The division protruding from the water signalized *her!*

To show she understood, she backed off from the ledge, crouched down in the shallow water of the cave until nothing but her upper neck and head protruded from the water, and then—trying to look as much like his crooked division as possible—approached him on the ledge.

He made noises. There was no way of being sure, of course, but she felt she was beginning to read the tone of some of the sounds he made; and these latest sounds, she was convinced, sounded pleased and satisfied.

He tried something else.

He made the "walking" shape on the ledge, then added something. In addition to the two limb-end divisions standing on the rock, he unfolded another—a short, thick division, one at the edge of that particular limb end, and moved it in circular fashion, horizontally. Then he stood up on the ledge himself and swung one of his upper limbs at full length, in similar, circular fashion. He did this several times.

In no way could she imitate that kind of gesture, though she comprehended immediately that the movement of the extra, short division above the "walking" form was supposed to indicate him standing and swinging his upper limb like now. She merely stayed as she was and waited to see what he would do next.

He got down by the water, made the "craft" shape, "swam" his "walking" shape to it, climbed the "walking" shape up on the "craft," then had the "walking" shape turn and make the upper-limb swinging motion.

The Youngest watched, puzzled, but caught up in this strange game of communication she and the diver had found to play together. Evidently he wanted to go back to his craft, get on it, and then wave his upper limb like that, for some reason. It made no sense so far—but he was already doing something more.

He now had the "walking" shape standing on the ledge, making the upper-limb swinging motion, and he was showing the crooked division that was she approaching through the water.

That was easy: he wanted her to come to the ledge when he swung his upper limb.

Sure enough, after a couple of demonstrations of the last shape signals, he stood up on the ledge and swung his arm. Agreeably, she went out in the water, crouched down, and approached the ledge. He made pleased noises. This was all rather ridiculous, she thought, but enjoyable nonetheless. She was standing half her length out from the edge, where she had stopped, and was trying to think of a body signal she could give that would make him swim to her, when she noticed that he was going on to further signals.

He had his "walking" shape standing on the "craft" shape, in the water out from the ledge, and signaling "Come." But then he took his "walking" shape away from the "craft" shape, put it under the water a little distance off, and came up with it as the "her" shape. He showed the "her" shape approaching the "craft" shape with her neck and head out of water.

She was to come to his craft? In response to this "Come" signal?

No!

She was so furious with him for suggesting such a thing that she had no trouble at all thinking of a way to convey her reaction. Turning around, she plunged underwater, down through the cave entrance and out into the loch. Her first impulse was to flash off and leave him there to do whatever he wanted—stay forever, go back to his kind, or engage in any other nonsensical activity his small head could dream up. Did he think she had no wisdom at all? To suggest that she come right up to his craft with her head and neck out of water when he signaled—as if there had never been a taboo against her People having anything to do with his! He must not understand her in the slightest degree.

Common sense caught up with her, halted her, and turned her about not far from the cave mouth. Going off like this would do her no good—more, it would do the Family no good. On the other hand, she could not bring herself to go back into the cave, now. She hung in the water, undecided, unable to conquer the conscience that would not let her swim off, but also unable to make herself re-enter.

Vibrations from the water in the cave solved her problem. He had evidently put on the "made" thing she had brought him and was coming out. She stayed where she was, reading the vibrations.

He came to the mouth of the cave and swam slowly, straight up, to the surface. Level with him, but far enough away to be out of sight in the murky water, the Youngest rose, too. He lifted his head at last into the open air and looked around him.

He's looking for me, thought the Youngest, with a sense of satisfaction that he would see no sign of her and would assume she had left him for good. Now, go ashore and go back to your own kind, she commanded in her thoughts.

But he did not go ashore, though shore was only a matter of feet from him. Instead, he pulled his head underwater once more and began to swim back down.

She almost exploded with exasperation. He was headed toward the cave mouth! He was going back inside!

"You stupid animal!" she signaled to him. *"Go ashore!"*

But of course he did not even perceive the signal, let alone understand it. Losing all patience, the

Youngest swooped down upon him, hauled him to the surface once more, and let him go.

For a second he merely floated there, motionless, and she felt a sudden fear that she had brought him up through the water too swiftly. She knew of some small fish that spent all their time down in the deepest parts of the loch, and if you brought one of them too quickly up the nine hundred feet or so to the surface, it twitched and died, even though it had been carried gently. Sometimes part of the insides of these fish bulged out through their mouths and gill slits after they were brought up quickly.

After a second, the diver moved and looked at her.

Concerned for him, she had stayed on the surface with him, her head just barely out of the water. Now he saw her. He kicked with the "made" paddles on his lower limbs to raise himself partly out of the water and, a little awkwardly, with his upper limb ends made the signal of him swimming to his craft.

She did not respond. He did it several more times, but she stayed stubbornly non-communicative. It was bad enough that she had let him see her again after his unthinkable suggestion.

He gave up making signals. Ignoring the shore close at hand, he turned from her and began to swim slowly south and out into the center of the loch.

He was going in the wrong direction if he was thinking of swimming all the way to his craft. And after his signaling it was pretty clear that this was what he had in mind. Let him find out his mistake for himself, the Youngest thought, coldly.

But she found that she could not go through with that. Angrily, she shot after him, caught the thing on his back with her teeth, and, lifting him by it enough so that his head was just above the surface, began to swim with him in the right direction.

She went slowly—according to her own ideas of

speed—but even so a noticeable bow wave built up before him. She lifted him a little higher out of the water to be on the safe side; but she did not go any faster: perhaps he could not endure too much speed. As it was, the clumsy shape of his small body hung about with "made" things was creating surprising turbulence for its size. It was a good thing the present hatchhole (and, therefore, First Mother's current resting cave and the area in which First Uncle and Second Mother would do their feeding) was as distant as they were; otherwise First Uncle, at least, would certainly have been alarmed by the vibrations and have come to investigate.

It was also a good thing that the day was as dark as it was, with its late hour and the snow that was now beginning to fall with some seriousness; otherwise she would not have wanted to travel this distance on the surface in daylight. But the snow was now so general that both shores were lost to sight in its white, whirling multitudes of flakes, and certainly no animal on shore would be able to see her and the diver out here.

There was privacy and freedom, being hidden by the snow like this—like the freedom she felt on dark nights when the whole loch was free of the animals and all hers. If only it could be this way all the time. To live free and happy was so good. Under conditions like these, she could not even fear or dislike the animals, other than her diver, who were a threat to the Family.

At the same time, she remained firm in her belief that the Family should go, now. None of the others had ever before told her that any of the legends were untrustworthy, and she did not believe that the one about the Lost Father was so. It was not that that legend was untrustworthy, but that they had grown conservative with age and feared to leave the loch; while she, who was still young, still dared to try great things for possibly great rewards.

She had never admitted it to the older ones, but one midwinter day when she had been very young and quite small—barely old enough to be allowed to swim around in the loch by herself—she had ventured up one of the streams flowing into the loch. It was a stream far too shallow for an adult of the Family; and some distance up it, she found several otters playing on an ice slide they had made. She had joined them, sliding along with them for half a day without ever being seen by any upright animal. She remembered this all very well, particularly her scrambling around on the snow to get to the head of the slide; and that she had used her tail muscles to skid herself along on her warm belly surface, just as the Lost Father had described.

If she could get the others to slip ashore long enough to try the snowy loch banks before day-warmth combined with loch-warmth to clear them of the white stuff . . . But even as she thought this, she knew they would never agree to try. They would not even consider the journey home to the sea until, as First Mother said, it became clear that that was the only alternative to extinction at the hands of the up-right animals.

It was a fact, and she must face it. But maybe she could think of some way to make plain to them that the animals had, indeed, become that dangerous. For the first time, it occurred to her that her association with the diver could turn out to be something that would help them all. Perhaps, through him, she could gain evidence about his kind that would convince the rest of the Family that they should leave the loch.

It was an exciting thought. It would do no dis-service to him to use him in that fashion, because clearly he was different from others of his kind: he had realized that not only was she warm as he was,

but as intelligent or more so than he. He would have
no interest in being a danger to her People, and might
even cooperate—if she could make him understand
what she wanted—in convincing the Family of the
dangers his own race posed to them. Testimony from
one of the animals directly would be an argument to
convince even First Uncle.

For no particular reason, she suddenly remembered how he had instinctively huddled against her
when he had discovered her warming him. The memory roused a feeling of tenderness in her. She found
herself wishing there were some way she could signal
that feeling to him. But they were almost to his craft,
now. It and the dock were beginning to be visible—
dark shapes lost in the dancing white—with the dim-
mer dark shapes of trees and other things ashore behind them.

Now that they were close er.ough to see a shore, the
falling snow did not seem so thick, nor so all-enclos-
ing as it had out in the middle of the loch. But there
was still a privacy to the world it created, a feeling of
security. Even sounds seemed to be hushed.

Through the water, Youngest could feel vibrations
from the craft. At least one, possibly two, of the other
animals were aboard it. As soon as she was close
enough to be sure her diver could see the craft, she let
go of the thing on his back and sank abruptly to
about twenty feet below the surface, where she hung
and waited, checking the vibrations of his movements
to make sure he made it safely to his destination.

At first, when she let him go, he trod water where
he was and turned around and around as if searching
for her. He pushed himself up in the water and made
the "Come" signal several times; but she refused to
respond. Finally, he turned and swam to the edge of
the craft.

He climbed on board very slowly, making so little

noise that the two in the cabin evidently did not hear him. Surprisingly, he did not seem in any hurry to join them or to let them know he was back.

The Youngest rose to just under the surface and lifted her head above to see what he was doing. He was still standing on the foredeck, where he had climbed aboard, not moving. Now, as she watched, he walked heavily forward to the bow and stood beside the "made" thing there, gazing out in her direction.

He lifted his arm as if to make the "Come" signal, then dropped it to his side.

The Youngest knew that in absolutely no way could he make out the small portion of her head above the waves, with the snow coming down the way it was and day drawing swiftly to its dark close. She stared at him. She noticed something weary and sad about the way he stood. I should leave now, she thought. But she did not move. With the other two animals still unaware in the cabin, and the snow continuing to fall, there seemed no reason to hurry off. She would miss him, she told herself, feeling a sudden pang of loss. Looking at him, it came to her suddenly that from the way he was acting he might well miss her, too.

Watching, she remembered how he had half lifted his limb as if to signal and then dropped it again. Maybe his limb is tired, she thought.

A sudden impulse took her. I'll go in close, underwater, and lift my head high for just a moment, she thought, so he can see me. He'll know then that I haven't left him for good. He already understands I wouldn't come on board that thing of his under any circumstance. Maybe if he sees me again for a second, now, he'll understand that if he gets back in the water and swims to me, we can go on learning signals from each other. Then, maybe, someday, we'll know

enough signals together so that he can convince the
older ones to leave.

Even as she thought this, she was drifting in, underwater, until she was only twenty feet from the
craft. She rose suddenly and lifted her head and neck
clear of the water.

For a long second, she saw he was staring right at
her but not responding. Then she realized that he
might not be seeing her, after all, just staring blindly
out at the loch and the snow. She moved a little sideways to attract his attention, and saw his head move.
Then he *was* seeing her? Then why didn't he do something?

She wondered if something was wrong with him.
After all, he had been gone for nearly two days from
his own People and must have missed at least a couple of his feeding periods in that time. Concern im-
pelled her to a closer look at him. She began to drift
in toward the boat.

He jerked upright suddenly and swung an upper
limb at her.

But he was swinging it all wrong. It was not the
"Come" signal he was making, at all. It was more
like the "Come" signal in reverse—as if he was
pushing her back and away from him. Puzzled, and
even a little hurt, because the way he was acting reminded her of how he had acted when he first saw her
in the cave and did not know she had been with him
earlier, the Youngest moved in even closer.

He flung both his upper limbs furiously at her in
that new, "rejecting" motion and shouted at her—a
loud, angry noise. Behind him, came an explosion of
different noise from inside the cabin, and the other
two animals burst out onto the deck. Her diver
turned, making noises, waving both his limbs at them
the way he had just waved them at her. The
Youngest, who had been about to duck down below

the safety of the loch surface, stopped. Maybe this was some new signal he wanted her to learn, one that had some reference to his two companions?

But the others were making noises back at him. The taller one ran to one of the "made" things that were like, but smaller than, the one in the bow of the boat. The diver shouted again, but the tall one ignored him, only seizing one end of the thing he had run to and pulling that end around toward him. The Youngest watched, fascinated, as the other end of the "made" thing swung to point at her.

Then the diver made a very large angry noise, turned, and seized the end of the largest "made" thing before him in the bow of the boat.

Frightened suddenly, for it had finally sunk in that for some reason he had been signaling her to get away, she turned and dived. Then, as she did so, she realized that she had turned, not away from, but into line with, the outer end of the thing in the bow of the craft.

She caught a flicker of movement, almost too fast to see, from the thing's hollow outer end. Immediately, the loudest sound she had ever heard exploded around her, and a tremendous blow struck her behind her left shoulder as she entered the underwater.

She signaled for help instinctively, in shock and fear, plunging for the deep bottom of the loch. From far off, a moment later, came the answer of First Uncle. Blindly, she turned to flee to him.

As she did, she thought to look and see what had happened to her. Swinging her head around, she saw a long, but shallow, gash across her shoulder and down her side. Relief surged in her. It was not even painful yet, though it might be later; but it was nothing to cripple her, or even to slow her down.

How could her diver have done such a thing to her? The thought was checked almost as soon as it was born—by the basic honesty of her training. *He* had not done this. *She* had done it, by diving into the path of the barbed rod cast from the thing in the bow. If she had not done that, it would have missed her entirely.

But why should he make the thing throw the barbed rod at all? She had thought he had come to like her, as she liked him.

Abruptly, comprehension came; and it felt as if her heart leaped in her. For all at once it was perfectly clear what he had been trying to do. She should have had more faith in him. She halted her flight toward the Uncle and turned back toward the boat.

Just below it, she found what she wanted. The barbed rod, still leaving a taste of her blood in the water, was hanging point down from its line, in about two hundred feet of water. It was being drawn back up, slowly but steadily.

She surged in close to it, and her jaws clamped on the line she had tried to bite before and found resistant. But now she was serious in her intent to sever it. Her jaws scissored and her teeth ripped at it, though she was careful to rise with the line and put no strain upon it that would warn the animals above about what she was doing. The tough strands began to part under her assault.

Just above her, the sound of animal noises now came clearly through the water: her diver and the others making sounds at each other.

". . . I tell you we're through!" It was her diver speaking. "It's over. I don't care what you saw. It's my boat. I paid for it; and I'm quitting."

"It not *your* boat, man. It a boat belong to the company, the company that belong all three of us. We got contracts."

"I'll pay off your damned contracts."

"There's more to this than money, now. We know

that great beast in there, now. We get our contract money, and maybe a lot more, going on the TV and telling how we catch it and bring it in. No, man, you don't stop us now."

"I say, it's my boat. I'll get a lawyer and court order—"

"You do that. You get a lawyer and a judge and a pretty court order, and we'll give you the boat. You do that. Until then, it belong to the company and it keep after that beast."

She heard the sound of footsteps—her diver's footsteps, she could tell, after all this time of seeing him walk his lower limbs—leaving the boat deck, stepping onto the dock, going away.

The line was almost parted. She and the barbed rod were only about forty feet below the boat.

"What'd you have to do that for?" That was the voice of the third creature. "He'll do that! He'll get a lawyer and take the boat and we won't even get our minimum pay. Whyn't you let him pay us off, the way he said?"

"Hush, you fooking fool. How long you think it take him get a lawyer, a judge, and a writ? Four days, maybe five—"

The line parted. She caught the barbed rod in her jaws as it started to sink. The ragged end of the line lifted and vanished above her.

"—and meanwhile, you and me, we go hunting with this boat. We know the beast there, now. We know what to look for. We find it in four, five day, easy."

"But even if we get it, he'll just take it away from us again with his lawyer—"

"I tell you, no. We'll get ourselves a lawyer, also. This company formed to take the beast; and he got to admit he tried to call off the hunt. And we both seen what he do. He've fired that harpoon gun to scare it

off, so I can't get it with the drug lance and capture it.
We testify to that, we got him—Ah!"

"What is it?"

"What is it? You got no eyes, man? The harpoon
gone. It in that beast after all, being carried around.
We don't need no four, five days, I tell you now. That
be a good, long piece of steel, and we got the locators
to find metal like that. We hunt that beast and bring
it in tomorrow. Tomorrow, man, I promise you! It
not going to go too fast, too far, with that harpoon."

But he could not see below the snow and the black
surface of the water. The Youngest was already moving very fast indeed through the deep loch to meet the
approaching First Uncle. In her jaws she carried the
harpoon, and on her back she bore the wound it had
made. The elders could have no doubt, now, about
the intentions of the upright animals (other than her
diver) and their ability to destroy the Family.

They must call First Mother, and this time there
would be no hesitation. She would see the harpoon
and the wound and decide for them all. Tonight they
would leave by the route of the Lost Father, while the
snow was still thick on the banks of the loch. They
might have to leave the eggs behind, after all; but if
so, Second Mother could have more clutches, and
maybe later they would even find a way ashore again
to Loch Morar and meet others of their own People
at last.

But, in any case, they would go now to live free in
the sea; and in the sea most of Second Mother's
future eggs would hatch and the Family would grow
numerous and strong again.

She could see them in her mind's eye, now. They
would leave the loch by the mouth of Glen Moriston
—First Mother, Second Mother, First Uncle, herself
—and take to the snow-covered banks when the water became too shallow . . .

They would travel steadily into the mountains, and the new snow falling behind them would hide the marks of their going from the eyes of the animals. They would pass by deserted ways through the silent rocks to the ocean. They would come at last to its endless waters, to the shining bergs of the north and the endless warmth of the Equator sun. The ocean, their home, was welcoming them back, at last. There would be no more doubt, no more fear or waiting. They were going home to the sea . . . they were going home to the sea . . .